The Werewolf of Priory Grange

by
Robin Bailes

The Universal Library Books

@robinbailes

Cover by Books By Design -
www.pikapublications.co.uk/BooksByDesign

Prologue - The Moor

Regardless of how good a shortcut it was, there were parts of the moor into which a sensible person did not stray by night. In these areas, the firm, tussocky ground gave way to sucking marsh, that looked solid enough from above, but was capable of tugging the unwary traveller down into its slimy depths never to be seen again.

In truth, these days the traveller would have to be very unwary indeed. In this era of health and safety, even Naughton Mire, a marsh that occasionally disgorged the corpses of horses, sheep and humans dating back centuries, could be made more user-friendly. The safe path through had existed for centuries, marked by chalk white rocks placed at regular intervals, but now those rocks had been replaced with illuminated bollards paid for by the Squire. At its fringes, where it bordered the path, the marsh was fairly shallow, so even if you took a bad step you would lose little more than a shoe. Only someone who ran headlong in - perhaps someone being pursued - was at risk of their life. And one thing that didn't change with the passing of the times was that, if you were so unwary as to get caught, you couldn't call for help. The moor was wild and empty, the village of Naughton that adjoined it was far from the marsh and, despite some valiant attempts, mobile reception and wi-fi stubbornly refused to take hold. No one would hear your screams. Which was why people did not take the shortcut from the east side of the moor to the school by night. And certainly not on a night like this.

Thunder rumbled with self-conscious portent, and the flashes of lightning provided the only light beside that of the bollards marking out the path, almost lost in the sheeting rain. Storms clouds roiled in the tempestuous sky, chucking down an ocean's worth of water, all of it apparently targeted on the hunched figure, plodding along the lonely path that snaked through the mire, his raincoat pulled up over his head.

Creighton had known that taking this route back was a risky decision. But then, venturing out tonight had been a risky decision to start with. He cast a glance up at the sky and, for a moment, the clouds edged aside to give him a glimpse of the full moon behind them. Perhaps he should have stayed at the school. But it had seemed like a good lead at the time and he had rushed out after it without stopping to think. If he had known that it would turn out to be a

4

fool's errand then he would never have left, but that was easy to say with hindsight. Driving would also have been a smart move, given the weather, but Long Road was washed out, the detour would have taken hours and he'd been in a hurry.

At the time, trekking across the moor in a torrential downpour had seemed exactly the right thing to do. But now, four hours later, tramping back in near pitch darkness with the full moon like a warning sign above his head, and with nothing to show for it but beginnings of bronchial pneumonia, he had to admit that this had been another mistake caused by his own rash tendency to act without thinking. His best course now was to get back to the school as fast as he could.

He should never have left. The school was the epicentre - that was where everything was happening and that was where his first responsibility lay. The school was the reason that Creighton had chosen the path back through the mire. With the moon already up, every passing moment was precious. He would never forgive himself if something had occurred in his absence.

Then again, the children of the Priory Grange School were all tucked up in their warm, dry beds, safe against the monsoon-like weather, and whatever horrors might prowl the moors by night. Which was more than could be said for Creighton.

The first howl was so low that Creighton managed to convince himself that it was the weather. The wind across the moor could make appalling noises by night, as if all the bodies claimed by the marsh were crying out for their lost lives with one voice, and tonight those cries seemed to have risen into screams. But the second was unmistakable, even through the roar of the storm; the long, keening howl of the wolf.

Creighton quickened his pace, the sodden earth of the path sucking at his feet almost as badly as the marsh. There was no sense in running yet, better to save his strength for when he might actually need it. He glanced about him, seeing movement in the darkness wherever he looked. That was ridiculous – of course there was movement; it was the rain and the wind, nothing more. He was a professional and he was still in control enough to know when he had actually seen something. It was not the first time he had been in this sort of situation, it went with the job. He concentrated on the bollards that stretched out in front of him, each one a beacon,

5

floating in the murky dark like a willow-the-wisp. Just get to the next bollard, then the next and then the next. That was all he had to do.

The howl sounded again, closer now and with an animal urgency. Then, off to his right in the mire itself, Creighton saw the shadow, illuminated for a moment by a flash of lightning that lit the sky from within, moving quickly, coming for him. Now was the time to run. He was in good shape, but you couldn't outrun a wolf.

"Damn it!" In his haste, he missed the path, and one foot sank ankle deep into the mire, sending him tumbling to the mucky ground. Yanking the foot free he dragged himself up, slicked with mud, and ran on as fast as he could, feet skidding on the path. He passed another bollard and fixed his eyes on the next. The row of lights ahead of him seemed shorter now; was he reaching the edge of the mire? Did it matter? Was the moor itself any safer?

Now the howl at his heels was contracted, no longer the lengthy call to arms, but a short, snarling warning. The wolf didn't need to hunt in silence, it delighted in letting its prey know that the end was near. Behind the crash of thunder, the whirl of the wind and the aggressive drumming of the rain on the muddy ground, Creighton could now hear feet behind him.

He should never have come out tonight. Bad decision.

The feet were getting closer; four paws rhythmically striking the path. And then just two...

Chapter 1 - The Universal Library

"Boris. Welcome back."

Passing through the double doors that led into the foyer of the Universal Library, the first thing that Boris saw was the smiling face of his boss, Carl. Genial, dapper, bald from an early age and wearing a pair of small, round glasses, Uncle Carl, as he was called by Universal staff (though never to his face), was one of those men who seemed to have been born 'old'. His appearance placed his age at anywhere between sixty and ninety and had not changed as long as anyone could recall.

"Good morning, sir," Boris replied, politely. It was always nice to see Uncle Carl out and about in the building, pottering around his domain like an anxious gardener in his greenhouse, but being met by him at the door was seldom a good sign.

"How was your break?"

Boris considered the question a moment. "Much needed. And much appreciated."

"I would imagine. Have you time for a chat?"

"Of course, sir."

Carl smiled his avuncular smile and led Boris through the twin sets of doors that led into the main library, a sort of aural airlock to soundproof it from the outside world. The Library itself was only a part of the Universal building. On higher floors there were labs and offices, common areas, a canteen, gym, shooting range, indoor assault course and the other vagaries of an organisation the precise purpose of which was kept on a strictly need to know basis. But, like many Universal operatives, Uncle Carl liked the Library best. It was the oldest part of the organisation, with texts that had been acquired when Universal was founded, centuries ago. It was also somehow reflective of Universal itself; quiet, undemonstrative, and above all concerned with the acquisition of knowledge.

The Library's design meant that, from no point inside it could you see its limits, giving it an air of the infinite, heavy shelving stretching on forever. The stacks rose to a height of around twenty feet, upper shelves accessed by wooden gantries served by tight spiral staircases at the end of each stack. The library did have a lot of books to store and so every inch of space had to be used, but aesthetics had also played a part in the design. Boris had always thought that the library looked exactly as someone would expect it to look. If you asked a person to describe a library which housed a large collection of rare and occult texts, then what they would describe would be the Universal Library, a symphony in dark oak and aged leather.

Neither Boris nor Carl said a word as they passed through the room, their feet cushioned by the soft carpet, the only sound around them the gentle turning of pages, the scritch of pen on paper, and the small, subtle noises somehow made by the books themselves. Reaching one of the columns that supported the roof, Carl opened a door and Boris followed him into the lift that ran through it, leading to the upper floors.

"Never had a chance to congratulate you on that Egypt business," said Carl, once the doors had closed and the lift had begun its silent progress upwards. "Fine work."

"Thank you, sir," said Boris, it seemed like a long time ago now. "I don't feel as if much of the credit belongs to me."

Carl shrugged. "You found the right person to help. Pity about her."

Boris nodded. "I thought she would join us."

"Staying in touch?"

"I got a message a few weeks ago," Boris replied. "She's on an archaeological dig in Eastern Europe. Still no interest. I checked."

Carl nodded, pursing his lips in thought. "I think her time will come. Some people are just a magnet for this sort of work and I rather doubt Miss Evans will be able to avoid it forever. We'll keep an eye."

The lift doors slid open and Carl led the way down a corridor, past a secretary typing dutifully, and into his own office. The room was dominated by a large oak desk, that had always struck Boris as being disproportionate to the small man who sat behind it, as was the leather swivel chair in which Carl now lost himself.

"Take a seat, Boris."

Boris did so.

"Do anything much with your time off?"

"Nothing special. Resting mostly."

"All healed up now?"

Boris nodded. His most recent mission had hit a fairly major mishap in the air over central Europe, a mishap that had resulted in his being seriously injured to the point of near death. Which was no reason for his not being back at his desk now, after a month's leave. 'Near death' was an occupational hazard for Universal agents. So was death itself, but you were not expected to keep working after the latter, except in certain special circumstances.

"Nice weather you had anyway," Carl went on.

"Yes, sir."

"Were you able to get out much?"

"A little. Took a few turns around the park. Like I said; nothing special."

"Well that's nice." Carl sighed and rolled his eyes. "I'm useless at this." He looked up at Boris, his face suddenly more serious. "Boris, I hate to send you back out on your first day back..."

"I'm more than ready, sir."

"Especially when you took a hit last time out."

"I'm quite fit."

"And so close to Christmas."

"It's not a problem."

Carl pulled a face. "I wish it wasn't."

"I mean that I'm ready for whatever assignment you have for me."

Carl nodded. "I know you are. I just wish the circumstances..." He tapped his fingers irascibly on the table-top. "Never gets easier, you know? No matter how many times..."

"Sir?" Boris had a horrible feeling he knew what his boss was about to say.

"We lost a man," said Carl. He suddenly seemed to have aged several decades in the course of one sentence.

Boris took the information in. It happened of course. More than anyone liked to acknowledge - Boris had lost a man on his last assignment. But, however dangerous the work, everyone liked to believe that each death was an anomaly, and that it would never happen again.

"Who?" he asked.

"Creighton," Carl replied.

"Good man."

"A little hot-headed sometimes," said Carl, reflectively. "Didn't always take the time to think things through. Maybe that... We don't know. In fact, there is a little too much that we don't

9

know. We don't even have a body."

"No body?"

Carl held up a hand. "We've no reason to be optimistic. The area where Creighton was stationed is a nightmare to search and we believe that, on the night he disappeared, he was passing through marshland. Plus," Carl sucked at his teeth, "the nature of his assignment does not always leave..." he swallowed, "remains."

"I see."

Carl got up from his chair and went to the large window behind it, giving a spectacular view out across the city of London.

"I look down there at all those people and... I sometimes wonder if they are better or worse off for not knowing just how many things, that they dismiss as legends, are really out there and really trying to kill them. Living in fear has little to recommend it, but is living in ignorance better?"

"I fear it would be chaos," Boris remarked. He'd had the same thoughts himself from time to time - they all had - but had always come to the same conclusion. "Look how people react when there's a bomb threat or something. Tell them that there are vampires out there and every goth teenager in Britain will be in danger of getting a stake through their heart."

"True." Carl shook his head. "Sorry. Beside the point. The assignment. You'll be heading up North tomorrow to pick up where Creighton left off, although we'll give you a different cover."

"Right."

"Your mission will essentially be the same; protect the innocent, find out what has been causing the deaths in the area and stop it. Obviously we also want to know what happened to Creighton, but I think if you find the answer to one mystery then you will find the answer to the other."

"Do we have any idea what's up there?"

Uncle Carl nodded. "We had a pretty good idea when we sent Creighton and he was able to confirm the what. Though not the who or the where."

Boris wondered if it was an inevitable side-effect of working in an organisation like Universal that you started talking in riddles.

"I know Egypt is your specialist area," Boris had been born in Britain and was the most English person that most people had ever met, but his parents were both Egyptian and he had made a special study of certain aspects of the culture. Specifically those aspects that had an irritating habit of getting up after four thousand years of peaceful death with murder and conquest on their minds. "But how much do you know about werewolves?"

Chapter 2 - Two Months Earlier

Two months prior to the conversation between Boris and Uncle Carl in the upper storeys of Universal's London headquarters, a train rattled its way through northern England, stopping at every out of the way station, disgorging a few people, and moving on. It was one of *those* trains - the ones that commuters fear as they make a long journey interminable, but which have to exist because, in spite of all evidence to the contrary, people *do* live in these tiny, isolated towns and villages, and if there is a station then the rail companies are obligated to serve it, however reluctant they may be to do so.

Lisa Hobson sat with her forehead resting against the window, staring at the passing landscape until her breath fogged the glass, then wiping it clean and staring some more. Her book (*The Woman in White*, Wilkie Collins) had lain forgotten on the table since the view from the train had become more irresistibly gothic than Collins' narrative, which she had in any case read before. What was it about that landscape that spoke, not just to Lisa, but to so many? What was it about hills stripped bare by hard winds; trees sullenly hunched against the rain; rivers that seemed to have hacked their way through hard rock to tumble down mountainsides? What was it about the lonely houses that crouched in the hollows of the landscape or stood stark against a slate grey sky? What was it about the solitary ravens, the huddled sheep, the ragged dogs that pattered down roads that were barely paths? What was it about the North of England that fed the imagination of all England, and fuelled its darkest dreams with tales of young women locked up in secluded houses, elderly men plotting murder, and handsome young bucks committing it?

Lisa didn't know the answer, but it gave her something to think about as the train muddled its ramshackle path through the ever more dramatic landscape. The funny thing was that it had this effect on Lisa even though she had no connection to it, outside of the books she read. She had never been this far north before, and would not have been going now if necessity had not demanded a new school.

Actually, Lisa would have argued that 'necessity' was the wrong word. She would have been quite content to remain at St. Leonard's and they would have been quite happy to accommodate her. As would Kingsbury or Dowes. Her secondary education had begun to seem like a tour of some of the best regarded boarding schools in Britain. Which was all very nice, but doing so in the middle of her final, A-Level year was hardly ideal - that sort of thing could have a detrimental effect on your results. And yet here she was again, leaving behind those friends she had briefly made at St. Leonards, to speed (if that was the right word for the pace this train could achieve) towards yet another new school.

The reason was seated opposite her, reading Matthew Lewis's *The Monk* (which he had borrowed from Lisa). It was not that Oliver Hobson was a troublemaker who got expelled from schools; he was well behaved, quiet, and kept himself to himself. It was not that he failed to meet the academic standards upon which such schools insisted, quite the reverse in fact, he was academically brilliant, possibly a prodigy, certainly destined for greatness. True, he did not fit in well with the other boys, which was odd for someone so gifted at sports. And he did not get on with the girls either, which too was odd for someone so strikingly beautiful. A shock of ash blonde hair set off his ascetic and yet somehow dangerous features, like a poet with past; Byron without the dodgy foot. But his social failure did not bother him, did not bother his teachers, did not bother the other students, did not bother his family; so it wasn't that either. No one could really say what it was but, with predictable regularity, the point would come when the head teacher would ask Lisa and Oliver's parents to come in for a quiet chat, at which it would be made clear that, while Oliver was a wonderful child, whom everyone liked and who was such an asset to the school, it might be best for all concerned if he found a different school at which to be an asset. The conversations were always polite, but couched in a way that made it clear this was not a negotiation. He was going.

And so Oliver would need a new school, and because their parents preferred the children to be together, Lisa would need one too. Lisa loved her brother, what with his being her brother and all, but she did resent her life being so much dictated by his. She was used to it. Oliver was special, he was the delicate orchid who required nurturing in a climate-controlled environment, while she was that green leafy thing no one recalled buying, which could be safely dumped on a window sill to be watered by anyone who remembered and trusted not to die. '*We have to make allowances for Oliver,*' was the mantra Lisa had heard her entire life. It wasn't cruelty or neglect, it was habit - he needed more attention and so got it. She had never been sure if Oliver was aware of the imbalance. He never mentioned it.

There was no denying that he was special; preternaturally brilliant at everything he tried, aesthetically pleasing since he was a baby, and somehow otherworldly, as if his thoughts existed on a different plane to those of people around him. Lisa was just Lisa; averagely brown hair, averagely attractive, average height, average build, average grades that promised an average future which would not be affected by shuffling her from school to school. If she had been given all the attention that was lavished on Oliver, then she would still not have surpassed her own basic averageness. The only thing that made her stand out was an above average younger brother, which was not the distinction she would have chosen for herself. In her dreams she had a stellar career (probably as an author, possibly as an historian), feted at parties and lectures where people told Oliver how lucky he was to have such a brilliant sister. In reality it seemed more likely that she would have an average career. Which would be fine but... it would be nice to excel at something, to be special in some way.

The train clattered to a nervous halt and Lisa wiped her breath from the window once more to read the station name.

"Allpeter." All the place names up here seemed to have been put together from words that had been left over from something else. "Just a few more stops."

Oliver lowered his book, revealing his grey blue eyes. "Yes."

"The school is sending someone to meet us."

"Yes."

"Are you looking forward to it?" It seemed a big sisterly thing to say - sometimes she got so caught up in her own feelings on the matter that she forgot to wonder what these constant changes of school meant to Oliver.

Oliver shrugged, looking for a moment like an normal teenage boy. "Just another school."

Lisa nodded; just another school. As Oliver retreated back behind *The Monk*, she looked about the train carriage, trying to guess something about the few people remaining on board. There were only five left besides themselves; an elderly couple who looked to have been on a day out to the big city and had lived in this area their entire lives; a teen wearing clothes that had been in fashion a decade ago; a hard-faced woman whom Lisa immediately branded with the word 'spinster' and immediately felt guilty about doing so; and a man. The man was the one who interested Lisa the most because he gave her the least. There seemed to be so much about him worthy of comment and yet he came across as oddly anonymous. His hair was sandy, his face active, his glasses slim and fashionable, his clothes neat but worn. He had a pair of large bags on the rack above his head and a case open on the table in front of him, from which he periodically took papers to read. Lisa strained to read something on the papers and then quickly turned the other way when the man looked up. Had he seen her? It didn't seem to matter; he went back to his reading.

Lisa went back to watching. The case and paper suggested a sedentary line of work but there was an obvious strength in the man's hands, and when his arms moved she saw muscles twist beneath the skin, revealed by his rolled up shirt sleeves. He was not bulky, but the man was clearly fit, with an athlete's body hidden beneath his sober attire. There was too, Lisa decided, a quiet charisma about him. For all his anonymity, he stood out, he made an impression, he had drawn her eye.

Idly, Lisa wondered for a moment if the man perhaps had a younger brother who exhibited all the same traits but in greater measure and flaunted them more openly. But the thought did not occupy her for long and she returned her gaze to the gothic landscape outside. Sooner or later they were sure to pass Dracula's castle (Bram Stoker).

It was about half an hour later that the train finally reached the village of Naughton, which, if not widely recognised as the middle of nowhere was surely a strong contender. Lisa and Oliver, weighed down under bags, stepped out onto the flagstoned platform.

"I think we're in *The Railway Children*," said Lisa, adding, "Edith Nesbit," as she looked up and down the station. Neatly pruned bushes in large ceramic pots flanked each doorway, the stonework had been scrubbed clean and the woodwork was all brightly painted. It was a station that someone cared about.

On an impulse common to every seventeen year old girl, Lisa checked her phone. The action drew peel of loud, cracked laughter

15

and Lisa looked up to see an elderly man who had probably been here since the time of *The Railway Children*, and had never changed his uniform.

"You'll not be able to use that thing here." The station master's voice sounded as if it had been mined out of one of the hills, while his language suggested that he had been placed here by Naughton's tourist board to keep up local stereotypes.

Lisa nodded. "No signal."

"And there's no 'signal' anywhere around here." Lisa wouldn't have been surprised if the man had crossed himself when he said the word 'signal'. People around here probably still thought a photograph would steal your soul, making a selfie a form of spiritual suicide. "You'll be for the school, I daresay?"

"Yes."

Lisa started at the reply, which had come from behind her and Oliver. She turned and found the anonymous man from the train standing silently there, showing impressively little regard for the heavy bags he was carrying.

"We are too," said Oliver.

"Aye," said the stationmaster, fulfilling his contractual obligation to include at least one 'aye' per conversation. "Our Malcolm will take you up."

"I wonder if Malcolm's a horse," whispered Lisa, not quite quietly enough as the old man cackled afresh.

"No, he's not a horse - less'un you listen to girls' gossip about the village." He paused to crackle with laughter then turned back to the station building. "Malcolm!"

"Here I am, Uncle Lester."

The figure that emerged, stooping to get through the door, might not have been a horse, but he clearly had some ox in his ancestry.

"Can I take your bags?" He politely addressed Lisa.

Lisa smiled. "Thanks."

Malcolm hoisted up Lisa's luggage with little effort, then picked up two of Oliver's bags as well before turning to the anonymous man.

"I'm fine, thank you."

"Right y'are. Follow me." He led the way through the station building and out into a cobbled yard in which an elderly minibus -

16

that was still probably the newest thing they had seen since arriving - was parked. Malcolm stowed their luggage and held the door open.

"Ladies' first." Lisa was starting to really like Malcolm.

Once they were all aboard, the engine kicked into unsteady life and they were off.

Lisa turned to the man who sat at the back, his expression unreadable. "I hope you don't mind me asking, but; you seem a little old for the school."

The flicker of a smile danced across the man's lips. "I'm starting as a teacher there. My name is Mr Tull. Who knows; maybe I'll be teaching you."

"What do you teach?" asked Oliver.

"Geography."

Lisa nodded politely, aware that, however utterly pointless a subject she personally considered geography to be, it was not a good idea to get on the wrong side of a teacher on her first day.

"I'm Lisa Hobson, this is my brother Oliver."

Mr. Tull smiled and nodded in the way that people tended to on learning that Lisa and Oliver were siblings. They were not physically similar.

"How come you're starting mid-term?"

Lisa shrugged. "It's kind of a long story. The short version is; that's just how we roll." She couldn't remember the last time she had started a school at the beginning of term. Mid-October was pretty good for the Hobson children. "How come you're starting mid-term?"

"I guess that's how I roll too."

"Really?"

"No. I was just trying to be the cool teacher."

Lisa shook her head firmly. "Don't. Nobody likes the cool teacher."

Mr Tull laughed. "I was wondering what sort of pupils I would be getting in an out of the way place like this. So far I am pleasantly surprised."

Truth be told, Lisa had been wondering what sort of teachers she would be getting. Her predicted grades were not stellar, but she cared about maintaining them and worried that a place like The Priory Grange - despite its reputation - would be a graveyard for teachers too old, out of touch or unemployable to get jobs closer to civilisation. It was hard to judge Mr Tull on so little acquaintance, but he seemed nice enough - which was at least a good start.

"How far is it to the school?" Oliver called up to the driver.

"Far," confided Malcolm (Lisa had secretly hoped he would start his reply with 'Bless you, young master'). "We've to go through Naughton and past The Grey Boar. Along the mill stream a ways, then over the bridge in sight of poor Ralph's Mill – there's only the log bridge by the village itself, you see. Then round, down and up across the moor. There's only the one road across the moor. Might be busy today."

Lisa wondered what 'busy' would mean in a place like this. The minibus rattled past an Inn (definitely an inn rather than a pub), the weather-beaten sign of which was still recognisable as a grey boar, then on past a line of houses that had stood here long enough for their stonework to acquire the same colour as the ground. These seemed to mark the village limits, the road became rougher, flanked by the mill stream on one side and a deep, steep-sided ditch on the other. Beyond these, out to either side of them, spread a vast expanse of uneven, tussocked landscape, rising to humps and hills here, falling from sight there. The moor.

Mr. Tull took off his glasses to clean them and stared out of the window. "*The land's sharp features seemed to be, the Century's corpse outleant, his crypt the cloudy canopy, the wing his death lament.*"

"Thomas Hardy," said Lisa automatically. "*The Darkling Thrush.*" And Mr Tull smiled, still staring out at their wild surroundings.

Lisa followed his gaze. There are landscapes for which the word 'bleak' might have been coined. The grass was rough and thick, more grey than green, not growing in an even carpet like that soft, southern grass, but clumping together in tight bunches, making the ground lumpen even where it was flat. A few low bushes and stunted trees dotted the scene, keeping their heads down and trying not to be noticed, their leaves shorn by wind and autumn to add brown and yellow splotches of leaf muck to the grey expanse. Brambles were strung out like barbed wire across a First World War battlefield, a thin, smoky mist adding to the illusion.

Looking out further across the moor the landscape seemed to buckle up. Sharp spines of black rock burst through the hardy

18

vegetation, climbing into bowed and broken hillocks or forging skywards in narrow spires and angular cairns. All bore the marks of the weather; the rocks worn by wind and rain into crags and claws, split into crevasses by seeping frost. Lumpen boulders lay about the bases of the jagged cliffs, having rolled down steep escarpments of loose stones, broken from the rock walls over long centuries, furred by moss and lichen. In the distance, taller hills rose into almost mountains, bordering the great bowl in which the misty moor squatted.

"Over there," Malcolm had observed his passengers' interest and took on the character of tour guide, "right over there in the distance, beyond Jag Head, you can just make out Naughton Mire."

Lisa shaded her eyes from the low sun and peered through the bus's grimy window till her gaze lit on a patch of land, greener than that surrounding it, almost verdant in the late afternoon light.

"Marshland, that is," said Malcolm. "There's a path through it from Squire Montford's – the young squire that is, now his father's passed - but you'd still be better off taking Long Road if you're going. That marsh has claimed its share of lives. Not so many these days," he admitted, as if the marsh's failure to kill as many people as it used to was a stain on its notoriety, "last one I can recall was old Jack Bridges, and he were drunk as a lord when he went in. Silly fool. But in my Granny's day there used to be about one a month. Stick to the road is my advice."

"Good advice," said Mr. Tull. His eyes shifted back to the mire. "Strange place for a school. More suitable for a prison."

"Victorian, it is, sir," said Malcolm. "House originally, then turned into a school. I don't know when. Reckon how they thought the moor and the marsh would stop children running away. As they had cause to back then," he added, as he remembered Lisa and Oliver. "I'm sure it's a much nicer place now."

"I'm sure it is." Mr. Tull nodded encouragingly at Lisa and her brother.

Lisa nodded back. It was a grim place in which to be exiled. A cold, damp place of open wastes, but somehow claustrophobic too, thick with the scent of ancient death. And yet, at least in Lisa's eyes, it had a strange beauty to it. The grandeur of the dark hills called to her, the emptiness of the moor seduced her with its silence, even the slick terror of the mire felt like a lure. Lisa would have been the first to admit that there might be something wrong with her - she blamed her taste in literature - but it was also something that made her different, and Lisa's life experience encouraged her to embrace anything that made her different, and wear it with pride.

The mini-bus reached a stone bridge, only just wide enough for it, crossing the mill stream.

"This is the only bridge for miles that'll bear a car," Malcolm returned to his tour guide voice. "There's the log bridge into the village and there's always talk of building another one – a proper one - so there's a more direct route for people visiting the school. But who's to pay for it?" He pointed back over his shoulder as they turned onto the bridge. "On your right, follow the stream down and you can see the old mill."

"Is it still in use?" asked Mr Tull.

Malcolm sighed. "Maybe it will be again. Maybe come the summer when we have the tourists in - they like a working watermill. But it's up in the air since poor Ralph's passing."

"The miller died?" Mr. Tull pressed.

"Aye," intoned Malcolm, leadenly. "Killed he was."

"Murdered?" Oliver's blue grey eyes widened with fascination.

Malcolm shook his large head. "Some animal. Gutted him. Horrible to see it was. Stomach ripped open like a wet paper bag." He seemed to remember that there were children present. "Though I'm sure he died quick. Found his body just down there, by the mill race."

Mr Tull craned his neck to look with, Lisa thought, a rather morbid interest. He settled back in his seat as the mill passed from sight, then gave a little smile as he caught Lisa looking at him. "A safe distance from the school."

"Still walking distance," Malcolm commented, cheerfully. "That's why Dr Lloyd don't let the children out past sunset. Which is early this time of year."

The bus set out across the moor road, built to take advantage of the flattest route from the village side to where the school stood in the shadow of the mountains, snaking its path between craggy, broken-backed hills, and sudden dips, where the land seemed to have collapsed in on itself under the weight of time.

Staring out at the pitted road ahead, Lisa wondered why

anyone would want to build a school in the most isolated place possible. It wasn't a cheering thought.

"Was the miller the only person killed by this animal?" asked Mr Tull.

"Aye," Malcolm replied. "Only man. Only human, I should say – begging your pardon, Miss. Plenty of sheep. Sir John lost five sheep up on the hills that night."

"The same night Ralph was killed?" wondered Mr Tull.

"Aye. And more the night after."

"Were the sheep gutted too?" asked Oliver.

"Oh aye." Malcolm nodded. "Those they found. Though some they never did. A lot of bits but not enough to add up to five sheep." He shook his head heavily. "Poor Ralph. Much missed in the Boar of a night, I can tell you. I'd say that's why no one's stepped up to run the Mill. Ralph had no kids you see. Wife long gone. The school will miss him too, you know."

"How so?" asked Mr. Tull.

"Used to be a regular place for trips did the Mill. 'Field trips' as they say. Not much to see about these parts - it's a long drive to take the children to a zoo, or a theatre or suchlike. But there was a working watermill, practically on their doorstep, that's been there since the middle ages they reckon, in one form or another. Or before. History that is. And he were always happy to go up to the school and talk about it, or about other local history. A good friend to the school was Ralph."

"How old was he?" It was hard for Lisa to be sure whether Mr Tull was being polite and humouring Malcolm, or if he was genuinely interested.

Malcolm rubbed his chin in thought. "Now I couldn't say to be sure. Not an old man, you wouldn't say. But not a youngster neither. Forties maybe? Fifties perhaps. Beard like a badger's backside, which makes it hard to tell. He was just Ralph to me. Poor Ralph." He was quiet a moment and then pointed out the window again. "You can't see it for the hills, but out that way is the Conliffe estate - Sir John Conliffe and his family - big landowners in these parts. Well regarded. Family been here since Domesday and they'll be here till doomsday. On your left…"

Lisa listened idly as they drove on, her gaze never leaving the moor.

You didn't see the school at first as you approached. It seemed to Lisa that it emerged from a shell of darkness cast upon it by the looming hills when the sun was low in the late afternoon sky. All of a sudden it seemed to detach itself from its surroundings, like a camouflaged soldier revealing himself. Time and weather had made the main building - an imposing slab of late Georgian/early-Victorian architecture - the same colour as the hills before which it stood. In this comparatively sheltered spot, ivy had managed to avoid the wind enough to get a toe-hold and clamber its way up the bricks here and there, clinging for dear life. Elsewhere, a grey-green lichen, that seemed to have coated every tree and rock for miles around, covered all bar the roof. It was the roof that stood out most - black, polished slate that shone as if it had been washed, and defied any plant life that tried to grow on it. To right and left of the main building, wings spilled out, contemporary - or nearly so - with the main structure, and beyond them, a scattered flotsam of outbuildings that had once been stables, smithies, sties, dairies and other assorted practicalities necessary to a house built so far from civilisation. In Victorian times that isolation must have been all the more profound. It was a lonely place for anyone to choose to live, and the plots of a hundred period novels avalanched through Lisa's mind - any one of them could have been set here, and most of them ended badly.

Though it was still afternoon, the light was already failing, and as the minibus approached, windows in the house started to light up with a dull, yellow glow. Peering up, Lisa saw the shadows of people moving behind the windows. Pupils or teachers? She could not tell, but one way or the other, these anonymous shadows would be her companions for the remainder of the school year. Not so long, but a lot could still happen in that time. School years were like dog years; you didn't get many but they were packed with incident.

"I'll drop you at the big house," said Malcolm. The minibus passed through the open gates that broke the high wall which circled the school. On a brass plaque, proudly displayed on one of the uprights flanking the entrance, Lisa read, *'The Priory Grange - Est. 1895. Private secondary school for boys and girls'*.

Chapter 3 - The Priory Grange

As Malcolm unloaded their bags, Lisa and Oliver stared up at the
school. It seemed far bigger up close than it had from a distance. The
grandly pillared frontage, served by a pair of sweeping staircases,
towered over them, designed to inspire awe and show off wealth.
Though to who, Lisa could not imagine. Who the hell was just
passing this way in the mid-nineteenth century?

Although, architecture was one of many subjects on which
Lisa unhesitatingly labelled herself as 'ignorant', she had a certain
acquired knowledge via the books she read, and was therefore aware
that, whenever it had been built, stylistically speaking The Priory
Grange was more Georgian than Victorian. But if you were going to
build yourself a house out here, where no one was ever likely to see
it, you could ignore fashion and build whatever the hell you pleased.

The main doors under the colonnaded portico opened and a
man emerged; balding, dressed in a dark blue suit and smiling as he
jogged down the steps.

"Good afternoon. You would be the Hobsons?"

"That's us." Lisa was well accustomed to this little ritual.

"Oliver and Lisa, yes?"

"Lisa and Oliver, yes."

"And you," the man turned to Mr Tull, "must be Mr Tull."

"Dr Bellamy?"

"The same."

"Pleased to meet you, sir."

"And you. Thank you Malcolm, please tell your Uncle Lester
to bill the school. Now let's get you all inside, it'll be getting cold
soon – colder I should say - and out here that really means
something. Can I help with anyone's bags?"

With Oliver trailing behind her, Lisa followed Mr Tull and Dr
Bellamy up the steps and in through the glass doors to an impressive
hallway within, lit by sconce lights and a brass chandelier that hung
low above them. Stone columns supported the high roof, below
which a landing ran around the top of the room, with doors leading
off it. On the walls were paintings that could have been old
headmasters, old residents of the building, or just been ordered from
a catalogue of 'Generic Victorian Gentlemen With a Stick Up Their
Butt'. They all held books or scrolls of some description and stared

off into middle distance as if something had just disturbed them.

"Always keep that door closed," commented Dr Bellamy, to no one in particular. "Creates a draught. Now," he spread his slim arms majestically, "welcome to The Priory Grange! We hope you'll be very happy here. First things first; Mr Tull, I know the Headmistress would like a word with you - I'll have someone take your luggage to your room. Oliver, Lisa; we'll get you settled in, then I'm sure Dr Lloyd would like to meet you as well. Now, where's Mrs... Ah, the very lady." From a side door to Lisa's right, a woman had entered to whom Dr Bellamy addressed himself. "Mrs Kerrigan, these are Oliver and Lisa Hobson, could you show Lisa to her room? Can you manage the bags or should I...? No? Alright? Very well. Oliver, you're with me. Mr Tull..."

Lisa could still hear Dr Bellamy prattling on in his convivial way as she was led through the side door by Mrs Kerrigan.

"How was your journey?" asked Mrs Kerrigan, a heavy set woman in her early fifties, whom Lisa instantly identified as the Suspicious Housekeeper, whose illegitimate son would turn up in chapter 5 but was ultimately a red herring and would have no bearing upon the plot.

"Long," admitted Lisa. "But okay. It's very beautiful country up this way."

Mrs Kerrigan nodded in a way that did not necessarily indicate agreement. "It has its charms. Did Dr Bellamy give you the lay of the school?"

"Not really."

"There's a map in your room. It'll take you a week or so to acclimatise yourself - and I mean that literally; the weather takes some getting used to - but the other girls will be happy to help you find your way. Very basically," Mrs Kerrigan read off an internal script, "the central block - the main house - is where most lessons take place and where the staff room is. The refectory is on the lower ground floor between the raised ground and the basements. The north wing - to which we are now heading - is the girls' boarding house; dormitories, studies, double and single rooms for older girls, activities etc. Also some classrooms. You have to pass behind the chapel to get there, which is what we are now doing. Chapel every Sunday morning, assemblies are also held there. The south wing has the same facilities for boys (except for the chapel, of course). The school went co-ed in the 1960s - relatively early for a school of this type. Most of the out-buildings are store rooms, sports related or guest accommodation. The old stable is now our gym. Most teachers live in one or other of the wings to be on hand in case of civil unrest." It was hard to tell if she was joking. "Any questions?"

"Will I get a single room?" It wasn't that Lisa was unfriendly or unwilling to make new friends, but she needed quiet in which to study so that she could make up lost ground. Besides, trying to make friends mid-term, when friendships had been long since cemented, was not best aided by being dumped into someone else's room in the hope that the two of you will 'get along' by force of proximity.

"You will," said Mrs Kerrigan. "Girls in their final year all get single rooms so they can study without distraction. Although they mostly study in each other's rooms anyway. I know you'll find the privacy beneficial, but I hope you don't close yourself away from the other pupils."

"I'll try not to." That was true too. While she wasn't here to make friends, Lisa did want to and she was pretty good at it – she'd had enough practice. She sometimes envied Oliver, who seemed not to care one way or the other, and so was less affected when they changed schools. She was a social person; she wanted to be liked and to be part of the crowd. Maybe that was why she struggled to be distinctive; because those two desires were mutually exclusive.

It did not seem as if a great deal of work had been done in converting the building from stately home to private school. Some of the rooms had been enlarged, others divided up with plasterboard walls, but the basic layout remained, and Lisa felt instantly and oddly at home in the maze of corridors and staircases through which she and Mrs Kerrigan wound. It was, again, a testament to her taste in books that this felt homey to her, even though most of the heroines who took up residence in those houses seemed to end up part of some dastardly intrigue.

They passed chattering dormitories, ringing with the sounds of the younger girls at play, at work, and sniping at each other - which is basically all children do at that age. They went through a common room, furnished with an eclectic conglomeration of furniture that seemed to have accumulated over the last hundred years, ranging from genuine antiques (the value of which had been seriously decreased by a century of graffiti and chewing gum), through kitsch vinyl from the nineteen fifties, all the way up to some blandly anonymous chairs that looked about a week old. Here, girls in their mid-teens read, watched TV, tapped away on laptops or chatted surreptitiously in corners. In a recreation room there were pool and table tennis tables, snack machines, bookshelves, board games and tea and coffee making facilities. Wherever they went, Lisa noticed that the loud chatter of teenage girls hushed at their approach and rose as they left, as if Mrs Kerrigan brought with her a cone of silence. It didn't matter what you were talking about – homework, lunch or meeting up with boys - no one wanted a teacher to hear. It was a prison mentality, common to most schools.

Going up a flight of narrow, worn, spiral stairs that had once, Lisa guessed, led to the servants' quarters, they emerged onto a landing with doors leading off of it.

"Sixth form rooms," explained Mrs. Kerrigan. "You're in here."

Lisa noted the number '6' on her door as she passed into the small but practical room. A bed, a desk and a wardrobe took up most of the space, the carpet between them worn to threadbare by years of anxious pacing by successive occupants, trying to drum fractions, Latin verbs or the dates of British monarchs into overcrowded brains. A window gave a view out across the moor, already vanishing into the dark of encroaching night.

"Lovely," said Lisa, feeling that something was required of her.

"Dump your stuff here," said Mrs Kerrigan. "I'll show you the facilities and then we'll head back down so you can meet Dr Lloyd."

At one end of the landing was the kitchen, which was a pretty grand name for a room that contained a kettle, a toaster and fridge with milk, butter and something that might, at one point in its ancestry, have been cheese. At the other end was a communal bathroom with sinks, toilets and showers. As they passed up and down the corridor, Mrs Kerrigan gave vague introductions to the girls they passed.

"Cristina, this is Lisa Hobson, she's the new girl in number 6. Make her feel at home." An attractive blonde girl with a sharp face and outrageously blue eyes.

"This is Lisa. Lisa, this is Fay who's in the room next to yours. I hope you're going to clean up those toast crumbs, they attract mice." A dark-skinned girl in the kitchen with challenging eyes and a sullen mouth.

"Zeffie, this is Lisa, she and her brother are starting this week, so show her around if she needs help." A plump, curly haired girl flopped on her bed, staring through the open door.

As the news of Lisa's arrival spread, more girls seemed to appear, peering from rooms with suspicious interest at the interloper, assessing Lisa until she felt as if she was in a dog show.

."Josie... Rosa... Elsa... Elena... Jane..."

The names faded and muddled and re-applied themselves to the wrong faces as Mrs Kerrigan tossed out introductions till Lisa gave up the idea of keeping track. She would get to know them soon enough in the process of living and studying alongside them. Or she wouldn't. One way or the other. Generally Lisa was pretty good at fitting in, but that just made her afraid of the time that she wouldn't.

Mrs Kerrigan looked at her watch. "I'd better get you back, Dr Lloyd is expecting you and your brother."

Dr Evelyn Lloyd, headmistress of the Priory Grange, was one of those women who takes to middle age as if she had been waiting for it. In her younger years she had probably been considered no more than average looking, but she had grown into a striking older women. This rather endeared her to Lisa, who liked the idea that a person's time might be 'still to come'. Her hair was jet black all save a white streak, which Lisa could not identify as natural or dyed, her skin was smooth, her eyes hard, her figure slim. There was a sternness about her that suggested she had always been destined to be a headmistress, and she spoke in clipped, brittle tones.

"How do you find the school?"

Lisa looked at Oliver just as he looked at her - he usually deferred to his sister when there was serious talking to be done. "It's very beautiful," said Lisa, falling back on cliché. "I like my room."

"Have you met any of the other girls?"

"Not 'met' exactly," Lisa replied. "Mrs Kerrigan introduced me to a few, but there wasn't really time for..."

"Quite." Dr Lloyd's gaze flicked over to Oliver. "And you, Oliver?"

"The other guys seem very friendly."

Did he mean that? Lisa wondered. It was unlike Oliver to give any concern to the friendliness of others. Perhaps he was just saying what the headmistress wanted to hear, but that too was unlike Oliver.

"I'm glad to hear it. You've both been given maps?" Lisa and Oliver nodded. "You've both been given your timetables?" Lisa and Oliver nodded. "I wish there was time to ease you in, but the term is already underway and, as you are no doubt aware, you will both need to work hard to keep abreast with your fellow students." Lisa and Oliver nodded. "Have either of you got any questions?" Lisa and Oliver shook their heads.

"The rules here are basic enough and no different, I'm sure, to any other school you have attended. With one exception." Dr Lloyd leant intently across her desk. "We allow pupils to go into the village at weekends or, on special dispensation, in the evenings during the spring and summer months. Generally, walking on the moor is also allowed (during the day, with permission) but at the present, that has been revoked. You *will not* go out onto the moor at any time. Do I make myself clear?"

Lisa and Oliver nodded.

They ate dinner in the gloomy refectory, which faced the mountains and so remained in near permanent shadow. By unspoken agreement they sat together, not quite ready to dive into the melee of getting to know people just yet.

"Do you have your own room?" Lisa tried to start a conversation.

"Sharing."

"I've got my own room."

Oliver nodded but seemed to have no further comment on the subject and Lisa gave up, turning her attention instead to the room, taking in the various cliques around the long tables. She had been to enough schools to understand how this worked; you had your class mates, your dorm mates, and your peer group. Your class mates were the people you shared the days with by virtue of your age and nothing else. You worked together and might talk outside of class if you needed help with 'prep', but that was it, unless you were also dorm mates.

In common with many boarding schools, Priory Grange did not simply put everyone of the same age together, believing that children would learn more if they were encouraged to socialise with those of different ages. They did learn more; how to avoid spit balls,

28

how to shower as quickly as possible before anyone else was up, and how to do the bigger kids' work for them. They also learnt division. By splitting the children into different dorms the inhabitants learnt to hate and fear their rivals, to compete with them on the sports field (which the school encouraged) and pick on them elsewhere (which was frowned upon).

Then there was your peer group. Your peers were your tribe. They were the friends you chose, regardless of age or dorm, the place where you were accepted and belonged. You would never betray them. To be part of a peer group gave you the right to treat those who were not, in whatever way you liked. It justified attacking those who were different. More than that; it rewarded it.

"What do you think of the place?" Lisa tried again to engage with Ollie.

He shrugged. "Just school, isn't it."

"You think you'll be happy here?"

"It's fine until the next one."

"Maybe you'll stay at this one." With only two and half terms left, Lisa was optimistic that this was where she would see out her schooldays, but Oliver still had a few years to go. It would be nice to think that he could spend them in one place where he fit in. It would be nice to think that he wanted to fit in.

"Maybe." It was pretty non-committal.

There was a loud clatter from across the room, followed by a peal of laughter and a round of applause. Lisa looked up to see a boy pick himself up from the floor, blushing bright red amongst the sarcastic jeers, and begin to retrieve his tray and cutlery. The broken remnants of his plate were scattered along with his food.

"Watch your step, Knaggs," laughed an older boy, and Lisa could not help noticing that the boy's leg was not fully under the table. She hadn't been watching, but it would have been easy for that boy to trip up the diminutive Knaggs. It was the sort of thing that happened and it seemed to find favour with the rest of the boy's table, who whooped and laughed like hyenas. Amongst the laughers seated about the table was the blonde girl Lisa had met earlier, laughing as hard as any of them. What had her name been? Cristina?

As the older boy stood up, Cristina stood with him, and together they walked across the spilled contents of Knaggs' tray, drawing more laughter from their table. Lisa noticed that Cristina's

29

uniform skirt seemed to have got shorter since they had been introduced, and wondered if it yo-yoed in length depending on the proximity of Mrs Kerrigan. Or possibly that of the boy. He was tall, blond, strongly built and walked with a swagger. He was not what you would call handsome - or at least not what Lisa would have called handsome - but there was a robust confidence in his rugged features and the way he moved that gave him... something. Perhaps charisma.

As the pair approached the table at which Lisa and Oliver were seated, Lisa saw Cristina's eyes light on her. She whispered something to the boy that made her giggle and him smirk. Lisa felt a hot and cold shudder up her back - the nasty sense that someone is laughing about you, and the panic of what might be the source of their amusement. The boy now looked directly at Lisa, no longer amused, but still smiling as he cocked his head to one side.

"Hi. You're new."

Whatever bad impression Lisa had of the boy, it was formed entirely on gut reaction, which was no way to judge a person, and she gave a friendly smile as she replied. "Yes. Hi. I'm Lisa."

"Larry. Larry Glendon." He was one of those people whose personality seems to be projected around them like an aura, almost a gravitational force. Despite herself, Lisa felt a desire to be liked by him.

"Pleased to meet you."

"Pleased to meet you," Cristina parroted from behind and collapsed into giggles.

Larry tried to suppress a smile, but not all that hard. "Yeah, right. 'Pleased to meet you.' May we take tea upon the veranda?"

Irritatingly Lisa felt herself blushing with embarrassment. He was a jerk. All schools had them and the best way to deal with them was to ignore them. But when you were new the bullies liked to come up and make an example of you, to show you who was in charge and to remind everyone else, and no one would defend you because they didn't know you and were just relieved that it wasn't them.

"Crissy says you're in number 6."

Lisa didn't answer, not knowing where this was going.

"Can you hear me?" Larry asked in a sing-song voice. "Can you hear me Lisa Pleased to Meet You? Do you think she's slow?"

30

he asked Cristina.

"I'm in room six." Lisa was infuriated at herself for the meekness in her voice.

"I'll remember," said Larry. "I'm up there from time to time. Keep your window unlocked." His way of saying that school rules about the segregation of boys and girls meant nothing to him. "Hey, don't be like that." He gave Lisa's arm a playful punch and cocked his head again. "Just having a lend of you. Doesn't mean anything. Just a little welcome to the school. Just wanted to say hi."

"Pleased to meet you," added Cristina from behind, making them both laugh again. And not just them. At some point, without Lisa noticing, more of their table had drifted over, ten to fifteen of them, boys and girls of varying ages, backing them up, moving behind them, faces peering over shoulders, jostling for position but always keeping behind their leader.

"Who are you?" Larry turned his attention to Oliver and Lisa felt her muscles stiffen. Making fun of her was one thing - she would tolerate it - but if this prize ass said *anything* against her younger brother then he would have her tray wrapped around his head. That was the deal when you had a sibling. Even one like Ollie.

Oliver looked up mildly, his grey blue eyes deigning to focus on Larry. "I'm Oliver. Lisa's brother."

"Pleased to meet you." Cristina was one of those who, once she had found a joke she liked, stuck with it.

"Pleased to meet you Oliverlisasbrother," said Larry, grinning at finding a new victim to torment. "I'm Larry."

Oliver looked them both up and down. "Okay."

He returned to his food.

Both Larry and Cristina looked a little nonplussed. Unsure how to react to someone who seemed, not just unimpressed by them, but actually disinterested. With a last look at Lisa, they moved on, their group trailing in their wake, running to keep up then falling back, afraid of getting too close.

Lisa had been glad to get a room with a view of the moor, but on a cloudy night, that meant a view of almost nothing. There were no lights across the moor, so when the sun went down, it was plunged into darkness. In the distance you could make out the faint haze of light that marked the village of Naughton, hidden behind the

31

rises of the landscape. But other than that, what Lisa had a view of was darkness.

She knew that she should have made an effort to socialise with the other girls on the corridor that evening. But after dinner she had really not been in the mood. It was the sort of thing that happened in every school - bullying that wasn't really bullying and yet somehow was. If that was the worst you got then you could considered yourself lucky, but it still burnt, and it was hard to brush away. Somehow it made you feel like less of a person. Tomorrow she could make a fresh start, make some friends, find a group that shared her distaste for the Larrys and Cristinas of this world. She had to. This would be a very lonely place to spend eight months with no friends to turn to.

Lisa's eyes returned to the moor. No wonder they had a rule about pupils not venturing out of an evening at this time of year. It was not that late yet, but a person would become completely lost in no time. Why the rule needed to be so insistently delivered was a mystery to Lisa - she loved the place but you couldn't have dragged her out there after dark. What was that line in *The Hound of the Baskervilles* (Sir Arthur Conan Doyle)? '*...Avoid the moor in those hours of darkness when the powers of evil are exalted.*'. But there are always a few people who insist on being rule breakers, who break rules because they are there.

She placed a hand against the glass, shadowing the light so she could peer out. Still nothing. She turned out the light in her room and tried again. Now, as the full moon's luminescence pressed against a thin patch of cloud, she could just make out the landscape, though the humps and bumps of the moor seemed to be composed of darkness itself and...

Lisa started. Something out there had moved. Her breath fogged the window and she wiped it clean before looking out again. Probably a sheep or something, though sheep didn't usually move that fast. Perhaps a stray dog that had gotten itself lost on the moor by night.

The wind whistled eerily through the hills. It sounded almost like an animal, howling in the night.

Chapter 4 - From the Diary of Lisa Hobson

October 23rd
I have decided to start keeping a diary again, and this time I am not going to let it slip and it is going to be a proper diary, recording my life here in this miserable hole. There are going to be proper, literate entries, like Marian's diary in *The Woman in White* (Wilkie Collins) or Mina Harker's in *Dracula* (Bram Stoker). Then years later they can be published as a shocking indictment of the public school system, or a glimpse into the formative years of a literary heavyweight (assuming I become a literary heavyweight). Practically every heroine in period literature seems to keep a diary so how hard can it be? Admittedly they had nothing else to do except sit in the window and embroider while waiting for the next male caller, but even so, it can't take more than half an hour a day and it's not like my social life is keeping me busy.

October 24th
    History sucks.

October 27th
    I never get to the Refectory in time for the pizza to be even warm. Is it possible it was never warm to begin with?

November 2nd
    Pizza cold again.
    Saw fires out on the moor after lights out. Apparently there are gypsies camped out there. Proper ones.

November 4th
    Just saw Mr Tull come through the gates absolutely covered in mud. Soaked up to his waist. Is this a geography teacher thing?

November 15th
    Reading back over the first three weeks of my diary entries, I find that I didn't exactly hit the ground running. It would be easy to give the whole thing up as a dead loss but I'm not going to do that, partly because I do actually want to do this right, and partly because I have no one else to talk to. I don't know why I'm writing this stuff

down, perhaps in the hope that it makes me feel better, or so that, when I'm older and feeling nostalgic for my schooldays, I can be reminded of how bogus nostalgia is.

I'd say that this was just an unfriendly school, but, wonder of wonders, Ollie has actually settled in rather well. More than that Ollie has made friends. There are words I never expected to write. I imagine Mum and Dad are over the moon about this - they may have actually found a school where Ollie can finish his GCSEs and stay through his A-Levels. I guess the ninth time's the charm. Sod's law it would be the place where I really don't fit in, but why the hell should that matter to anyone?

(Later) I got a bit pissy before. Now I've had a cup of tea and a shower (not together) I feel better. The truth is, I've got less than a year of school left, so moving really isn't an option. It's bad luck, but I can't blame Mum and Dad for keeping me here now I'm here. I can blame them for moving me here in the first place but that's a whole other thing. And it's not like I've made no friends at all. (I probably need to write this as if I'm reading it for the first time - I'm bound to forget stuff in the future.)

My first week was very difficult. Getting to know the other girls on the corridor hasn't been easy because everyone already knows each other - they all have a history and I am no part of it. The groups are set. Predictably, Cristina is the alpha dog (can a female be an alpha dog? Alpha bitch might be more accurate. In so many ways). I don't know if her and Larry Glendon are a couple - I don't really care. Sometimes I think they are, sometimes I think they'd just like everyone to think they are and that they're so much more adult than everyone else. There's a group they hang with (or at least a group that hangs around them begging for approval), I'm going to call them 'bullies' because that's essentially all they are - mostly from the sixth form, but weirdly with a few kids of other ages. Fay, Zeffie, Elena and Jane are all very much part of that clique. I hoped that I could get to know the other girls - all outsiders together - but it seems like, if you're an outsider, you don't fraternise with other outsiders, because that just makes you look worse. People don't like the bully group but they dream of being accepted by it. As the uber-outsider, no one wants to talk to me at all. I guess I can't blame them; if they talk to me then Cristina will pick on them even more. But it is very lonely.

34

One day, I think towards the end of my first week (which is actually when I started this diary and why I should have written this stuff down <u>when it happened</u>) I was heading back up to the sixth form corridor when I heard someone crying. I looked into the common room and one of the younger girls - Ollie's age or just under - was curled up in a chair sobbing to herself. I asked if she was okay and she looked at me like I was a monster.

"I'm fine." (I don't remember <u>exactly</u> what she said, but I want to do dialogue so I'll just write down the general sense of it.)

"You don't look fine," I said.

"She's fine."

I nearly jumped out of my skin when that voice came from behind me and I turned around to see Cristina striking a pose in the doorway. Cristina always looks like she's striking a glamour pose, I can't tell if it's deliberate or not.

"She doesn't look it," I replied. I'd been backing down to Cristina all week, but with this crying girl here I suddenly felt protective and more able to stand up, if not for myself, then for her.

"She said she's fine." Fay appeared behind Cristina, way more menacing than anyone with a name like 'Fay' has a right to be.

"She's crying."

"Sometimes girls cry. Maybe she's homesick."

"If she's homesick, she's not fine." (Now I come to write this down, I have to admit that I was talking about Gwen - her name is Gwen; I'll get to that - like she wasn't there.)

"The only thing to do about homesickness is have a cry and get it out of your system," said Cristina.

I took a chance. "Did you make her cry?"

Cristina raised a sharp eyebrow, making her looked like a suspicious weasel, and stalked across the room towards me, her heels clicking noticeably on the floor in the silence that followed my 'accusation'. She came to a stop less than a foot from me, Fay still hanging just behind her.

"What did you say?" Cristina bared her teeth as she spoke.

"I asked if you made her cry." I tried not to sound nervous - this was just some spoilt blonde girl, one good slap and she'd run off to Daddy. Or would she? Something about Cristina makes me nervous. Something in her eyes makes me feel like a field mouse having a staring contest with an owl – it doesn't matter who wins the contest, the mouse is dead either way. I was sweating so my blouse was sticking to my back.

"I wasn't even in the room," Cristina replied, her voice like cut glass.

"Then you're saying you didn't make her cry?" I held my ground but just barely - my legs were desperate to run away and it was all I could do to stop them.

"She doesn't need you protecting her. Do you Gwen?" That was the first time I heard her name, and the first time any of us had bothered to involve her in the conversation.

Gwen looked up with blind terror in her tear-reddened eyes. "Just homesick."

"That's right," said Cristina, her voice thick with false kindness. "Why don't you run along back to your dorm."

Gwen took off like bullet out of a gun.

Cristina turned her focus back to me. "Why don't you run along too?"

"Why don't you bite me?" I'd like to say that it took courage for me to say that, but all it took was a complete lack of thought - the words were out of my mouth before I could stop them.

Cristina smiled, showing sharp, white teeth. "One day, Hobson, I might just do that."

I'm not going to pretend to be any braver than I am in this diary - that scared the shit out of me. But I still felt like maybe I'd won a little victory, like I'd drawn a line in the sand and Cristina hadn't crossed it. Better yet, at lunch the next day when I was sitting in the refectory, alone as usual, Gwen came up to thank me and I asked her to join me. She did and we ate together. I know she's a lot younger than me, which is social suicide, but it felt good to have someone to talk to. Eventually I got up the courage to ask what she had been crying about.

"I was homesick." She wouldn't even meet my eyes.

"No, I mean really."

Gwen looked up at me, then looked back over her shoulder. It was the end of lunch, the room was emptying and none of the bully group seemed to be around.

"One night last week I couldn't sleep. I often can't. I get to worrying and then I just... you know? Anyway, I decided to go down to the chapel – I often sit in there when I can't sleep. As I left the dorm I heard a sound from the stairwell. I went to have a look and I saw Cristina and some of the other girls - the one who was there yesterday..."

"Fay?"

"Her, and some others, all going downstairs. I don't know why but - and I know I'm not supposed to - I followed them down."

"Where were they going?" I was engrossed in her story.

Gwen shook her head. "I don't know. When I got to the bottom of the stairs I looked down the corridor and saw Cristina at the far end looking straight at me. I ran back upstairs as fast as I could, jumped into bed and pulled the covers over my head."

"Then yesterday Cristina spoke to you about it?" I suggested.

Gwen nodded. "She grabbed me by the collar, shoved me back against the wall and said, 'You saw nothing. And if you ever tell anyone anything other than that, then I will come for you. You won't know when, you won't even know it's me. But I will come for you, and I will tear the flesh from your bones.'."

Having stuttered her way through this, Gwen sprang up and ran away. We've spoken since, and I think I can honestly call her the only friend I have here, but we've not talked about that night again, and I'm not going to press her on it.

It's now late, and although I had more to say, I'm wrapping up and going to bed. That was a proper diary entry!

November 16th

What I started off writing yesterday, and never came back to, was that Oliver has settled into Priory Grange better than any other school we've been to. Which isn't hard. Ollie's never settled in anywhere and has a complete block when it comes to making friends. He's smart, he's athletic, girls like him - until they get to know him - but the truth is he doesn't care. He treats anyone who tries to be friends with him with a sort of arch disdain. Now, for some reason, that's actually worked in his favour, and I wish I could be happier about it. It's not sour grapes that he's making friends and I'm not (although that does suck) it's the people he's making friends with.

Because we don't hang out a lot, I didn't notice till after my meeting with Gwen. I was coming out of the main doors of the big house (still struggling to find my way about the place) and, over by

37

the wall, I saw Oliver with Larry Glendon (the ass from dinner our first day and leader of the bully group) and a couple of other boys, whose names I don't know but all bully groupers. I know I'm not the best sister (I'll admit it, writing here) even if I sometimes think that's because Ollie's not the best brother. But siblings can be like that and still do anything for each other. For all that Ollie has driven me crazy over the years, I'm very protective of him and when I think someone might be picking on him then I get a hot prickling feeling up the back of my neck. I immediately headed for the group. Before I got close, I was shoulder-barged out of the way by someone else heading for them. It was Cristina, walking through me as if I didn't exist, this time with Elena in tow.

"Hey." Cristina sidled up to Larry casually and gave him a peck on the cheek. He gave her a confident smirk. Cristina then turned. "Hi Ollie." And she squeezed his thigh!

Oliver looked up towards her with mild interest and gave a barely perceptible nod to acknowledge her.

Cristina shook her head. "He's so damn cool."

"Nothing fazes Ollie," agreed Larry, and various of the group chipped in, making Oliver look up again, a knowing expression on his face.

As subtly as I could (probably not all that subtle) I changed direction away from the group. He wasn't being bullied, he was hanging with his friends and, unhappy as I was with his choice of peer group, I wasn't going to spoil it for him, given this is the first he's ever belonged to. I guess bullies aren't used to people not caring about what they say, and they find Ollie's total disinterest fascinating.

As I wandered away, my stomach in knots, I heard Larry say, "Isn't that your sister?"

"Yes."

"How come you're so cool and she's not?" asked Cristina.

I walked fast so as not to hear the answer my brother gave.

Since then, pretty much every time I've seen Oliver, he's with that group. I like that he has friends. I do. I am not just saying it to convince myself. And on the bright side, I really doubt he has become a 'bully' - Ollie doesn't care enough about other people to hurt them. But I still wish his first real friends weren't such horrible people.

Gotta wrap up. Some dumb, compulsory lecture.

(Later) The lecture was dumb as predicted – 'The Flora and Fauna of Naughton Mire, by Squire Simon Montford'. Who knew there even were squires anymore? Apparently he's a 'friend of the school' and gives a talk every term. Two things made it bearable; firstly that the Squire was hilarious – tripped over his feet, knocked over his notes, knocked his water over his notes, and talked like a character from a P. G. Wodehouse book. I liked him. Secondly, it was introduced by Mr Tull.

It's possible I have a little crush on Mr Tull. In fact, I lay awake for hours the other night wondering if I do, which is probably confirmation. Gwen mentioned him the other day, just in passing, and I went on about how cool he is. He doesn't even teach me.

Next to Gwen, he feels like the only friend I have here. He treats me like a grown up and - I think - he treats me differently to the other pupils. Is that a good thing? Is it a good thing that I'm thinking that? Crush or no crush; he's a nice teacher is all, and that wasn't why I started on this subject.

"This is Naughton Mire." Squire Montford started his lecture with a very green picture of the marsh. "Looks dashed beautiful, what?" (I swear, I'm not making this up; that's how he talks.) "And it is. Dashed beautiful. But a death trap to anything larger than a cat. Dogs, horses, sheep, pigs and - yes, by Jove - people; Naughton Mire has swallowed them all." There was a mass shifting in seats as a lot of the boys became more interested, hoping there would be some disgusting pictures of bog-bloated bodies.

"And yet," the squire went on, "insect life positively teems within it." The boys slumped back again. "I myself have identified five different sub-species of gnat. Let's look at them one by one…"

Interminable is an overused word, but an apt one in this case. The squire bounded about the stage, gesticulating wildly and beaming like a clown. He reminded me of a crane fly - another insect he talked about a lot - all gangly legs, no sense of direction, bumping into things. He remained oblivious to the boredom of his audience and to some members of it making fun of him. I saw the bully group, shaking with laughter as they passed notes and pictures, though Glendon himself remained oddly silent.

When the lecture had finished and the polite applause had faded, everyone trudged for the exit, too weary even to stampede. I was at the far end of a row so was one of the last out. I was almost free when I heard my name called.

"Lisa?"

It was Mr Tull, and I'll admit to feeling a little flutter at him calling me back out of all those children.

"Have you got a moment? If you're not busy."

"Sure," I nodded, casually.

"Great. Just give me a minute." As I stood to one side he turned back to his guest, still flushed from the exertion of his lecture. "Thanks for doing this, sir. I'm sure the children enjoyed it."

"Good show," the squire enthused. He was a much younger man than his manner, his vocabulary, and pretty much everything about him suggested, probably still in his twenties. "Happy to help the wee ones gain a bit of enthusiasm for the Mire. Long as they don't go poking about there, what?"

"I think you underlined its dangers," smiled Mr Tull. "And I have learnt my lesson."

"Jolly glad to hear it."

"If you hadn't shown up when you did it might have cost me more than a pair of trousers and my best boots."

"You wouldn't be the first," the squire admonished.

"But there *are* safe routes?" Mr Tull pressed. "You surely haven't amassed all this knowledge just from standing on the edges."

"Oh, by Jove, no," Squire Montford stressed. "Much study. And yes, there are safe ways. Most of the locals have a working knowledge of the Mire's secret pathways – passed from father to son, don't you know." He beamed with a twinkle in his eye. "Angling for a tour?"

Mr Tull held up his hands. "Geography teacher. I'd be lying if I said it didn't fascinate me."

"We must set a date," the squire enthused. "Anything to stop you charging in half-cocked again."

"Oh no. One near death experience was enough."

The men shook hands as they said goodbye. Maybe it shows how much of a crush I have that I still like Mr Tull even knowing his interest in tedious marshland.

Mr Tull turned back to me. "Sorry about that. Did you enjoy the lecture?"

"Sure."

40

Mr Tull shook his head, clearly not fooled. "It really is an interesting subject, you know. And the squire is an expert, well worth listening to. Anyway, what with you not doing geography, I haven't had a chance to ask how you're settling in."

"Okay." I lied, wondering what this was about. "You?"

He shrugged. "It's a strange school."

The relief I felt was immense. "So it's not just me?"

He shook his head. "There's something different here to any other school I've been to." He eyed me cautiously. "Your brother seems to be making himself at home."

That didn't take long. For a moment I had thought maybe he'd noticed that I was unhappy. But no; it was about Oliver. It's always about Oliver.

"Yeah."

"Do you know much about the group he's hanging out with?"

"No."

"But you don't like them?"

"No. They're..." I wanted to say 'bullies' but you don't grass. I've been in enough schools to know that, and to know that it seldom makes things better when you do.

"Yes?" Mr Tull urged me on.

"Just not my type of people I guess."

He looked disappointed. "If you saw them doing something wrong – something unusual - I hope you would tell a teacher."

"Of course," I lied.

Mr Tull pulled a wan smile. "No you wouldn't. I don't know why I said it. You'll regret it later in life, we all do, but no amount of me telling you that will change anything."

Maybe I should have told him about some of the bullying I've seen - it would make me unpopular but it's not like I've got any friends to lose.

"I'm just sorry Ollie's hanging out with them."

Mr Tull nodded. "Well, you have to make allowances. Human beings still have tribal instincts in their DNA. We are, in essence, pack animals, desperate to belong and to find our place in that social hierarchy. Be grateful that you're too smart to fall for it."

"Oliver's smarter than I am."

Mr Tull smiled. "In some ways, perhaps. But in others, very definitely not." He paused a moment while I glowed with pride. "I

41

wonder if you would do me a favour, Lisa."

"Of course, Mr Tull." I tried not to bite his hand off in my eagerness.

"If you see anything unusual happen around here, let me know."

"I..."

"I'm not asking you to grass anyone up," he added hastily. "I'm not talking about the run of the mill horrors that happen in school - I wish you would tell me about those, and you should, but I know you won't. I'm talking about..." He paused as he tried to decide what he was talking about, running a hand through his sandy blond hair. "I think you'll know it when you see it - and you may never. Just keep an eye out. You've got a very sharp mind," (I'm pretty sure he said very) "and an unrivalled experience of boarding schools - you've seen it all. Tell me if you see something here you've never seen before."

I'm still wondering if I should tell him about Cristina and her friends sneaking out, and the threat Cristina made against Gwen. But is that weird? Or just nasty people being nasty? What's weird?

As I left, Mr Tull called after me. "And keep an eye on your brother."

I don't see why I should. He's fine, he's got plenty of friends. Who's looking out for me?

November 17th

Now I'm wondering if Mr Tull spoke to me yesterday for a reason. Like; did he choose that particular day for a reason? Or maybe so the whole 'weird' thing was in my head because he spoke to me, so I started reading stuff into stuff, like Catherine in *Northanger Abbey* (Jane Austen). Or perhaps I just wanted to come up with something to report to him because then I'd feel like I'd done what he asked. I haven't made up my mind yet and I'm writing this now, at the end of a day spent thinking about it, in the hope that writing it down might give me an answer. Whether it's what Mr Tull was talking about or not, it definitely warrants recording.

After dinner yesterday evening (ate with Gwen. Oliver was sitting with Larry and the bully group again), I headed back to my room to get some work done. I made a cup of tea in the kitchen and managed to share a few words with Josie (when there's no one else

42

about I think we're almost on the point of being friends), then went back to my room to work. I heard the other girls; the usual laughter, chatter and music. It's got so I can recognise tones of voice, so even when I can't hear words, I can tell when someone is being picked on by the sneering tone. But it wasn't a loud night - everyone has work to do and just cos you're a bully doesn't mean you don't care how your exams go.

I was still distracted by my conversation with Mr Tull, so I had trouble focussing on what I was doing and ended up working quite late. When I finished up, I glanced at my watch and found it was close to eleven already. Working by the light of my little lamp, I hadn't noticed how dark it had gotten, and now I got up to draw the curtains and go to bed.

But when I reached the window, something outside caught my eye. There was a light, down by the main gates. On an impulse - or mistaking myself for Sir Henry Baskerville - I put out the lamp, plunging the room into total darkness, then hurried back to the window. The light was a torch, its powerful beam cutting a wedge out of the uniform blackness that cloaked the moor. It passed through the gates and headed out along the road that led to Naughton. There are strict rules about going out after dark (or at all), but I'm sure people break them all the time. (Not because there are cool places to go after dark around here, but just to say that you'd done it.) But it would take someone seriously brazen to sneak out after dark through the main gate, with a torch that looked like Blackpool Illuminations. It took someone very confident or very stupid.

Or it wasn't a pupil.

Tearing myself away from the window, I ran to one of my bags that I still haven't got around to unpacking yet, filled with that stuff we all have, which we cart around with us from home to home and probably never use, until it takes up permanent residence in a drawer alongside light bulbs that proved to be the wrong voltage and batteries that you can't remember if they're spent or not. I pulled out my pocket telescope and returned to the window.

To my surprise, the light had now left the road and struck out into the moor itself. Even more against the rules. By day, a person could get lost on the moor, by night, navigation was almost impossible as all landmarks became invisible. I'd been told that a lot of those kids who snuck out, got caught because they couldn't find their way back until daybreak. Again, the possessor of the light had to be stupid or very confident. Perhaps this was a path they had walked many times before. I raised the telescope to my eye but, owing to its cheapness, all I got was a larger light and a still indistinct figure carrying it. They also seemed to be carrying a plastic bag.

As I was wondering who it could be, something disturbed the figure - the moor is full of weird noises. They turned, and the torchlight briefly illuminated the face. The telescope finally paid off as I recognised Dr Lloyd, looking pale and nervous.

Whatever she had heard seemed to be nothing as she turned back again and continued on her original trajectory across the moor, walking quickly and confidently, backing up my guess that she had walked this way before.

But what was that way? I watched until the light was out of sight then tried to do a bit of mental geography, but my knowledge of the surroundings is very limited. I've been driven across the moor once, but since then I've been confined to quarters. I still can't guess where she was going.

For a long time I sat on the bed, reading *The Castle of Otranto* by Horace Walpole - it may be very influential but so far, I've read better) and checking the window regularly. I must have fallen asleep like that, because when I started awake, my place lost in *Otranto*, the clouds had cleared and the full moon was high in the sky. I peered onto the moor: nothing. I checked my watch: just after three. I undressed, checked the window once more then drew the curtains and got into bed. As I slipped into sleep I heard the wind howling across the moor, sounding almost animal.

Suddenly I was wide awake. A horrendous noise had started me from sleep, coming from outside, from the moor. An inhuman sound, like nails on a blackboard, drawn out into grating and guttural squeals. Leaping up I pulled the curtains open and peered out. The moon lit the moor but I still saw nothing that could explain that sound. There it was again, rending the night, echoing across that empty expanse like the death throes of some tortured animal, a cry wrenched from its soul. My blood ran cold and my teeth seemed to itch with fear. I couldn't tell where it was coming from, I just wanted it to stop, which it finally did.

I slept only fitfully then, tossing and turning. In the early hours of morning I heard footsteps from the corridor and whispered laughing. I wondered if anyone else had heard what I had and had also struggled to sleep, but I was afraid to ask.

At around half five I got up and looked out the window again. I hadn't expected to see anything but, to my surprise, there in the still dark of the late autumn morning was Dr Lloyd, walking back towards the school. She no longer carried the bag she had earlier. I watched cautiously through cracked curtains as she entered the gates and went straight to the main house.

So what have I learnt? Dr Lloyd goes across the moor late at night with a bag of something. I don't know where she goes but wherever it is she leaves the bag there and then comes back early the next morning.

Doesn't amount to much really does it? She's well within her right to do these things and when you put it all together I guess there's nothing 'suspicious' about them. I've nothing to connect her to the noises I heard and it's far more likely those noises came from nocturnal animals going about their business – I'm not a country girl and I can't even say if what I heard was animals fighting or making baby animals. I heard two cats going at it once and it was like the end of the world! Strange sounds in the night – like Emily in *The Mysteries of Udolpho* (Anne Radcliffe).

And yet I can't help wondering. Maybe because it came so quick on the heels of my conversation with Mr Tull. Should I tell him? I feel better grassing up a teacher than I would a pupil. On the other hand he might just tell me not to be so silly, and that that wasn't what he had in mind at all.

I'm not sure writing this down has helped me decide. I'll try sleeping on it. Should sleep well after last night, totally zonked.

November 18th

Great news! (And about time.) Dr Lloyd has lifted the ban on sixth formers going out across the moor during the day. We have to be back by sundown and there's a whole bunch of other restrictions (no idea how she expects to enforce them) but we can go for walks. I've been wanting to explore the moor since I got here and I can't wait. Perhaps I can figure out where Dr Lloyd might have been going two nights ago. I'll take a walk out in that direction for myself and then decide whether or not to tell Mr Tull.

I feel like things are looking up.

Speaking of Mr Tull, he must have been out early this morning as I saw him coming in through the gates first thing looking exhausted. Maybe he has a girl in the village. That's going to prey on my mind.

Chapter 5 – One Man and His Dog

There was, Lisa recalled, a line in *The Hound of the Baskervilles* (Sir Arthur Conan Doyle), '*The fresh beauty of the following morning did something to efface from our minds the grim grey...*' She couldn't remember it exactly, but the general message was that everything looked a hell of a lot better in the light of a new morning. She wondered if there was a name for having the exact opposite reaction.

In the evenings when she could shut herself away in her room to focus on schoolwork, and when the moor was shrouded in atmospheric darkness, Lisa found that she could better cope with being at the Priory Grange. In the quiet gloom she could forget her worries. But then the morning came, and she had to leave the safety of her room to face another day of chill weather, persistent drizzle and unpleasant neighbours. Everything looked worse in the morning, no matter what Dr Watson had to say on the matter.

That said, this particular morning did at least have a few things to recommend it, most notably that she had study period all afternoon, which freed her up to go walking on the moor. It might not have fallen quite within the strict spirit of 'study' but, Lisa argued with herself, getting work done in her room was not always easy when there were other people about. On the moor there was at least peace and quiet to think, and thinking was an essential part of study.

That was flimsy justification to say the least, but it would do for someone who was going stir crazy and had been gazing out for weeks at the romantic landscape of her dreams but been prevented from exploring it. And, were further justification needed, she had been told by Mr Tull to keep an eye out for anything unusual, and a trip across the moor might tell her whether Dr Lloyd's nocturnal journey came under that heading. So she was practically going out on the instructions of a teacher.

After an interminable morning in class, Lisa changed into more suitable clothing and signed out in the day book.

"Going somewhere?" asked Mrs Kerrigan, somewhat unnecessarily Lisa thought.

"Just for a walk on the moor."

Mrs Kerrigan nodded. "The perimeters of the marsh are well

marked, but if you feel the ground starting to get soft then for goodness sake, turn around." It had been years since the marsh had claimed any victim, leave alone a pupil, but it was always a concern.

"I will."

"And be back well before dark."

"I will."

Mrs Kerrigan nodded in a way that suggested she was much happier when pupils sneaked out, because it devolved her of blame if anything happened to them.

Stifling the urge to run, Lisa walked away from the north wing, passed the main house and went through the main gates. A wire fence flanked the road on both sides on the approach to the school, and it occurred to Lisa that that was why Dr Lloyd had followed the road a ways before cutting across the moor. She now did the same, and felt a shudder of excitement at following in the footsteps of her quarry.

Stomping up the tussocky incline, Lisa paused. Acres of undulating wilderness spilled out before her, forbidding and yet welcoming, a landscape that seemed unchanged since the Iron age, brooding under a slate grey sky. A tremendous weight seemed to lift from her shoulders. The Priory Grange and everyone in it faded to a bad dream that she could now shrug off. Maybe it was being out of those claustrophobic confines, maybe it was her love of the moorland landscape, or maybe it was just the refreshing feeling of being outdoors, but Lisa felt as if she had come home. The sharp wind blew in her face, bringing with it a sting of light rain, blanching her cheeks, but she could not have been more at ease. She felt like laughing. Or possibly dancing. But decided against either. You could take the girl out of the school, but the paranoia of being seen doing something embarrassing was not so easily dispelled.

Happy though she was to be out here, Lisa did now find a slight problem with her plans. The moor looked very different down here at ground level to how it had from her window at night. She had vague idea of the direction in which Dr Lloyd had walked but it was hard to keep going in any consistent direction thanks to the undulations of the ground. You tried to head one way and ten minutes later found that you were curving wildly off course. You weaved your way around gorse thickets, random cows, pools of murky water, and muddy tracks where sheep had ploughed their way

48

through *en masse*. Hillocks reared up to force a detour, ditches appeared suddenly in front of you, the earth split to reveal the rock within which rose to make a craggy wall blocking your path.

On reflection, Lisa decided that if she got onto high ground then it might be easier to replicate the view from her window, so rather than *going* where Dr Lloyd had gone she would be able to *see* where the headmistress had gone. A high ridge of runkled ground - the foothills of the more mountainous regions to the west - attracted her attention (and gave her an overwhelming urge to start yelling 'Heathcliffe!' from their summit). It was a longish trek, and the afternoon was starting to wane as Lisa plodded up the steep slope, chest heaving, shoes caked in mud, sweating heavily and yet chilled to the bone. For a while, during the final ascent, when the hillside began to resemble the great north face of Everest, Lisa's boundless enthusiasm for the moor started to seep away, but it returned with a rush when she reached the top and saw it spread out below her.

"Wow," she breathed. When Malcolm had driven them across it, the moor had not seemed that big. But when you were in it, and when you got up high enough to really see it, only then did you get a sense of its true scale. Areas that she had come to think of as being at the fringes of the moor suddenly revealed yet more moor beyond them. The hills no longer seemed a perimeter wall, but just a topographical blip in the middle. There, nestled like a child's toys on a brown carpet, was the village of Naughton - Lisa could make out the train tracks winding away from it. Down and to her left she could see the lush green of Naughton Mire, and she shuddered at the memory of Squire Montford's lecture. And there... There was a man on horseback coming towards her.

Lisa's first thought was to run. Then she wondered why on earth she should do such a ridiculous thing. This was not the wild west; people approaching on horseback did not portend of anything terrible. Which did nothing to make her any less nervous as the rider came closer, moving with no great sense of urgency, but now clearly making for her.

The horse was a magnificent animal. Lisa knew nothing about horses except that 'magnificent animal' was considered the standard compliment, and this horse was impressive enough to warrant it. She now saw that its slow pace was dictated by a medium-sized dog, padding along beside it, its tongue lolling, wearing an expression of manic happiness. Then there was the rider. He was younger than Lisa had expected, probably not much older than her. For a moment, she wondered if he could even be a pupil of the Priory Grange, though the horse and dog seemed to preclude that. He wore a flat cap, from under which, unruly dark hair fought to escape, and satisfyingly rustic clothes. If she had had to guess, Lisa would have put him down as a blacksmith's apprentice or stable hand, the sort of character who has a brief but intense affair with the lady of the manor in chapter seven and is given a beating with a stout cudgel. He was also, Lisa's brain tactfully noted, very handsome. He had a rugged charm about him that went well with his clothes, and with his arriving on horseback in the middle of a moor. Lisa wondered if it was possible that she had in fact passed out from exhaustion halfway up the ridge and was having an hallucination inspired by some of her favourite books.

"Hi." Lisa was actually quite proud that she was the first to speak.

"Afternoon." The boy's accent (boy? man? Lisa could go either way) wasn't as pronounced as Lisa had expected, but frankly she could see a positive side to that.

With the effortless grace of an experienced rider, the boy swung a leg over the neck of his steed and dropped to the ground, an effect only slightly marred by almost landing on his dog.

"Dammit, Moose. Careful."

"Moose?"

The boy gave a lopsided shrug. "You don't like the name?"

"Just wondering why."

The boy took the dog's head and guided its permanently happy face toward Lisa. "See? Moose. Right away. That was the name that popped into my head when I first saw him."

"Okay." It certainly hadn't been the name that had popped into Lisa's. "What type of dog is he? (I'm assuming 'he')."

"Bit of this and a lot of that," grinned the boy. "Moose the mongrel." His eyes flicked up and down, giving Lisa a quick once over and apparently liking what they saw. He stood up. "And what's your name?"

"Lisa. Lisa Hobson."

"It's pretty."

"It's boring."

"Well my parents named me Talbot, so I wouldn't go around complaining about boring."

"Fair point," Lisa smiled.

The boy gave her a look of mock effrontery. "What? You don't like Talbot? I'll have you know that name's got history."

"You mean your father didn't like it either?" suggested Lisa.

Talbot laughed and nodded. "Or my grandfather. Generations of pissed off Talbots, determined to settle the score by inflicting it on their sons. It's like a family curse. Or a plague on the firstborn."

Lisa laughed. He had a nice voice that suited his appearance, and a nice sense of humour, as well as being nice looking. All in all... nice. When was the last time she had laughed like this? When was the last time she had chatted to someone like this? Gwen was a friend, but there always seemed an edge to their conversations, perhaps because of the age difference. This was comfortable, easy, immediate.

Lisa checked herself. Pleasant company had been severely at a premium recently so she might be overreacting. You didn't give the farm away just because it had been a while since you'd met someone who was actually friendly.

"What about the horse? Does he have a name?"

"Forrester."

"He's handsome."

"He takes after his master," said Talbot.

"Really? Who owns him?"

Talbot laughed again. "Fair enough. You win that one. What are you doing up here anyway? I don't recall seeing you around before and... well we don't get a lot of new faces up here."

"I'm at the school," admitted Lisa, making sure that she added, "Final year."

"Ah." Lisa had watched Talbot's face go on a little journey through discovering that she was still in school to the reassurance that she was old enough to be almost not. "Enjoying it?"

"No. Although I guess there are worse places to be." She looked out across the view again, letting the wind blow through her hair and hoping that it made her look windswept and interesting, and not just a mess. "It is beautiful."

"In its way," Talbot agreed. "I've lived here all my life, but from up here it can still make you look."

51

For a few moments, which Lisa enjoyed more than any she had spent since arriving in Naughton, they surveyed the scene in silence.

"If you don't mind me asking," Talbot went on, "what are you doing up *here*? The school kids - if you'll pardon the expression - don't usually stray this far. They go to the village or they find someplace out of sight to have a smoke (or something else they're not supposed to be having). And you don't look like you planned on coming this far."

Lisa frowned. "What makes you say that?"

"Your shoes."

Lisa looked down at her feet. She was wearing shoes, she knew she was, but it was no longer possible to verify, so caked were they in mud.

"Probably need a new pair."

"Probably. So... why are you up here?"

Did Lisa want to entrust the details of her mission to a stranger? She did like Talbot, but she had only just met him and was not one hundred percent sure that she trusted him. Which wasn't the end of the world - strangers you met on the moor riding magnificent horses were not meant to be trustworthy on sight, they were meant to prove themselves trustworthy with time, after you had got past their gruff, dark exterior. Maybe it was best to just leave his question unanswered and see if he noticed.

"What's out there?" Lisa pointed in the rough direction in which she thought Dr Lloyd had been heading the other night.

Talbot followed her finger. "Not much. Which is the case pretty much any way you point. There's the mill."

Lisa recalled Malcolm's guided bus tour. "Ralph Matthews' mill?"

"I suppose we're calling it his till someone else steps up. He's dead, you know."

"I know. Anything else?"

Talbot considered the question, his brow attractively furrowed. "Oh; there's the mine."

"Mine?"

He pointed. "Underneath that hill there. Abandoned now. Least as far as I know. Slate mine from the nineteenth century. Never yielded much to be honest. How come you're interested?"

Lisa shrugged as casually as she was able. "Just trying to get

52

my bearings. New place. New surroundings. I thought I might take a walk out there one of these days and I was wondering what there was to see."

"Well, if you need a guide..."

He left it hanging and so did Lisa, though there was a lot more going on inside. He was awfully handsome, and he rode a horse and had a dog and was a salt of the earth working man who strode about these hills letting the wild wind cleave across his rugged features and ruffle his untamed hair. Maybe that was too little to base yet another crush on, but it was a hell of a lot better than the pampered public school snobs with whom she was incarcerated.

"What are you doing up here?" asked Lisa, moving the subject away from her own still unexplained presence.

"Checking on the sheep," said Talbot, unaware of how much his answer thrilled Lisa. It wasn't quite blacksmith's apprentice or stable hand, but a shepherd who tended his flock from horseback was still a serious tick in the 'humble yet proud' romantic cliché column. "Something spooked them a few nights back and they're all over the place. They usually find each other pretty quick (sheep are like that) but then they just stay wherever they are. And that could be just about anywhere."

"How hard can it be to find a flock of sheep?" asked Lisa.

Talbot clicked his tongue and shook his head. "Townie. Trust me, there's all kinds of places they can hide out here." He paused. "You want to help me look? If you don't mind getting your shoes even muddier."

Yes, said Lisa's mind instantly. The rest of Lisa was a more circumspect, but a look at her watch confirmed she had a little time yet. "Sure. If you think I can help."

They walked along the ridge, Talbot leading Forrester by his bridle while Moose ran along beside Lisa, to whom he seemed to have taken a fancy. Truth be told, Lisa's dating experience was pretty limited. What with sitting exams, moving schools and a natural shyness that sometimes came across as diffidence, she had never really had much to do with boys. Talbot was somehow different; though she found him more instantly attractive than other boys she had dated (for want of a more accurate word), she felt at ease around him, as if she was talking to a friend. Did that mean he wasn't interested and they were in the famous 'friend zone'? Lisa hoped not, but also found that she wouldn't necessarily mind too much if they were, as long as they could keep hanging out. Or maybe it was the setting that made things comfortable. This wasn't meeting up behind the changing rooms or sitting together at lunch (the two staples of in-school dating), they were looking for sheep. It wasn't an obviously romantic activity, and certainly wouldn't be recommended for a first date by any of the best dating guides, and yet, to Lisa, it seemed like the ideal way to get to know a man. It was very romantic indeed.

Right up until they found the sheep.

"Hell's teeth," breathed Talbot.

Lisa said nothing but looked the other way. She prided herself on not being a girlie girl, and would never have described herself as squeamish, but this... It was more than she could stand.

The bodies of the sheep had been hideously mutilated. At least three of them had been physically torn in half - and 'torn' was definitely a better word than 'cut'. The head of one had parted company with its body, all saving a thin shred of stretched flesh, and now stood on its ragged neck, eyes wide and glassy, staring at Lisa. Most had simply had their bellies ripped open so their gory insides spilled out onto the ground, turning the dirt to ruddy mud. Limbs had been pulled from parent sockets; gobbets of crimson flesh were scattered about; blood-soaked wool hung in tattered garlands from the bushes. At a glance it would have been impossible to tell how many sheep there were there in that muddled and mismatched mess of ovine dismemberment, but at least ten, Lisa guessed. All apparently slaughtered in a frenzy and with vicious intent.

A cloud of ravens, which had taken off when Talbot and Lisa arrived, spooked by their approach, now started to return, landing on the ground and hopping closer. This feast was clearly a few days old, greening at the edges, moving with maggots, but that did not concern them.

"What the hell did this?" breathed Lisa, risking another glance, revolted but unable to resist the urge to look.

Talbot shook his head. "I don't know. The same thing as last month. There's something on the moor. A wild dog. Maybe something escaped from a zoo."

"I thought that was an urban legend."

"It happens. Big cats and the like. Maybe a wolf. Some

54

animal."

"Maybe the same thing that killed Ralph Matthews?" Lisa suggested.

"Maybe. Come on, you don't want to stay here."

Normally Lisa would have objected to being treated like a child or a fragile woman, but in this case she was happy to allow herself to be led away. There had been something about the scene that had gone beyond the simple, bloody horror of it. It was chilling in another way that she could not quite put a name to. Animals killed to eat, didn't they? Although she would have guessed that those sheep were missing some bits, there was a great deal left that had not been eaten. And what sort of animal needed to kill that many sheep to feed anyway? As she had stared at the carnage, the thought had insinuated its way into her mind that whatever had done this horrible thing, had enjoyed it.

Her thoughts strayed back to a few nights ago and the hideous sounds she had heard from the moor. The sounds of sheep being torn apart? It was certainly possible.

For a long while they walked in silence, not with any particular direction in mind beyond 'away'. This was not how it was supposed to go, Lisa considered, when you met handsome strangers on the moor. It was not supposed to end in dead sheep. It had certainly put a dampener on things between them - if there had been 'things' between them.

"I should head back to school," said Lisa, finally. The afternoon was wearing on and darkness stole up quickly at this time of year.

"Of course," Talbot nodded. "I can walk you back if you like."

"Is it on your way?"

"Not remotely. I'd actually be going a very long way out of my way, and yet I'm still offering. Because I'm that kind of a guy."

Lisa had still not made up her mind what 'kind of a guy' Talbot was, but she laughed and felt a bit better again. It would be so easy to get caught up in this situation. And given the general unhappiness of her existence at the Priory Grange, it would be pretty understandable, wouldn't it?

A lifetime of being 'nothing special', of being the 'also ran', of being 'average', hovered at the back of Lisa's mind. It was nice to meet someone who seemed to think that she was more than all those things.

"I can walk myself back," she said, finally. "But I do appreciate you being that kind of guy. All the guys I meet are rich, spoiled brats."

Talbot nodded, an odd look on his face. "I suppose so. It's that kind of school."

"Well, I'm there too."

"But you're not enjoying it."

"No."

"I feel I probably should clear one thing up," Talbot continued, taking a deep breath. "It occurs to me that, without any ill-intent - and in fact quite unintentionally - I may have misled you through my appearance and the fact that I was looking for sheep and so on."

"They're not your sheep?"

"Well, yes, they are," Talbot hedged. "An awful lot of stuff around here is mine. At least, my family's. I don't think I told you my surname, which is Conliffe. Whether or not that means anything to you..."

What was it Malcolm had said during the drive from the station? Something about the 'Conliffe Estate' and 'Sir John Conliffe'.

"Your family are the local landowners?"

Talbot pulled a face. "One of the local landowners. Not the only one; there's the Montfords, the Byingtons. But one of the larger ones to be sure. I'm guessing that maybe you had me down as a sort of farmhand, maybe a poacher or something. The honest toil type. I'm afraid I'm actually quite wealthy."

"Right."

"So the bad news is," Talbot continued, "I probably qualify as one of the rich, spoiled brats you were talking about. The good news is that; those brats at your school? I could buy and sell them."

"That wealthy?"

Talbot threw up his hands in a 'what can you do' kind of gesture. "Embarrassingly so. You have to be very rich to dress like this." He displayed his coarse, working clothes, and Lisa couldn't help laughing. He was right of course. The rich dress well because they can, but the very rich dress poorly for exactly the same reason. "I hope this isn't a tremendous disappointment."

Lisa sighed theatrically. "I'm afraid it is."

56

"Thought so."

"But I would feel bad knocking a man back on the same day he lost his sheep."

Talbot grinned, a spark of optimism in his eyes. "So if I were to, for instance, suggest seeing you again sometime?"

Lisa's heart pattered excitably in her chest - men so seldom asked her out. It was exciting. "I would consider it."

He wasn't what she had assumed, but that was her fault for making a whole bunch of assumptions based on literary clichés. He had not lied to her or even misled her, he had been honest and friendly and decent from the start and he was still that person - nothing had changed. That said, there was a guilty corner of disappointment in Lisa. She had wanted the story. She also wanted to be the type of person who was attracted to 'honest toilers', as Talbot had put it. It was disappointing to find out that she was attracted to the uber-wealthy. It felt as if she had let herself down and failed to live up to her own standards. But when you came down to it, a person was a person, and a nice person was a nice person. The snide tormenting of the rich kids at the school seemed no part of Talbot's nature. How you were born and with how much money did not dictate what type of person you were; everyone is free to make that decision for themselves.

"I've got to go up to London for a little while," said Talbot. "Maybe as long as a month."

"That's not so long."

"Can I write to you?"

Lisa laughed. "You can call if you like."

Talbot laughed back. "Not round here you can't. No mobile signal and the landline is a bit dicey. If you're going to be here a while, get used to pen and paper."

"Then, yes. You can write."

"Can I see you when I get back?"

It was a very honest and open question, suggesting that there was no pressure on Lisa and she retained the right to say no.

"Yes."

The sun was barely visible behind the hills as Lisa hurried back through the school gates. The bottoms of her trousers were caked in mud and her shoes were probably not salvageable. Her clothes were wet from the rain that had started in earnest on her way back, her coat was torn from where she had snagged it on a bramble, her face was pinched with cold and her hair had been re-styled by wind and rain into something resembling tumbleweed. But she felt better than she had for a long time.

"Been for a walk?"

Yesterday, if her favourite teacher had seen her in such a state, Lisa would have been mortified, but now it seemed less important.

"Seems like the squire's lecture inspired you more than you let on?" Mr Tull suggested with a smile.

"Maybe," Lisa shrugged.

"See anything interesting?"

"I don't know about interesting." Lisa described what she had found on the hill, skirting around the presence of Talbot.

Mr Tull pulled a face. "Sounds revolting. Out on the ridge above the mire?" He pointed vaguely.

"Yeah."

"Right." He nodded to himself, thoughtfully. "I might tell Dr Lloyd. Don't need the younger children seeing that." He hurried off.

Back in the north wing, and still buzzing with the events of the day, Lisa took the steps up to the sixth form corridor two at a time.

"You look like you've been dragged through a hedge." Cristina greeted her as she reached the corridor.

Lisa smiled back. "Yeah. But after a shower I'll look better, and you'll still be... well; you."

She entered her room, considering that that had been a perfect end to a perfect day.

As she sat in her room later, the mud washed from her skin and her hair newly brushed, Lisa decided to tell Mr Tull about seeing Dr Lloyd walking out the other night. Perhaps it wasn't important, but now she had established that there was nothing out that way but an empty mill and a disused mine, it seemed more suspicious. Also, Lisa had seen first-hand how potentially dangerous the moors were. Something must have compelled Dr Lloyd to take that risk. And after all; what was the worst that could happen? Mr Tull could dismiss as her as a foolish girl, but that no longer seemed quite so terrible.

'Perhaps I am fickle...' Lisa wrote in her diary that evening, as she tried to order the events of the day. But although it was Talbot

Conliffe who dominated the diary, her dreams that night were of blood and torn flesh. The lifeless eyes of sheep stared at her, and in the background, those terrible screams echoed in her sleeping mind.

Chapter 6 – Excerpts From the Diary of Lisa Hobson

November 20th

I decided to act on last night's resolution straight away, before I changed my mind, so I spoke to Mr Tull before classes began.

"What can I do for you, Lisa? Not found more dismembered sheep I hope."

"You know how you told me to look out for anything out of the ordinary?"

He raised his eyebrows. "Don't tell me you've spotted something already?"

That immediately made me nervous again. He clearly wasn't expecting anything. Was I making the thing with Dr Lloyd more than it was just because he asked me? I almost chickened out, but stuck with it.

"I don't know if this is anything - I'm still not really clear what I'm supposed to be looking for - but..." And I told him what I'd seen earlier this week.

Mr Tull listened carefully, seeming far more interested than I thought he would, and when I'd finished he said, "Are you sure about where she was heading?"

I shrugged. "I've no idea where she was heading. But I'm sure about the direction."

He nodded. "Good answer." Then he shrugged and grinned. "Well, I'm sure Dr Lloyd just enjoys a nocturnal stroll, but thanks anyway. And do keep your eyes open. I'd rather you told me something completely innocent, like this, than ignored something important."

I felt like a complete idiot, like I'd wasted his time, and I couldn't stop feeling like that for the rest of the morning. So, at lunch, I went back to see him again to apologise. His classroom was empty when I got there, so I checked the back office. That was empty too. But as I was about to leave, I caught sight of something on Mr Tull's desk. Open across it was a map of the moor with lines drawn on it and four circles in red ink.

Of course, he's geography teacher and they're entitled to draw lines on maps, but my strong impression was that the red circles were around the mill, the mire, the hill where Talbot and I found the dead sheep, and the fourth <u>might</u> mark the mine Talbot had pointed out. The first had a cross slashed angrily through it in black biro, while the others were question marked.

As I was leaving I bumped into Josie. "Mr Tull's not in there is he?"

"No."

She shook her head. "He missed a class this morning. He's gonna catch hell from Dr Lloyd."

He must have left straight after I spoke to him. Where did he go?

(Later) Just saw Mr Tull coming back across the moor. It's a big moor, I guess he could have gone anywhere. But from what I could see, he was taking the same route as Dr Lloyd did the other night.

Nothing else to report.

November 21st

I had planned to go out today and follow the same path as Dr Lloyd and Mr Tull - maybe even find Mr Tull's footprints, which would surely still be visible in the mud of the moor - but the weather has taken a turn for the worse. Rain, gusty winds, hail; the works. Any footprints will be long gone, and even if I thought I could bear it, Mrs Kerrigan has forbidden anyone going across the moor until the weather eases. Don't know when that'll be.

The weather hasn't stopped Mr Tull from going out again, I guess heading for Naughton village, since he drove.

November 23st

I don't know the details (I never know the details) but Mr Tull is in trouble with Dr Lloyd. There was the missed class the other day, but rumour is that they also had an argument over something in Naughton.

November 25th

I have lapsed from writing regular entries, perhaps because the curious events of the previous week have died away. I never intended this diary to be anything other than a diary - certainly not a record of some spurious investigation that's all in my head (feeling *Northanger Abbey* again – not even a book I'm that fond of). I need to get back to normality.

I went to the post room at lunch, not expecting anything, and found a parcel. Opened it, thinking it must be a care package from Mum and Dad, and found a pair of hiking boots. Seriously expensive. Inside one of the boots was a note: 'If we're going to look at the mill and the mine then you'll need these. Talbot.'

The weather is slowly improving, but I'm now minded to wait until Talbot gets back before exploring further. I did sort of promise.

This afternoon I saw Mr Tull going out across the moor with Squire Montford, both wearing welly boots, chatting and laughing. I guess Mr Tull is getting his guided tour of the mire. Really can't understand the appeal. Mr Tull always seems to be going somewhere recently, out across the moor or to the village. I guess geography teachers get excited when they're surrounded by all that geography. Or maybe he's doing some Christmas shopping.

December 1st

I'm still torn by what to think about Ollie's 'friends'. I shouldn't put the word in inverted commas, because they clearly are his friends, I just don't like to think of them that way. I saw a kid with a pile of books, walking to class, and five of them, led by Elena, started shoving him, trying to make him drop the books. They'd dash in to push him then fall back, giggling and watching him totter, the five of them circling him, attacking from all sides as the poor kid got more and more flushed and upset until the books spilled to the muddy ground. He probably got in trouble with a teacher for that, but I bet he didn't say how it had happened.

I could have stepped in to help but I didn't. I told myself it wouldn't make any difference, and it almost certainly wouldn't, but shouldn't I have tried? It's so hard to stand up to bullies when they're in a group. I don't know if it's because they outnumber you or because you secretly want to be part of it; to be in on the joke. I've never seen them unhappy. Which doesn't seem fair.

But that was my original point. I don't like Ollie hanging around with them - though I haven't seen him bullying anyone - but he is happier than I've ever seen him, and more alive than I've ever seen him. He looks like he's woken up. Seeing him with that group, with Glendon and Cristina and the rest, he looks like a different boy to the one I've always known; running with them, laughing and play-fighting. He's still the one who doesn't kowtow to Glendon - Ollie's always aloof. I guess I'm pleased about that.

December 6th
Not a brilliant day. Managed to catch up to Oliver at lunch to talk about Christmas.

"What about it?" he asked, hunching away from me into a doorway. He was beaming like a Cheshire cat when I stopped him, his eyes wide and glassy, but as soon as he saw me he seemed to contract into himself.

"I thought maybe, since we're out in the middle of nowhere, we could ask permission to go shopping in Naughton together one weekend? I doubt there's much, but we could pick up something for Mum and Dad."

Irritable tics flicked across Ollie's face. "Think Mum and Dad'll care? They sent us here. They know it's not exactly Regent Street."

"Nice to make the effort though."

He backed further away. "Pretty busy."

"With your friends?"

"Something wrong with that?"

I wanted to scream 'YES!' but couldn't. "Of course not."

"Well then." He shrugged. "I mean; yeah, you're right. It'd be nice. Maybe don't have to go together though."

"Sure. I can go with Gwen."

"Whatever. I've gotta go." He glanced quickly up and down the corridor before hurrying out past me then breaking into a run, and I realised that he didn't want to be seen with me. That was what all his strange behaviour was about.

(Later) Is it possible Ollie is on something? Does that sound crazy? Does there need to be some malign reason for him being happy and full of life? Am I just jealous? He just seems so different. Then again, I always wanted him to be different – to be more normal. Now he's normal; a jerkish teenager like any other. And I'm still not happy.

December 10th
Haven't written much recently. Not much to say - though I know that's no excuse. Life continues normal. Work, study, Cristina being a bitch. Got another letter from Talbot (got a few in fact) and

63

the fact that he is forced to send me letters rather than email, text, facebook or something, just enhances my stupid romantic notion of our 'relationship'. I like that he wants to keep in touch as he had to go away so soon after our one meeting, but the tone of some of his letters is starting to bother me. We really don't know each other that well yet. How do I say 'cool it' without making him think I don't like him? I think it'd be easier in person, and I think he'll respect my wanting to go slow. Everything will be easier when he's back, but it's starting to sound like he'll be coming back up north at the same time I'm heading down south for Christmas, putting a two month gap between our meeting and our first 'date'. That puts quite a lot of a pressure on it.

It's kind of nice to be writing about girlie stuff rather than mysterious headmistresses and dismembered sheep.

There was an argument outside the south wing (the boy's wing) this afternoon. Apparently, Glendon and some of his group were trying to go out onto the moors, but thick clouds have made today very dark, and Mr Tull told them they couldn't go. Rather than doing as he was told (or pretending to then sneaking out, like he normally would) Larry snapped back at Mr Tull, who gave him detention. Larry then flew off the handle, yelling and snarling at Mr Tull, even threatening him. I was watching from a distance (felt like most of the school was) but I could see the veins standing out on Larry's face and the tendons popping in his neck. I honestly thought for a moment he might take a swing at Mr Tull. Glendon was sent to see Dr Lloyd and the grapevine says his parents will be sent an official warning.

Mr Tull himself is still in the doghouse with Dr Lloyd. Still no idea why.

Maybe it's my imagination but it feels like there is tension in the school. More than usual. There's another big storm coming, that's for sure.

December 17th

It's lunchtime but I am still shaking from what happened this morning, and can still feel the pain on the back of my hand.

The weather has been horribly close recently, like there's a weight of weather waiting to happen, teasing us with constant rain, pressing down on us before it finally explodes into something more epic. I find nights like that very difficult to sleep through, or maybe there's stuff on my mind. Either way, I slept fitfully and woke around five thirty feeling horrid. I went for a glass of water and almost slipped over in my fluffy bed socks. The floor of the corridor was wet.

At first I thought the roof was leaking - which seems bound to happen sooner or later - then I saw the foot prints. Wet, bare footprints led from the landing door to Jane's room. Had she been outside?

I only took a moment to decide – although it was against the rules, I went out of the door and crept down the stairs, following the prints by the dull, yellow glow of the low energy security lights set into the wall. They led almost all the way down through the building, and I remembered Gwen's story of how she had seen the bully girls of the sixth form going down those stairs the week I arrived. Jane must have been really drenched to leave prints all the way back up to the sixth form corridor. On the first floor, the prints turned left and I was plunged into darkness as I followed them (or at least went in the direction from which they seemed to come). They stopped at a window in the third form locker room, looking out straight along the rain-slicked roof of the garage where teachers' park. Just beyond it, barely visible now, was the wall of the school.

Of course, Jane could have come down here to smoke – it was a good window for that. But it was hard to shake the feeling that, if you wanted to sneak out by night, this was the best window from which to do it. It was not overlooked and it was only a short run to the wall from the garage. Also, if Jane had come down here to smoke or meet a boy or anything like that, why would her feet be wet?

With my mind turning over the possibilities, I went back the way I had come.

The corridor was silent when I crept back in. I stole back to my room like a ninja in pink bed socks and closed the door gratefully behind me. Immediately I felt a breeze. Had I left the window open?

"Hello Lisa."

I started in terror at the male voice that came from the shadows in the corner of my room. Larry Glendon leant forward, a shaft of greyish, early morning light through my curtains catching his face, illuminating bared teeth and narrowed eyes.

"Crissy tells me that you've been snooping."

Before I could recover myself enough to answer, Glendon leapt toward me, bounding across my bed like an animal, grinning horribly. I tried to shriek but no sound came as I wrenched the door open and hurled myself into the corridor, Glendon's laughter seeming to follow me out.

"Going somewhere, Lisa?"

Instantly Fay and Zeffie were to my right, waiting for me.

I made a dive for the exit, but suddenly Jane blocked my path. She lunged at me, and I blundered blindly back down the corridor. Glendon came out of my room, still grinning, and the three girls converged behind him, their unblinking eyes boring into me as they stalked closer.

With nowhere else to go, I ran into the kitchen. Elena and Cristina seemed to be waiting for me. Cristina was making toast, holding a knife so the blade lay carelessly across the top of the toaster. It was just a butter knife - you could barely cut water with it - but it was the most threatening thing I had ever seen.

"Something wrong, Lisa?" Cristina smiled, revealing her small, sharp teeth. She looked at Jane, who had arrived in the doorway behind Glendon. "Next time, remember your damn towel."

"One of you could have leant me yours," Jane pointed out, poutily, and Glendon instantly cuffed her about the face so she shrank back – that would teach her to talk out of turn.

I now noticed that all of their hair was in that straggly, recently dried state. "You were all outside."

I don't know if I thought attack was the best form of defence or if I was just speaking my mind, but apparently it was the wrong thing to say.

Moving fast, Elena slipped behind me, poking at my arm with sharp nails, forcing me away from the wall. At the same time, Jane, Zeffie and Fay closed in, surrounding me.

"You gonna tell people?"

"You gonna tell anyone, Lisa?"

"Who are you thinking of telling?"

Someone tugged at my T shirt. Sharp nails scored my bare arm. I yelped as my hair was pulled from behind.

"What's wrong?"

"Why don't you call for help?"

66

"Come on."

"What's wrong with you?"

Their short, sharp questions darted at me, pricking me, not giving me a chance to speak. Then suddenly, Zeffie slapped me – not hard or full palm, but light and quick, enough to make me jump. I started again as Fay slapped from the other side, then Jane and Elena, all of them, their hands darting in for any available part of my face. You forget how much a slap, even a little one, can hurt, and four girls doing it at once seemed more painful than it should have been. But it was made the worse by the situation, by the sense of threat, by their ganging up on me, and above all by Glendon, leaning against the door frame, laughing at my distress. I tried to block the slaps, but they kept pulling my arms away. I wanted to run – they would have caught me but at least I would have made it hard for them, rather than standing there and taking it as my cheeks grew red and hot, and tears welled up in my eyes.

"She's crying."

"My God, she's crying like a little baby."

They laughed as they slapped me, urging each other on with laughter, goading one another.

The toaster popped up, but no toast came out. Cristina suddenly stepped towards me and I squealed, jerking my hand away as a sudden unbearable pain shot through it. On the back of my hand was a raw, red burn mark, where Cristina had pressed the heated butter knife against it.

The girls fells back as Glendon stepped forward, as close as he could come without touching me, his breath hot on my forehead, overwhelming me with his presence, his whole attitude one of domination.

"Look at me. Look at me." He spoke quietly but with command. "I said, look at me." The edge in his voice forced my head up to meet his gaze. He stared down at me and I tried hard not to sniffle and sob. "Have we got a problem here?"

I shook my head helplessly.

"Good."

He walked to the door, the girls obediently following. I wanted to scream that they were only brave when it was six against one. But I didn't. Because it was still six against one.

Last to leave was Cristina, who paused in the doorway and

looked back at me in disgust, apparently as appalled by my spinelessness as I was. "Why can't you be more like your brother? You could have joined in, if you'd played the game."

Once I was sure they had gone, I shuffled back to my room, no longer trying to stop the tears that came silently. In the corridor I saw doors open a crack, Josie and Rosa had both been watching and listening. The doors closed. I wondered if they had been through something similar.

Not long left now to Christmas holidays. Just need to get through these few days and everything will be better. Family Christmas. Talbot back in the new year. Holding my breath for the end of term.

I won't write again today.

(Later) The storm has hit. Holy hell how the storm has hit.

(Later) Dr Lloyd went out tonight! She took her car, but still, in this weather she's nuts.

And now, minutes later, Mr Tull goes out on foot! Practically running. Is he following her? Is that why she's mad at him – she caught him doing it? Why not take his car?

December 18th

I don't feel like writing but I think I have to write this now while the events and my impressions of them are still fresh. I don't know where to start so please excuse these somewhat unfocussed recollections. (Don't know who I'm asking to excuse me. Me, I guess.)

The storm which had been massing for days, turning the moor into permanent night, broke just after lunch yesterday, and broke hard. The first peal of thunder was so loud that I honestly thought a wall had come down or something. The lightning made the clouds look like they were being lit from the inside - like there was a battle going on in the sky. Out on the hills we could see forked lightning jagging to the ground - something I've never seen before. But it was the rain that was really something else. It wasn't like rain, not like individual drops, just an unstoppable sheet of water, deluging down like God was trying to wash away the whole damn school, and good luck to Him. In the ninety seconds it takes me to walk from the main building to the girls' wing (because I still haven't learnt my damn way through the corridors!) I was soaked to the skin - hair plastered to my face. Even the books in my bag were drenched and are still drying out on my heater. Honestly this is the sort of rain where you imagine someone, somewhere is busily herding up two of every animal - and if I keep citing God in my descriptions it's because that's how it felt; this was a <u>Biblical</u> storm.

Normally in bad weather, no one's allowed to leave the school but lessons continue uninterrupted - why wouldn't they? But the electricity kept going on and off, a window was shattered by something, water started to come in thought the roof of the art room and rise up from the floor in the refectory, and so classes were abandoned and everyone sent back to their dorms where a register could be taken and teachers could keep an eye on everyone at once. I thought I would be able to get on with some studying, but the sixth form corridor being right up under the roof, it sounded like someone was playing *Wipeout* on the ceiling. The constant hammering of rain against the slates, against the windows even as the wind rattled them in their frame, only drowned out by the occasional thunder. It was like trying to work during the battle of the Somme. I gave it up as a bad loss.

It must have been around then that I saw Dr Lloyd drive out and Mr Tull go out shortly after, looking in a major hurry. Wish I knew why.

The only good news was that our roof seemed to be holding - there was no water coming into the dorms so nothing prevented us from going to bed, although the noise from outside seemed to preclude sleep. Still, trying to maintain a sense of routine and normality, Mrs Kerrigan made sure everyone observed curfew, which meant we were all in bed by eleven. I lay awake, as I guess most of the girls did, listening to the tumult without. I maybe cried a bit to myself; still fragile from that morning.

Around midnight the storm slackened somewhat, as if the sky was running out of water to chuck down on us. I got out of bed and looked through the curtains at the nocturnal landscape. Just as I did, the clouds parted for a moment to reveal a full, yellow moon, casting an eerie glow down onto the moor.

I can't be sure of what I saw. I can't be sure that I actually <u>saw</u> anything. It may all have been my imagination. But my strong impression in that moment, before the clouds again covered the moon, was that I saw an animal running. Not a sheep or any other

69

farm animal, and if it was a dog then it was the largest I ever saw. It was shaggy and soaked through by the rain, its head hung low below its muscular shoulders, sniffing the ground. As I watched, it came to a sudden halt and threw back its head. The clouds covered the moon again, removing the light but, behind the rain and the wind, I heard its long, drawn-out howl. When the moonlight returned it was gone.

I spent long minutes at the window, desperately peering out, trying to catch some further glimpse of whatever it was, but no luck so went to bed. As I closed my eyes I was ready to write the whole thing off as my imagination, but then I heard another howl, then another and another. The rain had dropped a bit but the wind was still high. Could it have been that I had heard? Of course it could, but I didn't think it was.

I slept only fitfully and started awake in the early hours, so I was aware of the kerfuffle in the school before most others. The first I knew something was wrong was from the sounds outside; voices and footsteps and an engine starting. I got up to look out. The storm had blown itself into nothing, leaving a clear, fine start to the day - the best for a long while - the sun beaming down on the sodden earth beneath.

Down and to my right I could see a small group of teachers, including Dr Lloyd and Dr Bellamy, standing outside of the south wing. They looked to be in earnest conversation and their gestures had an almost desperation to them. As I watched, I saw Mr. Knowles hurry away from the group to a car, its engine idling, get in and drive away, splashing through the puddles as he went. The rest of the group broke and headed off in different directions, moving with urgent purpose.

No one knew if classes would be back to normal today - the school rumour mill said that many rooms were water-damaged - so there was an air of apathy hanging about the place that would usually have been swiftly quashed by teachers. But those teachers we saw were just passing through, hurrying urgently by. Something was waiting to break. Not long after, we were all summoned to an emergency assembly in the chapel, and Dr Lloyd stood up in front of us all, looking red-eyed and tired.

"Mr Tull is missing." I felt my stomach contract sharply. "He went out last night, but it now appears that he never came back. Has anybody seen him since last night?" Presumably this was just on the

70

off chance, but Dr Lloyd scanned the room desperately for a raised hand. "Very well. It is possible that he spent the night in the village or in one of the houses or farms around the moor, the phone lines are down so Mr Knowles has driven out to check, but if this proves fruitless then we must assume he was caught out on the moor in the storm. He may be in trouble. We have already contacted emergency services but they are obviously very busy. In the meantime, all lessons are cancelled, you will be organised into search parties and we will comb the moor."

There was an air of chaos to the organisation of the search parties. Suddenly teachers who had spent years, even decades, corralling kids into line found themselves at a loss, the stresses of the day taking their toll. I was put into a group headed by Dr Bellamy, which I was pleased to find included Gwen. It also included Larry Glendon. He didn't look at me, acting as if the other night never even happened. We were all buddied up (Gwen and I hastily grabbing each other), counted, recounted, told to stay in the same pairs, and marched out of the gates across the moor.

Despite the seriousness of the mission, I could not help being quietly proud of my new hiking boots, which made me one of those better prepared for this. I haven't had a chance to break them in yet but they already feel comfortable and they fit like a glove (no idea how Talbot knew my size).

Our group headed up into the hills not far from where I met Talbot.

"Spread out!" called Dr Bellamy. "But stay in sight of each other. Don't go too far."

Given the number of pupils, it had seemed to me that we had a really good chance of finding some trace of Mr Tull. But once we got up high, and the whole of the moor was spread out beneath us, I realised how slim those chances actually were. Looking back and down, I could see the other parties, lines of children fanning out in search formation. All together at the school we had seemed a pretty expansive search party, but the moor swallowed up such numbers with ease. They looked like insects, lost in the harsh landscape. It was easy to forget the scale of the moor but it was also easy to forget its complexity. The number of humps, bumps, hills, mountains and random spires of rock. There were old mines, animal dens, natural caves and one's dug by our stone age ancestors. The vegetation might be sparse but it was dense and thick, hiding anything that might be concealed within its tangle of twigs and branches. Then, of course, there was Naughton Mire. The truth was that Mr Tull could be ten feet away and we would still miss him.

As we approached the steeper slopes, there in the shadow of a bare cliff, hugging the wall for protection, we saw a Gypsy encampment.

"Alright, everyone stay together!" Dr Bellamy was one of those men who thinks the best of everyone, but with other people's children under his care he felt the need to be circumspect, even if being so suggested a prejudice he did not necessarily harbour.

I couldn't help staring and wishing I could go closer. It was the type of gypsy camp you assume doesn't exist anymore, or perhaps never did; horses, caravans, handkerchiefs tied about their heads, chickens wandering about.

"Stay here." Dr Bellamy strode towards the encampment and a tall man with a weathered face came out to meet him.

"He doesn't look happy," whispered Gwen.

We couldn't hear what was being said, but the man's gestures were sharp and brutal, against Dr Bellamy's more conciliatory ones. But as the man angrily waved the Deputy Head away, another figure from the camp approached, calling and gesturing for him to wait. From what I could see she looked about a hundred; small, wizened, bent almost double and walking with a stick that was as twisted as she was. Her skin was leathered by exposure, and she seemed to be about 75% shawl. She beckoned Dr Bellamy down to speak to him, while the younger man stood behind with his arms folded, exuding the universal body language of 'in a huff'. When the old woman was done, Dr Bellamy nodded polite thanks and re-joined us.

"They've promised to keep an eye out. Alright, on we go."

The search party headed on up the hill, the gypsies watching us as we went. We seemed to be objects of considerable fascination. The old woman in particular scrutinised each child, as if she was looking for something.

To make the search even harder, the bad weather had made the moor even more difficult to traverse than usual. My hiking boots stood me in good stead as we clambered up the hill, but virtually everyone else ended up with muddied knees and hands as their feet skidded away from beneath them, and poor Dr Bellamy slipped onto his backside and slid halfway back down the slope, yelling, "Don't go too far without me," as he disappeared over a hummock like an unambitious ski jumper. I was disappointed to note that Glendon was not among the slippers. Though his shoes did not look suited to the terrain, he clearly was, proving himself irritatingly sure-footed.

After reaching the top of the hill we began to fan out, going back down in a circular pattern, trying to cover as much ground as possible. After an hour or so of hunting, a shriek from the far end of the line made us all start, and the carefully ordered line broke into a dashing horde, following the sound. The source of the scream was one of the younger girls - Jenny I think her name is - and as we rushed up, she and her buddy stood, arms around each other, shivering and crying.

Several of the girls turned away from the sight, and a few of the boys too, and I think more would have if they had not been trying to look tough or impress Glendon.

"Oh dear," said Dr Bellamy, as he arrived. "Alright, let's move on. Whatever happened here, it's not what we're looking for."

I wondered if Jenny had seen the furiously dismembered sheep and thought it was the remains of Mr Tull. I might have, if I hadn't seen this before, only not so fresh. There were more this time. The sheep had found themselves a place to hide from the worst of the rain and wind, sheltered by a rocky overhang, but that had just made it easier for whatever it was that had attacked them. Steeled by my previous encounter, I looked a little closer than most and saw something in amongst the blood and torn flesh. Most of the ground was churned up, and that which wasn't had been washed by the rain, but in one spot I could see a clear footprint. Perhaps it was a dog, it was too large for a fox. But putting it together with the silhouette I had seen on the moor through the storm, and the howls I had heard, there was only one word in my mind; Wolf.

I'm still wondering if I should be telling someone about that print. The horrible irony is that the person I would have told is Mr Tull

I don't know why I've let this entry get side-tracked by things I heard in the night that could have been dreams, or by dismembered farm animals. Maybe I just don't want to reach the point of saying the thing I have to say.

No trace of Mr Tull was found. Not by us; not by the villagers who came to help, led by Squire Montford, looking genuinely upset by the loss of his friend; not by the emergency services when they finally arrived (several roads were flooded making their journey difficult and circuitous). Any footprints there might have been would have been eradicated by the rain. The search will continue tomorrow but I don't think anyone is looking for a living man any more.

I don't know why this is hitting me so hard. Mr Tull felt like one of the few allies I had in this wretched place, but that just sounds like a selfish reason. I'm crying now. I can't seem to stop, and I feel the need to write it down because I want to remember that I cried. It's the only thing left that I can do for Mr. Tull.

Chapter 7 - The Cathedral

For Lisa Hobson, the days following the disappearance of Mr. Tull passed excruciatingly slowly, made worse by the sight from her window of the search parties in high viz jackets, wending their dejected path back to Naughton each evening. Though she tried not to hope, each day felt as if she lost her favourite teacher afresh.

The Christmas holidays arrived with an eruption of relief, which Lisa instantly felt guilty about but could not suppress. Though she enjoyed the festive season (Oliver seeming back to his normal, distant self) she kept an eye on the news from the north. Despite weeks of searching, no trace of Mr Tull's body was found. The official version was that Mr Tull had tried to shelter from the storm and had slipped into a ravine or gotten lost down a cave, though gossip in the Grey Boar preferred to blame the mire, embellishing its ghoulish reputation.

It was all very sad and very plausible, but made no attempt to answer what Lisa felt was the main question; why had he gone out at all? Why had he not driven?

But she was not the only one who had seen him and everyone agreed that he had gone of his own volition, so there was nothing to investigate. A tragic accident, and the real truth would likely remain unknown.

But Lisa still found it hard to accept, perhaps because of the other odd stuff that had been going on. None of it pointed to an explanation, but, to her mind at least, it suggested that another explanation might exist.

A week after Christmas, Lisa turned eighteen. She was an adult, and adults took action. By the time she returned to school, a plan had formed in her mind, one that she intended to carry out at the first opportunity.

"How have you been?" asked Talbot, as he and Lisa struggled to hear each other over the crackly landline. "It's great to hear your voice."

What a nice thing to say. Although Lisa again wondered at the speed things were moving between them, or at least the speed with which Talbot might expect them to move.

"I've been pretty bad," said Lisa, honestly.

"I heard about the teacher. Did you know him well?"

75

"Not really. I mean; you don't know your teachers do you? But he was one of the good ones. Started the same day as me and Ollie."

"Your brother, right?"

"Yeah." Lisa had not written back to Talbot as often as he had written to her, but she had filled him in on a few of her life details, including family.

"Well, I'm sorry." He didn't know what to say, but what did you say? "You still want to meet up?"

"Definitely." She might have said that with way too much enthusiasm. It gave the wrong impression. "You said we could walk out across the moor?"

"Towards the old mill. I remember."

Was he disappointed that she just wanted to go walking? It was so hard to tell over this wretched line. Well, either way, that was what was happening.

"Great. And you'll need to bring a torch."

They fixed a time and place to meet, and promised to catch up more when they weren't trying to make themselves heard over the wheezes and crackles of a line which was only slightly better than a pair of tin cans and a length of string. Lisa hung up and stopped with her hand still on the receiver. Had she just made a date? Was that was this was? She had very clear ideas about what they were going to do, to the point of this being an investigative mission. She also had very clear ideas about stuff they were not going to do, because she really didn't know Talbot that well and her parents, for all their comparative lack of interest, had been very clear on how good girls behave.

But she was spending a day out with a boy, just the two of them. And there was an attraction. His behaviour had made it pretty clear that he was attracted to her and there was little point in her denying a reciprocal attraction to him.

It sounded like a date. Albeit a very unconventional one.

"The mines?" asked Talbot, as they strode across the moor, trying to ignore the sharp wind that chased the colour from their faces, Moose trotting along beside them like a hairy chaperone.

"Yeah," nodded Lisa. "That okay?"

Talbot shrugged and gave the lopsided grin that Lisa had spent many a night thinking about in his absence. "Whatever you want.

It's your day."

Yeah, this was definitely a date.

When they had met, it had not slipped Lisa's notice that, while he was sensibly attired for the landscape and weather, Talbot had also made an effort, and looked very good. They had hugged and there had been a peck on the cheek - Lisa was pleased that Talbot tried for nothing more - but above all there had been enthusiasm. Lisa hadn't realised how much she had missed this brief acquaintance until she saw him again and felt a leap, not just of excitement, but of familiar pleasure; the joy of seeing a friend. Talbot had become cemented in her head as a beacon of happy times in a wilderness of grey, school-based misery. His face too had lit up on seeing her approach, and within moments they were both pouring out stories of what they had been doing since each had seen the other last. There had been none of the 'How have you been?' awkwardness of their phone conversation. They were like two old friends who could simply pick up where they left off. For them to be like that after so little time, Lisa thought, was pretty special.

She almost regretted the necessity of telling him that they were not going for lunch at whatever passed for a restaurant in Naughton Village, nor to sit on the riverbank and gaze romantically into each other's eyes. They were going down a disused mine.

"You don't mind, do you?"

Talbot shook his head firmly. "Moose and I are up for anything you want."

Lisa gave Moose a pat as he walked alongside her. He had sprang up on her when she first arrived, apparently as pleased to see her as his owner. She shot a sidelong glance at that owner now, and decided to chance it. "I'm sure it's not the date you had in mind."

Talbot shrugged, completely unphased by her reckless use of the 'D' word. "I guess I don't know you all that well, but I got the impression that whatever I had in mind for a first date, this wasn't going to be that."

Now he had used the word himself. That seemed to confirm it.

"That said," Talbot went on, "I was wondering; are we going there for any particular reason?"

Lisa squared her chin. "We're looking for the body of a geography teacher."

Talbot took this in. "Okay. *Definitely* not the first date I had in

77

mind, but okay. Do you mind if I ask; is there a good chance of us finding one?"

What were the chances? Presumably the emergency services had known that the mines were there and would have looked at them. But how closely? Given the amount of ground they had to cover. In the back of Lisa's mind lurked the idea that Mr Tull had been following Dr Lloyd that night. That surely meant either the mines or the mill, and the mill was easy to search. Which left the mines. It was a long shot. But it was worth a look, and she felt she owed it to Mr Tull to do everything she could.

"No," she admitted. "But you don't know if you don't look."

Talbot nodded. "Words to live by."

"Are you making fun of me?"

Talbot held up his hands. "Just learning to roll with things. I get the impression that's going to a valuable skill around you."

"I promise next time we'll do something normal."

You could have lit ball rooms with the wattage of Talbot's smile. "I only heard 'promise' and 'next time'. Moose, you're my witness."

Moose barked and Lisa laughed.

It was a long walk across the moor but it did not feel it. However grim the purpose of their journey might have been, that purpose did not kick in until they reached the mine and for now they were just a young couple out for a walk together, and Lisa was quite happy with that.

They walked close enough that their fingertips brushed as they strode on, and when Talbot gently encouraged Lisa's hand into his, she did not resist. Though she did shoot him a knowing glance.

"That was pretty smooth."

"Beginner's luck, I swear."

"Yeah, right."

Talbot did not strike Lisa as someone who struggled for female company. He was confident, easy in his own skin, happy to be liked or disliked for who he was, at the discretion of his companion. It was appealing, and it made Lisa wonder; why me? Or perhaps it was not *just* her. Perhaps he had a girl in every town he visited. Perhaps, while he had been in London he had been writing letters to her, resting the paper on a naked woman sprawled across his bed, like John Malkovich in *Dangerous Liaisons* (original play by Christopher

Hampton).

Then again, maybe he liked her. It was not *so* far-fetched was it?

"What's your favourite book?" Cliché question, but literature mattered to Lisa and she was holding her breath a little. If he said *The Da Vinci Code* then she would have to turn around and go back.

"*Titus Groan*," replied Talbot.

"Mervyn Peake," Lisa said automatically, as celebratory fireworks went off in her head.

"The first Gormenghast book," Talbot clarified. "People call it fantasy and it's not. Nothing wrong with fantasy but *it's not*. It just shows what happens to a culture in extreme isolation."

Lisa nodded. Mervyn Peake's masterpiece was not grouped with the traditional gothic novels but it earned an honorary spot in her mind, and was in any case frickin' awesome.

"It's a great story," Talbot went on, "but - and I'm not a great reader or literary savant - there's something about the writing. It's like poetry that's been pressed between the pages, you know? Like pressed flowers. Is that dumb? Is that the sort of observation that gets you kicked out of A-Level English?"

Lisa had not previously known that it was possible to become physically aroused by someone discussing *Titus Groan*, but it was a discovery she was pleased to make. "Actually I think you summed that up pretty well."

"What's your favourite?"

"*The Woman in White*," Lisa beamed. "Wilkie Collins. I want to be Marian Halcombe."

Talbot shook his head. "I'm ashamed to say I haven't read it."

"I'll lend you a copy."

Everyone should read *The Woman in White*, of course, but Lisa also liked the implied intimacy of sharing books. As far as she was concerned it was a form of safe sex, and *The Woman in White* was long enough that by the time Talbot had finished it... She felt her cheeks growing red as her imagination got ahead of her, and was grateful for the biting wind.

"Is that the mill?" Lisa pointed to their right at a small collection of buildings, just coming into sight in the distance beyond one of the moor's irregular hillocks.

"That's it," said Talbot, a hint of melancholy noticing in his voice. "Poor Ralph."

Lisa stared. She had not seen the place since that first day when they had driven by on their way to the school. Now she stopped to think of it, Mr Tull had taken a real interest in it and in the fate of 'poor Ralph'.

"Something about this place," she observed, misquoting *Once Upon a Time in the West*. "Something to do with death."

"That's life, isn't it?" said Talbot, more cheerfully than the statement seemed to warrant. "You live, you love, you die. May as well make the best of the first two."

Was that a hint?

"Where are the mines?"

"Not far now." Talbot pointed ahead to where some of the hills had been torn into rugged quarries, augmented by spoil heaps spilling from their sides.

Twenty minutes later, the pair arrived at the hills and Talbot led the way to where a jagged slice seemed to have been cut from the slope, leading down to a dark hole that bored into the hill.

"Watch out for the rails." Talbot pointed to the ground where the rails on which the old mine cars had run, carrying up the gleanings of slate, still protruded through the dirt and scrubby grass.

Lisa shivered as a blast of cold air whistled down the cut.

"Acts like a wind tunnel," commented Talbot, and Lisa managed a nod and a smile.

Suddenly, all the easy comfort of their journey here was gone in the cold reality of the morbid task they were here to perform. But it seemed to Lisa that there was more to it than that. Though they were not in the mine yet, something in the air made it seem as if a shroud had descended over them. Something to do with death.

"Come on." Determined not to be cowed by the atmosphere and not to play the weak woman with her strong man, Lisa led the way towards the mine's entrance.

"So we're really doing this, huh? That's cool." Talbot followed.

At the mine's entrance was a heavy, iron gate, rusting but still solid, a thick chain and padlock passing through it, but unfastened. Lisa gave the gate a push and its hinges shrieked as it swung back into the darkness.

"Seems a bit pointless to have it at all."

"Kids used to come in here," Talbot explained. "The council thought it was dangerous so they put the gate on. So the kids got bolt cutters. So the council replaced the chain, and so on. After about the fifth time the council said pretty much the same as you."

"What?"

"Seems a bit pointless to have it at all. Once they stopped locking it, people stopped going in. Human nature." He turned to Moose who was hanging back and whining unhappily. "Moose - stop being silly - I don't think you're going to like it down there so you're going to have to wait here and I'm going to have to tie you up. Not because I think you might wander off - I trust you - but because I think you might follow me. Or possibly Lisa - it's hard to know where your loyalties lie when she's around. Also, on the very off-chance that something happens to us down there, then having you here will mean the search parties will at least know where to look, so you'll be fulfilling an essential function. Now I've explained all this to you, I hope I can tie you up without that reproachful expression of- dammit, Moose you're doing it already. We talked about this."

Lisa petted Moose as Talbot produced a leash from his pocket and tied the dog up. "It's for the best."

The dog did not seem happy, though Lisa thought that was as much to do with the place as being tied up.

"You tell him," said Talbot.

"Moose," Lisa knelt to address the dog, nose to nose, "we're doing this because we love you." It was hard to say if Moose accepted this but he licked Lisa's face, which seemed to suggest that, even if he did not understand, he was willing to forgive.

"Come on."

They entered, the mediocre yellow haze of Lisa's torch cutting into darkness, revealing a low tunnel, water dripping from the roughly cut ceiling. It was quickly joined by the brilliant white beam of Talbot's torch stretching far ahead of them.

"Good torch."

"Thanks."

Again, Lisa took the lead, but this time Talbot put out a hand to stop her.

"Let me go first. My torch is better."

"You could give me your torch. That's what a gentleman

would do."

"Guess I'm not a gentleman." Even in this light, Lisa could almost sense Talbot's smile. "Please let me lead. When I brag about this afterwards I've got to be able to say I led, or the other guys will make fun of me."

"They go first when they take girls down mines?" suggested Lisa.

"Invariably. If the girl goes first then it's like you've just castrated the guy right there in the mine."

Lisa returned his smile with one of her own. Though there was a knot of nerves bundled up in her stomach and the creepy atmosphere of the abandoned mine still laid thickly across her, they were still capable of a witty back and forth. It wasn't much, but it made her feel better.

"Stay close," said Talbot as they began to walk down the tunnel, the muddy grit making a sucking, scrunching with each step they took. "Was that condescending?"

"I don't know. To be honest I'm sometimes exhausted keeping track of the things I'm *meant* to be offended by, so I usually just get upset about things I actually am."

"That's an awfully smart thought for a pretty little thing like you."

"Bear in mind that in this light I can't always tell when you're joking and I have a mean right hook."

"Noted. I…"

Suddenly Talbot stiffened, his whole body shaking where he stood.

"What is it, what's wrong?!" Lisa gasped.

"Water drip. Went down the back of my neck."

Lisa giggled.

"It's not funny. Wait till it happens to you."

"Don't make me take the lead."

They walked on into the darkness. Every now and then Lisa glanced back to see the bright, white rectangle of the entrance, but it soon vanished with the curve of the tunnel, and they were left with no light but the torches. The wind blew sharply, and Lisa switched hands with her torch, so her right hand could have a turn in her pocket. Then, up ahead, Talbot's bright light discovered a divergence, the tunnel breaking into two branches.

82

"Left or right?" asked Talbot, he was now a disembodied voice with a torch beam emanating from around waist level.

Lisa shone her torch into his face, feeling more comfortable being able to see him as they spoke. "Sorry. Not blinding you am I?"

"With that? No. Left or right?"

"Toss a coin?"

Talbot fished in his pocket and flipped a coin. It landed with a splat somewhere in the darkness.

"Yeah, that was never going to work."

"Sorry."

"It was only fifty pee. Left or right?"

Lisa sighed. It was her expedition so it was her choice but she felt a sudden weight at having to make it. Were these tunnels dangerous? Was she leading Talbot unbeknownst into danger, when he would have been quite happy for them to make out someplace quiet?

"Right."

Talbot shone his torch down the tunnel, revealing it to be blocked by an old cave-in. "Left it is."

"Next time, we check that first."

"How about we just take every left, that way we can find our way back easily."

"Good call." The idea of getting lost in here had never really occurred to Lisa. How many times did these tunnels sub-divide? It seemed to her that, even if you took every left, you could still get good and lost. Was it possible that had happened to Mr Tull? No. He was too smart for that.

Talbot's torch gave such a clear view of what was ahead that Lisa had turned hers to the ground so she could see where she was walking, looking out for stuff to trip over. Near the entrance, the floor surface still showed, in muddy streaks and rivulets, where the rain had streamed in, but the deeper they went the less that became the case. Mostly it was a mess of mud and silt and whatever else had accumulated in over a century of abandonment. People dumped rubbish down here, animals had nested, the rotting detritus of the mining operation lay about, slowly deteriorating. But amongst it all...

"Look!"

Talbot stopped when Lisa grabbed his arm and looked to where her torch pointed.

83

"Is that a footprint? Like a dog or something?"

"Big dog," said Lisa, her words falling like lead in the gloomy atmosphere of the mine. Talbot's torch beam found her face and Lisa waved the bright light away. "What are you doing?"

"I wanted to see your face."

"Why?"

"Well, aside from the obvious aesthetic advantages, I think there's something you're not telling me."

"And you decided to blind me as punishment?"

"Don't change the subject. Were you expecting to find that?"

"No," said Lisa, honestly. "But I did see the same type of print in amongst the dead sheep the morning after Mr Tull went missing."

"That's a longish way from here," Talbot mused.

"That's why I didn't expect to find it here. Though of course, this print could have been here a while. It's sheltered."

Talbot stooped and gingerly touched the print. "Dry." Which didn't confirm anything, except that the print hadn't been made recently. "If there's one then there should be more."

Although the ground down this far was comparatively safe from rain run-off, nowhere was completely safe because the tunnels sloped downwards and the rain just kept running. It grew less as it was absorbed into the mud, but still. In addition, the walls ran with moisture and the ceiling dripped continuously, leaving spatter patterns on the floor that destroyed any impressions that might have been there.

Talbot looked at the ceiling. "I remember Ralph told me that the water that drips from the ceiling, seeping through the cracks in the rock, was rain about six months ago. That's how long it takes to travel down."

"It's always raining around here," nodded Lisa. "We're lucky to find one footprint when the floor is like this."

But they did find more. It took some searching, but here and there, between the water damage and other litter, more prints, some complete, some partial, emerged,.

"Not what we came here looking for though is it?" commented Talbot. "A big dog."

"No."

"And yet I get the sense you're connecting these things. Mr Tull and the big dog."

"A big dog?"

"Not a big dog?"

"Aren't there stories about some sort of animal on the moor?" Lisa hedged in the direction of her suspicions - which still remained pretty vague even to her. "Something escaped from a zoo that might have killed Ralph?"

Lisa could hear Talbot shrug. "Yeah. But there isn't a moor in Britain that doesn't have a story like that."

"Seems like a lot of dead sheep for a big dog."

Dogs were descended from wolves of course, and some were still trained to kill by barbaric and unpleasant humans, but for the most part, that side of their nature was a relic. A big cat on the other hand, or a wolf; they were designed by nature to kill.

Talbot seemed less convinced. "A dog without an owner, not knowing where its next meal's coming from, it can go feral and be as dangerous as a wolf."

Lisa had to acknowledge total ignorance on the subject. "Maybe. But whatever it is, it would need a den wouldn't it?"

"Potentially." Talbot shone his torch on down the tunnel. "Are we going on?"

Suddenly it seemed a whole lot colder than it had moments ago.

"We can go a bit further."

They walked on, perhaps a bit slower than before, and certainly quieter. The chatter had reduced to a handful of words, only when necessary. The walls of the tunnel seemed to close in about them until...

"Holy hell," murmured Lisa.

The beam of Talbot's torch showed the tunnel opening up ahead of them, and suddenly they found themselves in a cathedral of rock. The roof was almost too high for Talbot's powerful torch, while Lisa's had become completely useless. Jagged pillars, carefully worked around by the old miners, towered from the floor, supporting the ceiling. The walls were broken into irregular shelves and cuts, knuckles and corners; sharply edged here, carunculated there. Everywhere had been worked furiously with explosives and then hand tools to pry forth whatever the ground had to offer.

"Guess they found some slate here," said Talbot, his voice weak with wonder, lost in the immensity of the space. "Watch your

85

step."

To their right, the floor plunged away beneath them where the miners had followed the seam downwards, almost undermining themselves. Talbot picked up a stone and tossed it down, listening to it bounce and rattle against the walls till it found its way to the distant bottom, the echoes of its passage slowly dying away.

"You wanna know something weird?" asked Lisa.

"What?"

"This is the first time I've felt claustrophobic." The vastness seemed to swallow her, so she felt she was shrinking in upon herself. "This place is incredible."

"I can't believe I never knew this was here." His torch found her face. "Thank you." Lisa blinked back at him. "What are you thanking me for?"

"Without you I never would have seen it. And I'm really glad I got to see it with you."

Lisa froze as he took a definite step towards her, his hand finding hers in the darkness and gently drawing her. What she might have done had he continued, as had clearly been his intention, she was not sure, but his progress was arrested by the loud crack that came from beneath his foot as he stepped.

"What the hell was that?" Talbot frowned, irritated to have been interrupted while making his move.

"You trod on something." Lisa directed her torch downwards. "Looks like... oh."

It was a bone. And it was not the only one.

"Big dog with a big appetite," mumbled Talbot, the words seeming slurred and numb as he stared at the boneyard they had unveiled. There were probably not that many animals there, comparatively speaking, maybe as few as ten. But you did not really appreciate how many bones there were in an animal's body until you saw them all piled up, picked clean. Or mostly so.

"They're not human," said Lisa, with the certainty of one who had paid attention in GCSE biology. And of one who is hanging onto her sanity by a thread.

"This would explain the missing animals," said Talbot. "There were always sheep unaccounted for. Or bits of them, anyway. And some cows elsewhere. A horse too I think. All sorts. You're sure there's not..."

He left the thought unfinished but Lisa knew exactly what he was asking. The truth was that she couldn't be sure. In that pile of bones, how could she be sure that there was not one human one? What there was not, was any sign of a geography teacher killed less than a month ago, and that absence was the only thing that was keeping her on the quiet side of screaming.

What would she have done if she had actually found what they had come down here searching for? What sort of idiot was she to have thought that this was a good idea? Could she smell rotting flesh on the air? She was sure she hadn't when they had entered yet now the fetid stink seemed to linger at the back of her throat so she could not shift it.

"Let's get out of here."

Talbot didn't take any convincing. But as they turned back toward the tunnel, a sound reached their ears, echoing from up ahead of them. Footsteps.

Shrill panic raced through Lisa and she looked at Talbot to see his face as frightened as hers in the torchlight. He looked at her for guidance and Lisa could only whisper. "Hide."

Hurrying across the floor of the cathedral, torches to the ground, looking for trip hazards, they rushed to the far side of one of the massive pillars that held up the roof and huddled against it.

"Turn it off," hissed Lisa, and the brilliance of Talbot's torch vanished. Lisa took a breath and turned out her own, plunging them into the most profound darkness she had ever known.

It did not last long. The footsteps took on a new quality as they entered the cathedral, their echoes rebounding expansively about the chamber. A torch beam, closer to Talbot's than Lisa's, shone like a searchlight and Lisa bit her tongue to stop herself from screaming. Without meaning to, she grasped Talbot tightly and felt his hand on her hair in reply, soothing her, even though his racing heart, which she could feel pounding against her chest, told her that he was as scared as she was.

The footsteps stopped and the torch beam descended to the floor. He had found the bones.

"Hmm." It was a low, subtle sound, and yet in the silence of the cathedral it seemed to boom.

A clicking and clattering followed, a noise of bone on rock that made Lisa's skin crawl, as the stranger examined the grisly pile.

Eventually the footsteps resumed. They were hard to pinpoint as each echoed and re-echoed in the chamber, so they seemed to come from all around at once, but it seemed to Lisa that the unseen visitor was taking a stroll about the room's perimeter. Did he know they were here? Was he looking for them?

Clearly Talbot was thinking along the same lines, as Lisa now felt a light pressure on her shoulders, edging her backwards. If they could move silently and keep that pillar between them and the stranger then they would remain unseen.

But so would he.

Without exactly meaning to do so, Lisa resisted Talbot's backward urging. She wanted to the see who had come in. Just a glimpse, then they could go back to hiding. She would not get much of a look in this light but, suddenly, seeing whatever she could mattered. She was eighteen years old and in her life had taken as few risks as possible. None really. What compelled her to take one now she could not say. Past Talbot, she could see the torch beam shining against the cathedral wall. The stranger seemed to be interested in one particular spot, and Lisa thought she heard his footsteps quicken as he approached.

There. Though he was just a shadow, vaguely delineated against the light of his torch, she had got her first look at the stranger. He approached the wall, keeping his torch on that same spot, onto which he now placed his hand, running his fingers across the rock.

"Hmm."

As Talbot's urgent pushing finally overcame Lisa's curiosity and the pillar again interposed between them, Lisa managed to get one final look. The man - she could now be relatively sure it was a man - angled his torch against the flat surface and the reflected light cast his body into fuzzy silhouette. He was average height or just above, with a slim build and appeared to be sensibly, but smartly, dressed for this kind of expedition. His movements were quick and precise, wasting neither time nor energy.

Only now did Lisa allow herself to be pushed from view, in fact encouraging Talbot - now her curiosity was sated she wanted to be out of sight again and was astounded by her own inviting of discovery. But urgency breeds carelessness. From the ground at Lisa's feet, a stone rattled. Dislodged by either her or Talbot. It rolled away from them before coming to rest. Lisa felt Talbot stiffen against her as they both froze. Were they out of sight? She could not see the man's silhouette any more though she could still see a hint of the torchlight on the wall. Where was the man? Was he listening?

"Hmm."

The silence was deafening as Lisa held her breath, her heart pounding at the back of her throat. She could feel Talbot's hands on her, protective but tense, as if he was afraid the very movement of his muscles could give them away. His heart pulsed against her, quicker and quicker, until she felt she could hear it alongside her own.

"Hmm."

The man seemed to dismiss the idea that he had heard anything, and the sound of his footsteps returned; deliberate, but casual. Nothing to suggest he was coming for them.

Lisa felt Talbot's gently exhaled breath, warm on her face. She squeezed his arm, needing to communicate her relief to him somehow.

As the man continued his slow circuit of the room, so Talbot and Lisa continued theirs of the pillar, keeping it always between them, only moving when he moved so any noise their carefully placed feet made was disguised by the loud echoes of his hard soles on the rock floor. As they came full circle, the man arrived back at the door. The light from his torch flashed about the room, giving it a final once over.

"Hmm."

And with that, the footsteps started again, but now moving away, their echoes losing the broad quality that the cathedral had given them as the man passed back into the tunnel.

Lisa and Talbot remained in frozen tableau, clinging tightly to each other, afraid to move as the darkness settled upon them once more. It was only when the sound of the footsteps had finally died away, that they dared to let go of each other and allow their muscles to relax.

"Ow," murmured Lisa.

"Are you alright?"

"Yeah, just... tight." She massaged the stress from her muscles, strained by being held tense for so long.

Talbot's torch flicked on and Lisa squinted, shocked by the

sudden brilliance of the light.

"Who do you think that was?" asked Talbot, his voice still low.

Lisa shook her head. "I guess it could have been anybody. Probably just a tourist."

"You got a better look than me," said Talbot, perhaps a hint of reproach in his voice. "Did it look like a tourist?"

"Maybe." Lisa sighed. "Not sure he acted like one."

She flicked her torch back on and made her way across the room to the stretch of wall in which the strange man had been so interested. It was difficult to find - the encompassing darkness made it easy to lose your bearings - but eventually Lisa found what she was pretty sure was the right area. She ran her fingers across the rock as the man had.

"Hmm."

"Anything?" asked Talbot, not sounding that interested. Lisa had a hunch that this whole expedition had palled for him - the sexiness of exploring in the dark together did not seem to be yielding the results for which he might have hoped.

"Scratches.".

"Like tool marks?" The walls were scarred with marks left by the miners.

"Maybe." She didn't want to start an argument, but these looked more like claw marks left by an animal. They were not deep, barely visible in fact - the man clearly had good eyesight - but there they were; 4 thin lines, like nails on a chalkboard. "Let's get out of here."

Talbot was as keen to go as Lisa, but neither of them felt inclined to walk fast. Though their strange companion had not seemed the type to dawdle, they had no wish to bump into him on the way out. There was, Lisa thought, no reason to assume ill intentions. There was no reason to assume it had been anything other than a passer-by with an interest in the region's industrial archaeology. And yet...

There was too much in Lisa's life at the moment that came under the uncomfortable heading of 'and yet...'. Stuff that bothered her but which she could not put her finger on. It was not a situation she liked. It was common to the novels she read and it never ended well.

The pair's steps unconsciously speeded up when the light of

the entrance became visible ahead of them, and they practically ran the last twenty feet out into the fresh air to be greeted by an enthusiastic Moose.

"Good boy!" Talbot enthused. "Well done."

But though Lisa patted the happy dog, she was less effusive. "He must have known."

"What?"

"He must have known that we were in there." She shook her head as if trying to dispel an unpleasant realisation but finding it stuck fast. "The man. He can't have missed Moose. And why else would a dog be tied up out here?"

"Guard dog?" suggested Talbot. They turned their gaze on the mongrel who gave them a soppy head tilt. "Perhaps not."

Lisa nodded. "He must have known."

It was a further credit to the rapport that the pair had built up that the walk back across the moor was not a grim one. There was a lingering chill to be dispelled, but they shrugged it off and chatted like old friends. Talbot insisted on walking her back to the school and Lisa was in no frame of mind to argue. She liked to think of herself as an independent, modern woman, but when you had just had a close encounter with a shadowy figure in an abandoned mine, then it was probably okay to break out old stereotypes and let a man be a bit chivalrous.

It was nice. And that was the predominant word in Lisa's mind. There was clearly something between them, and something that went deeper than nice, but she was not sure if this was the time to explore it. For her, for now, 'nice' was about the limit. How would Talbot react to that?

They passed through the school gates, Talbot walking in as if he owned the place, easy confidence radiating from him. They were, Lisa noticed, observed by Larry Glendon and some of his group, who followed the couple with their eyes as they strolled towards the north wing. Ollie was among them, and Lisa instantly wished he wasn't. It was hard to tell what the bully group thought, and Lisa did not want to care what people like that thought, but unfortunately what people like that thought affected her everyday life. Nice though it had been to have Talbot walk her home and have the chance to chat with him for longer, perhaps it would have been better to keep the whole thing *sub rosa* till she knew what it was. Especially given what she was about to do.

"So this was fun," said Talbot as they reached the foyer that led into the Girls' wing.

Lisa couldn't help laughing. "Bits of it. Yeah."

"I was thinking next time, maybe something less dark, grim and soul-chilling. Maybe a movie."

"Well..."

"There's no cinema in Naughton, but I can drive us into town. Or we could ride even. Do you ride?"

"Well..."

"Of course Moose couldn't come," Talbot continued, unconcerned.

"Talbot..."

Talbot stopped.

Lisa took a deep breath. She hadn't really been expecting him to stop and now found she didn't have anything ready to say. "I like you."

"Good. You should. I'm likeable. And the feeling is more than mutual."

"But..." Lisa struggled for words. What was a person supposed to say in a situation like this? A question that might have been easier if she had a better handle on her own feelings. She drew Talbot to one side, into the shelter of the building and out of sight of prying eyes. "I'm just not looking for a boyfriend - for anything really - right now."

Talbot nodded. "Okay. 'Right now' are the words I'm going to focus on there. 'Right now' implies that I can ask again. I can be patient."

Lisa smiled wanly. "That's not the impression I get of you."

"Well, I'm used to getting my own way," Talbot admitted.

"Sorry to disappoint you. And if I misled you..."

"Maybe a bit."

"Then I'm sorry for that too."

"How about I try to convince you?" Without warning, Talbot swooped in to kiss Lisa, his lips brushing against hers, his arm curling about her waist to pull her against him.

"No!" Lisa hissed the word, violently, pushing him away and jolting her head back from him.

Talbot let her go and pulled away. "Sorry. I shouldn't have..."

92

"No."

"I didn't mean to..."

"But you did."

Talbot shot her a guilty glance. "Lisa, please don't..."

"It's done. You should go."

He looked as if he had more to say, more excuses to make. Talbot Conliffe was not a man accustomed to people saying 'no' to him, and no doubt this sort of tactic had worked for him in the past. But he had badly misjudged things today, and the result had left both with a sour taste in their mouths. Without trying to plead his case more, Talbot turned and walked away, leaving Lisa to hurry into the North wing.

Damn it.

On a day when it had, on occasion, felt as if she might be in real and significant danger, it was this ending that left the most livid scar on Lisa as she ran up the stairs to her room to sit on her bed.

Damn it.

Maybe she should have let him kiss her? Hadn't he earned that? Hadn't she led him on to nothing?

No. No, that was all crap. She hadn't wanted him to kiss her, she'd been very clear about not wanting a relationship and even if at points during the day she had led him to believe otherwise, a person has a right to change their mind without unwanted affection being forced on them. He was in the wrong.

Which wasn't about to stop her from feeling bad, because she had liked him and because that kiss might have been very welcome somewhere down the line. But now…

What happened next?

She still liked him, but this had confused matters considerably. At best it would be a while before she could trust him again.

Lisa heaved a sigh. Who would have thought that a search for a dead body could have ended so badly? She looked out of her window. Darkness was already falling.

Chapter 8 - As Darkness Falls

Damn it.

Truthfully, Talbot had known that he had done the wrong thing as soon as he had moved, but he had kept going until Lisa spoke because you had to lean into your mistakes. And because sometimes it did pay off. But not today. Not when it mattered.

Damn it.

This was what you got for going after a girl with some standards and some class, rather than... well rather than that girl he'd met in London while he'd been away. He regretted that now. Call it an inevitable consequence of being handsome and rich and confident all at the same time. Well, perhaps not inevitable.

He'd regretted it at the time actually, because he did like Lisa very much. Though he was not entirely sure why.

Rather than walking home across the moor immediately, Talbot sat on a bench by the school's main gate and stared morosely out in front of him. Perhaps Lisa would notice he hadn't left yet and would take pity on him. But most likely not.

"You still love me, don't you?" he said, as Moose licked his hands.

She was pretty, of course - Lisa, that was. But in Talbot's experience there was not a paucity of pretty girls in the world, there seemed no danger of running out and Lisa was not the prettiest he had met. Yet she was the most attractive. She attracted him. She was independent and strong-minded and interesting and funny. All good things he liked, because he was not as shallow as recent behaviour might suggest. But they were also all things that other girls displayed. There was nothing unique about intelligence.

She was Lisa. That, in the end, was what it came down to. Nothing more sophisticated than that, and if he could not quantify why being Lisa made her more attractive to him than other girls who were not Lisa, then there was something special in that too. Liking Lisa, Talbot considered, was like having faith in a deity; if you could explain it rationally then it wouldn't be faith.

If it had been any other girl he'd screwed up with, then he would have chalked it up to experience and moved on, but moving on from Lisa was not an option. He would have to find some way of getting back into her good graces. Did women find persistence attractive? Every romantic comedy he had ever seen suggested they did, but in real life most of the men in those films would have ended up with a restraining order against them. He would write to her. She had liked the letters when he was away in London. There was an old-fashioned streak in Lisa that made such gestures appeal and he could use that. He would write to her.

"What do you think, Moose?"

Moose barked.

"I agree. She's worth the effort." He tousled the dog's head. "Weird one too though."

Today had certainly demonstrated that. What on earth had that been about? They'd gone looking for a dead body and he'd damn near ended up becoming one. And yet, that too was oddly attractive. It was nice to be around someone whose behaviour he couldn't predict. Yeah; he really had to come up with a way of winning her back.

But it could wait until tomorrow. He stood up. Darkness had fallen as he had been sitting there.

"Hey, you!" Talbot looked up to see a group approaching him, headed by a tall boy with blonde hair. "What are you doing here?"

"Leaving," said Talbot, turning to the gate.

But the boy blocked his path, backed up by his friends behind him. "You're not supposed to be here at all."

"And now I'm leaving." Talbot's voice was conciliatory but within, his temper was rising, his guilt and anger at himself finding a new focus.

"Oh you think that do you?" The boy pushed Talbot back and the group around him laughed, as groups will when a bully starts to pick on someone – an attractive blonde girl, a curly haired one who seemed to be angry even when laughing, and a boy with hair blonde enough to be white, laughing joyously at Talbot's expense. "You came in with Hobson didn't you? Not surprised she's had to slum it in the village to find anyone who'll spend time with her." He pushed Talbot again.

"Don't push me."

"Or what?"

One of the good things about Talbot was that rather than using his 'position' to lord it over those less fortunate, he used it as a cushion. He never got angry with people, because he was better off

95

than they were and nothing they could say or do would change that. They could call him all the names they wanted but he would still be richer, better looking and just generally more at ease with life. But that easy comfort with who he was had evaporated after he had done something dumb to Lisa and been forced to face a side of himself he didn't like. Right now, Larry Glendon looked a whole lot like that side of himself.

Talbot nailed Glendon on the nose with a perfect straight right that would have made his boxing coach weep with happiness. The bully fell to the ground, the group around him suddenly silenced, toothless without their alpha.

"Remember this moment, next time you're tempted to be a dick," suggested Talbot, and strolled off through the gates with Moose bounding after him.

"You'll regret this!" The anger in the voice that screamed at Talbot from behind, sounded more animal than man. A serrated anger, that could tear flesh. "You'll regret it!"

Talbot ignored it and walked on. He had enough to feel guilty about, and was not going to waste any of it on a bully who had got what he deserved.

The dark expanse of the moor by night was enough to give anyone the willies, but Talbot had been born and raised here. He had been walking its paths since he was old enough to walk and the moor held no fears for him. Besides, he was too preoccupied to be scared. He walked slowly, with a heavy tread, taking time out on occasion to kick at any rocks that were incautious enough to lie in his way.

Guilt is a mobile emotion, one that describes a circular path, and right now his was arcing away from himself. Yes, he probably should not have gone for the kiss with Lisa, but didn't girls like to be kissed? He knew lots of girls who very specifically liked to be kissed by him, and it would only take a phone call to make that a reality. Perhaps Lisa ought to consider that before she started making rash decisions. He did not want to lose her but surely she ought to be far more worried about losing him. The world was only supplied with one Talbot Conliffe - if she lost that one then she would spend the rest of her life regretting it.

By the time he got back home, the guilt would probably have found its way back to himself, but in the solitary self-righteousness of his walk across the moor, Talbot managed to convince himself - more or less - that he was in the right, and that a message from Lisa, apologising for her feminine flightiness, would be waiting for him when he got home. And if not, well maybe one of those other girls would be getting a call.

This optimistic thought kept him warm as he traversed the cold moor, and he was halfway home when a sound made him stop.

"Did you hear that?"

Apparently Moose had, as the dog had stopped and pricked up his ears.

The sound reached them again, wafting across the moor, a long, low animal noise, like the howl of a wolf.

"Must be the wind," said Talbot, although the fact that he felt the need to say this out loud to his dog, revealed that he was more worried than his attitude might have admitted.

The next howl sounded nearer, and there was no longer any way to mistake it for the wind. Despite its drawn-out length, it sounded urgent. It had purpose.

Talbot began to move faster, even breaking into a jog, Moose hurrying along beside him. It was stupid to be frightened; he'd walked this route so many times. But presumably Ralph Matthews had thought the same thing.

Ralph had been ripped to shreds when they found him.

Talbot began to run, his heart thumping in his chest, his breath ragged and uneven. He tripped and fell, tumbling down the side of a ditch, plunging a foot into a puddle of cold water and cursing angrily. Dragging himself up and out he continued to run.

There was nothing to be scared of, he told himself.

Another howl. This one was unbearably close, and sounded somehow satisfied, as if to say; Gotcha. There was an edge to it, as if the animal was angry and that anger fuelled its hunt.

Talbot ran as fast as his legs would carry him, fear piercing him like ice. It was behind him now, he could hear it, hear the feet pounding the ground. It was gaining. It was faster than him. And he couldn't run much longer.

Chapter 9 - From The Diary of Lisa Hobson

January 16th

    Talbot is dead.

    Something is wrong here. Terribly wrong.

January 17th

    Don't want to write, but need to remember this. Glendon bumped into me at lunch. Literally. Knocked over the glass on my tray.

    He cocked his head at me in that infuriatingly smug way. "Heard about your boyfriend. Sad stuff. But that's what you get when you mess with the big dog."

    Doesn't that sound like something? Like he knows something? Even like he <u>did</u> something? Josie told me that Talbot punched Glendon that night. I don't know what I'm thinking here. Is it possible that Glendon has a dog or something kept out on the moor? Or have I just read *Hound of the Baskervilles* (Sir Arthur Conan Doyle) once too often?

    So confused.

January18th

    Ollie was allowed up to my room yesterday. It's the longest we've spent together since we arrived. He listened to me and hugged me and told me how sorry he was. We've never been close but this was like having a brother again.

    Little things keep setting me off. I saw *The Woman in White* (Wilkie Collins) on my shelf. I said I'd lend it to Talbot, now he'll never get to read it. Ollie held me while I cried.

    I don't want to stay here, but I don't want to run away from it either. I've been given a week off school to go home and - I don't know - recover? As if that's an option. I don't know what good it will do but I'm grateful for it.

Chapter 10 - The White Wolf

But first there was the funeral.

The eulogy was delivered by the gangling Squire Montford, who had been here all too recently following the death of his father. He tripped over his feet on his way up to the pulpit but was surprisingly affecting. The words, 'Quite a chap,' had never carried such sombre reverence.

After the ceremony, Talbot's father, Sir John, came up to Lisa.

"Miss Hobson, yes?"

"Yes." Lisa struggled to form the word.

"I wanted to say…" The man swallowed and Lisa could only imagine what was going on inside him on a day like today. "I wanted to say how glad we were that he found a girl like you."

Lisa didn't know how to respond.

"Talbot was always… I don't know what you call it these days. He wasn't a shy boy. Could be a bit of terror with girls to be frank. But he liked you. I'm glad he had that. That he got to know what it meant to care for someone, before…" The poor man couldn't finish the sentence.

"I liked him too," Lisa managed to choke out.

"Even better." He looked wretched, as if his fragile self-control was all but shattered. "Just wanted you to know."

It was a long, slow drive back from the little graveyard in Naughton, where Talbot was buried alongside his illustrious ancestors, and when she got back, Lisa had no desire to face anyone. The freezing, January rain had driven everyone indoors and she took advantage of it to get some alone time. The rain ran down her face to soak her hair and clothes, but it felt wrong to care about getting wet when Talbot was…

It had taken a physical effort for Lisa to write the reality in her diary - that single devastating phrase - and since then she had struggled to acknowledge the reality of it. Now she was not sure what she was supposed to do, here at the school or with life in general. What would happen if she just didn't leave this bench? The world would keep on turning. Just as it had with poor Talbot torn to… She forced the thought from her chaotic mind and trained her eyes on the muddy gravel of the path in front of her.

Sealed in her own world, Lisa did not notice the caretaker's approach until he spoke.

"Miss Hobson?" He had only started at the school this term and had struck Lisa as a thoroughly creepy individual, but for once she was glad to see him, not least because of the company in which he came.

"Moose?"

The dog practically threw itself at Lisa and she wrapped her arms around him, burying in her face in the pungent aroma of wet dog, her tears mingling with the mud in which he was covered.

"Careful," warned the caretaker in his gentle, west country tones. "He's hurt. I called a vet, but I thought perhaps you might be the one to look after him. I don't have time."

"Where did you find him?" asked Lisa, from within the bundle of damp hair.

"I was out for a walk on the moor. He were cowering in a hollow. Reckon he'd been there days. He's got a nasty wound, see. Injured animals hole up and lick their wounds till they get better. Or don't."

Lisa finally removed her head from the dog so she could look at him. Though Moose looked happy to see her, there was no mistaking that he was in a poor state. He was thin and dirty, and there were numerous bloody scratches in his skin, which she had not at first noticed through his coat. His left hind leg wobbled, struggling to hold his weight.

He had fought for his master.

She hugged the dog again, before turning back to the caretaker. "Let's take him inside and warm him up."

As they entered the North wing, Mrs Kerrigan met them, a look of polite horror on her face, like a Duchess who'd spotted someone using the wrong spoon. "Mr Rains, where do you think you are taking that animal?"

Lisa realised that this was the first time she had actually registered the caretaker's name, she had always thought of him simply as 'the caretaker'. What a terrible thing to learn about yourself.

"Sorry, Mrs Kerrigan." Mr Rains seemed to shrink in the teacher's presence.

"Get it out of here."

"Yes, Mrs..."

But Lisa interrupted. "He's been hurt, he needs somewhere to warm up."

"Now Lisa..." Mrs Kerrigan began.

"This was Talbot's dog. If you'd like to explain to Mr and Mrs Conliffe that you let their late son's beloved pet die, then you be my guest. But I am going to do everything I can to save him."

Mrs Kerrigan could only splutter as Lisa pushed past her. Since Talbot's death, Lisa had been treated with kid gloves, as everyone had known there was something between them - though what was a matter of some speculation - but it was her attitude that did the trick in this instance. A part of her that burned brightly insisted that she would not lose the dog as well. There was precisely one thing left that she could do for Talbot; not let his dog die.

The vet's verdict was that the injuries were serious, but would heal with proper care, and that if they had not found Moose when they did, he would certainly have died. Lisa turned to give credit where it was due, but Mr Rains had gone back to his mopping. There are many kinds of hero.

As the vet took Moose away, Malcolm arrived in his mini-bus to take Lisa to the station. Seated on the train that bore her swiftly away from Naughton, the school and the oppressive presence of the moor, Lisa pondered on the moments and events on which lives turn. Before Mr Rains had arrived with Moose, she had been planning to leave the Priory Grange. She had been lost in sadness and mired in inactivity. Now she felt the need to act. A week away would do her good - a week not thinking about any of it - but when she returned... Suddenly it seemed as if there was more she could do for Talbot than just looking after Moose. And perhaps for Mr Tull as well.

"That's a good place to start."

It was a week later, Lisa was back at school and was spending her first afternoon back facing her fear by walking the moor, with the newly returned Moose gambolling beside her.

"Is there a connection between Talbot's... between Talbot and Mr Tull?"

Moose's only response was to snuffle hopefully about the entrance to a rabbit burrow.

"One disappeared," Lisa continued – you weren't talking to yourself if there was a dog there, which made it *not* crazy, " the other... didn't. There's more similarity between Talbot and Ralph

Matthews."

If there was some large animal loose on the moor then there was probably a limited amount she could do about it, but...

"I can't shake the feeling they're connected."

Moose shook his face free of soil and moved on.

"They both..." she had to get used to saying it sooner or later, "...*died*, after making trips across the moor." More than that. "Is it possible Mr Tull was going to the mine that night?"

Lisa would have been prepared to swear that Moose shrugged.

"I think he went in that direction before; after I told him about Dr Lloyd. And she did go out that night." What else? "They were both engaged in some sort of investigation; Talbot of Mr Tull's disappearance, Mr Tull of where Dr Lloyd was going (potentially)."

She paused. Everything which linked the victims was also true of her. She decided not to think about that.

"What else did they have in common?"

Moose barked.

"Yes," Lisa exclaimed. "You're right. Mr Tull argued with Glendon and Talbot punched him."

What was it that odious creep has said? '*That's what you get when you mess with the big dog.*'

Lisa shivered.

Was it too fanciful? It didn't amount to evidence. Glendon unquestionably had a temper and a viciousness that went beyond ordinary bullying, but Talbot had not been killed by a man, he had been torn apart. What if he *did* have a dog hidden somewhere out on the moor? She had noted the possibility in her diary but mentally dismissed it because that *was* the plot of *The Hound of the Baskervilles* (Sir Arthur Conan Doyle).

"Which doesn't mean it isn't true." She had stopped walking and Moose hurried back to urge her on, he was a dog who preferred to be moving. "We need to consider this logically."

Lisa started to walk again, the dog bounding happily beside her.

"Why would Glendon do something like that?" Moose didn't have an answer and neither did Lisa. Motive might have to wait.

"He's a vile individual but that doesn't seem enough." If 'bully' equalled 'killer' then every school in the world would be littered with corpses.

"If he does have a dog, where could he hide it?"

Moose whined as he prodded his nose into a thistle and Lisa recalled hearing that sound before.

"The curious incident of the dog at the mine." Moose had been very uncomfortable at the mine entrance. "Did you smell another dog?"

Though he seemed to know that he was being addressed, Moose could give no more lucid response than sticking up his head and panting.

"If there was a dog in the mine," Lisa continued with her train of thought, "surely we'd have seen it. Or heard it."

Moose bounded off after a moth that he had disturbed into flight.

"Maybe Glendon had taken it for a walk when we were there? No, you're right, that would be a hell of a coincidence. But the mines are pretty big," Moose hurried back, having been outwitted by the moth. "We barely looked around any of it. It could have been down another tunnel. You could set up a light, some food and water. All that."

It was tenuous. But not impossible.

"Would explain the bones. And the gate would keep it in."

It would be too much to say that it all tied up neatly, but life seldom does.

"Not impossible." Lisa looked down at Moose, who was pushing his head under her hand in that way dogs do when they want to be petted. "So what next?" She submitted to Moose's will and scratched him behind the ears. "He's got to feed it sometime. Spend time with it." Maybe give it some article stolen from its next potential victim so it could hunt them down?

Lisa knelt down to look Moose in the eyes as she tousled his hair.

"I could follow him."

Moose licked her face.

Back at the school, Moose was returned to the caretaker's basement - Mr Rains had agreed to house the dog as long as Lisa fed him, watered him and took care of whatever came out the other end - and Lisa headed up to the sixth form corridor.

Returning to the school after her week away had not been easy, all those emotions she had put on hold had come rushing back. And yet, it was in a far better frame of mind than she might have expected that Lisa went to bed that night. Perhaps it was all ridiculously far-fetched, but the investigation gave her something to focus on beyond the cold, immutable reality of what had happened. It gave her something to do.

She had to bide her time waiting for an opportunity. School did not allow for long periods of sitting by the window, watching the comings and goings through the gate. Though her focus had shifted, Lisa did not abandon her school work - she had worked too hard to chuck it all in now, little though it seemed to matter these days. One day she saw Glendon coming back through the gate and cursed her luck that she had not been watching when he left. But that was the problem: he could leave at any time and that would not necessarily be when Lisa was watching. In addition, he had a vested interest in not being seen, as keeping a dog on the moor was against school rules (not any specific rule, but in principle). The chances were that he snuck out when no one else was watching. It also occurred to Lisa that while her room afforded her a conveniently commanding view of the main gate, a man making a surreptitious exit might hop over the back wall instead. The more she thought about it, the less watching the gate seemed likely to yield results. Watching Glendon would afford her a better chance.

This did not go brilliantly either. There is a reason that spies and the police receive training in covert surveillance - because it is difficult. On more than one occasion, Glendon spotted Lisa watching him and made fun of her (*'Got a thing for me have you? No offence but you're not my type. I like pretty girls.'*). It was better he think Lisa had developed a crush than guess the real reason for her interest, but the thought still made Lisa feel as if the skin wanted to crawl off her body and hide under her bed.

One thing she did notice was that Oliver seemed to be less a part of Glendon's crew than he had been. Perhaps there had been an argument while she had been away. Perhaps he had seen them for what they were. More likely, Ollie being Ollie, he had simply tired of them. Either way, it was nice to have something positive to write in her diary, even if it took her no closer to her current goal.

Finally, after two fruitless weeks, the break she needed came through pure chance. During study group, taking place after class

104

was finished for the day, as Mr Knowles was expanding on themes of male inadequacy in *Macbeth* (and revealing an uncomfortable familiarity with them), Lisa's gaze wandered out of the window to the moor. It was the constant of being at Priory Grange - the moor was always with you - but today there was something to see. In the waning light of early evening, a figure was walking away from the school, one whom Lisa could instantly identify from his distinctive gait. Larry Glendon even walked like a smug twat.

"Sir?" Lisa's hand shot up.

"Yes, Lisa?" Mr Knowles looked over.

"I'm feeling a little nauseous. Would I be able to go to the infirmary?"

"Yes, yes, go." Lisa was a good student, one whom teacher's tended to believe, and there was still a degree of understanding leniency in how she was treated following Talbot's death. Lisa usually hesitated to exploit it, but in this circumstance she was sure that Talbot would have forgiven her.

Leaving hastily but hurriedly, Lisa made sure she was out of earshot and then broke into a run, down the stairs, through the entrance hall and on out through the main gates to the moor. As she ran, the thought did occur to her that this was, almost certainly, a dreadful idea. If it had been hard to follow Glendon unnoticed in school, it would be even harder in the wide open spaces of the moor. Plus, she was wholly unprepared for such a venture; she was in school uniform right down to her unsuitable shoes, and still clutched her books and notes for class. The sun would soon be going down, leaving her exposed to the freezing temperatures of the moor after dark, against which a smart blazer and knee length skirt would be damn-all protection .

But she might never get another chance and she had waited long enough already. *And* he had been heading north-east; the direction of the mine.

Was it possible that she was right?

If she was, then she was following a multiple murderer to the place where he kept his murder 'weapon', with no more defence than her A-Level notes and course texts. It was hard to believe that Sir Charles Baskerville would have been all alright if only he had been armed with copies of *Macbeth* (William Shakespeare) and Virgil's *The Aeneid.*

As she had started out far behind him, Lisa moved as quickly as she could, while still cautiously attempting to stay out of sight. Unable to see her quarry, she simply made for the mine and was delighted when Glendon became visible up ahead. He was still going the right way.

Now he was in her sights, Lisa fell back as much as she dared. As long as he was visible, that was all that mattered. But if he was visible to her, then she was visible to him. All he had to do was turn around and this whole enterprise would be for nothing. She scuttled from stunted tree to wind-scoured boulder, and hunched low in ditches and hollows, where stagnant water filled her shoes and soaked her feet. When it seemed Glendon might turn, she hurled herself full length to the cold, hard ground, pressing her face to the dirt.

But even after going to such lengths, as they finally approached the mine with the sun creeping ever closer to the horizon, Lisa's resolve began to falter. Not because she was afraid of being caught - she was pretty sure she could handle Glendon, who struck her as all mouth when his followers weren't there to back him up - but because of the last time she had come this way. She tried hard not to think about it, but there were, inevitably, emotions stirring within her.

From a safe distance, squatting uncomfortably close to the ground behind a prickly bush, Lisa watched Glendon enter the crevasse which led to the mine entrance. He did not pause, Lisa noticed, did not even slow. He had been this way before. He knew where he was going. Lisa gave him a minute, then followed, her heart thumping against her ribs like it wanted to get out.

What if she was right about everything? She had been right so far. Was it so far-fetched to think she might be right about the rest? What if there was a big, vicious dog in there that had killed perhaps three people and more sheep than you would have thought necessary? What if Glendon had trained his dog to kill those people? Would he stop at her?

That was the part of the theory that was currently holding the least water with Lisa. Vicious though he was, was Larry Glendon capable of murder? Also; how had this started? Had Glendon brought a pet dog to school with him, which he kept in an abandoned mine, because school rules forbade pets, and then, following some sort of argument with Ralph Matthews, decided to train it up as a killer? Then, after discovering how easy it was, he used it to revenge himself on any who angered him. Suddenly it all seemed a bit improbable.

Reaching the entrance to the mine, Lisa peered in cautiously. Because she had left so abruptly, she of course had no torch with her, not even her phone. She could set fire to her copy of Virgil's *The Aenid* (Dido had fallen well short of her expectations of how a heroine should behave), but she didn't have any matches. Glendon, presumably, did have a torch, but there was no sign of its light in the darkness of the tunnel. Either that or he had switched his torch off when he heard someone coming, making Lisa a big, clear, unmissable silhouette against the entranceway. That wasn't a happy thought. Lisa took a deep breath; she was not about to turn back now.

Her feet squelched and crunched in the mix of accumulated material that formed the floor of the mine tunnel. She hadn't noticed the noise when she had come this way the first time, because of course she had been in company. The thought made a lump rise in her throat which she swallowed down again - not now, she had to focus on what she was doing. At frequent intervals, she turned back to look at the increasingly distant light of the tunnel mouth - although 'light' was a relative term now, as the sun was setting. As the tunnel curved, what little light there was vanished, and Lisa was enveloped in total darkness, unable to see her hand in front of her face. It felt suddenly colder, and it had been close to freezing already. She walked on with hesitant steps, one hand out in front, the other following the clammy, uneven rock of the wall. Her foot snagged on something and she fell forward, managing to regain her footing before she hit the floor. She straightened again and listened for any sound of her prey. Nothing. She moved on, then came to a stop as her forward hand touched something. It was uneven, cold and lumpy, a mixture of rock and mud. Had the tunnel turned? She felt around, and for a moment experienced a surge of blind panic as it seemed that she was closed in, before realising that, in the dark, she had gone down the caved-in tunnel where she and Talbot had flipped a coin on their first excursion here.

She recalled that moment in *The Castle of Otranto* (Horace Walpole) when Isabella was in the cave and her lamp went out;

'Alone in so dismal a place, her mind imprinted with all the terrible events of the day...'

This was stupid.

How could you follow someone you couldn't bloody well see? She was just as likely to fall down a mineshaft as she was find Glendon. And to what end? What would she do if she found him? Probably beg him to get her out of there in one piece. There was only one way out of the mine (as far as she was aware), waiting outside would be just as good. Surely he wouldn't come all this way if he didn't plan to take this hypothetical dog for a walk. Even if it had been provided with a light, the poor thing could hardly be kept forever underground until he needed it to kill someone.

Lisa started back the way she had come.

That was when she heard foot falls. Fast-moving like someone running, possibly more than one person. Or possibly a dog. They were coming from deeper inside the mine, and they were coming her way.

Darting back into the blocked-off branch of the tunnel, Lisa crouched and held her breath, straining her eyes to see something as the noise got closer. The running feet, accompanied by thick, exerted breathing, passed by the end of the tunnel, heading for the outside. Before she could think what she was doing, Lisa headed after it. Probably this was still stupid, but she had come all this way and she wouldn't give up now she had actually found something.

But as she turned back down the tunnel towards the entrance, a light started from behind her - a torch beam slicing through the dark. Lisa looked back, expecting to see Glendon, but instead she saw, faintly visible by light reflected from the walls, the figure of the man she had seen down here on her last visit, the stranger who had so terrified her and Talbot.

Hot and cold stabs of panic seared through Lisa and she broke into a run, full pelt, dropping books and notes as she went.

"Hey!"

The voice from behind just made Lisa increase her speed. She could hear his footfalls as well now, sharp and echoing, chasing her.

"Rats!"

An instant after the unlikely curse, she heard the thump of someone tumbling to the floor of the mine, having tripped on an unexpected copy of Virgil's *The Aenid*. Nice to know it was good for something. Up ahead of her, Lisa could now see the tunnel entrance, a light grey patch in a sea of black. She tore out into the open air, skidded to a halt and tugged at the rusty iron gate. It moved unwillingly, screaming on seized hinges as it went, but finally clanging shut. Lisa grabbed the heavy chain and wrapped it round and around the old fastenings, tying it into a knot. It would not trap the man in there, but it would give her time to get away.

As she heard footsteps approaching from the darkness of the tunnel, Lisa took off again, sprinting away from the mine as fast as her legs would allow onto the moor, as night fell.

At first Lisa ran straight back the way she had come, but then thought better of it. The man had got a better look at her than she had got at him, and she was currently dressed in a pretty distinctive school uniform. If he was intent on coming for her, then he would know where she was going and would know what route she would take. Picking up her speed again, Lisa bent her path towards the mountainous hills (or possibly actual mountains; she was sketchy on the distinction) on the horizon. This route would add at least a half hour to her journey, probably more, but that didn't matter - she was in trouble with Mrs Kerrigan either way if she got caught.

After about five minutes she quit running and slowed to a brisk walk. She did not feel safe yet, but Lisa was not one of nature's runners, and if she kept on at this pace then she would be adding heart attack to the list of things out to kill her today. The slower pace unfortunately gave her the opportunity to think about what had happened and about some of the decisions she had been making recently. What had possessed her to do this? What had she thought she would find? She could remember asking herself similar questions when she went to the mine with Talbot. And look how that had wound up.

Was her rashness responsible for Talbot's death?

Was that why she was so keen for Glendon to be responsible? Because then it wouldn't be her fault?

To add to her general feeling of moroseness, it started to rain, pattering to the ground around her and soaking Lisa's inadequate clothes. Despite the full moon, holding its own through a veil of cloud, the darkness was choking, shrouding her, making the walk back still more funereal. Why was it always full moon at times like this?

109

And then, drifting across the empty expanse of the moor, came the sound of an animal howl.

The sound made a shiver run down Lisa's spine. But as she looked up at the moon again, even the shiver froze and her blood turned to ice. Standing on a ridge, high above the moor, silhouetted against the low, pale body of the moon, was an animal. It could have been some unusual breed of dog, but as it threw back its large, shaggy head and let loose a clear, ululating howl into the night, there was only one word in Lisa's mind: Wolf.

It stood, posed like that for a long moment, its strikingly white fur seeming to blend with and reflect the light of the moon, making it almost luminescent. Then, on an instant, it was moving. Like a waterfall spilling over a cliff edge, the white wolf cascaded down the steep slope, building speed as it went.

For a heartbeat, Lisa was frozen, staring in terrified fascination. Then, as if a spell had been broken, she took to her heels, all exhaustion forgotten. It was coming in her direction. A long, high howl echoed across the moor. And then, with a chill of pure horror, Lisa heard the call answered. Another howl. Then another. And another.

This wasn't a lone wolf. It was part of a pack.

Perhaps it was her imagination, whetted by adrenalin, light-headed exhaustion and fear, but Lisa was sure the howls were starting to converge on her. She sprinted as hard as she could - faster than any gym teacher had every been able to coax out of her - muddy shoes slipping on the coarse, wet grass. Who knows what causes a person to look behind them in situations like this, but Lisa found she couldn't help herself. At first she saw nothing, but then her eyes began to pick out the patches of darker movement against the black backdrop of night. Here and there the moonlight caught the gleam of their open slathering jaws and wide, staring eyes. Lisa gulped at the back of her throat as she caught sight of the closest wolf, a grey one, bigger than the others, its red eyes piercing into her.

The sight almost hypnotised her, and meant that she didn't see the slope coming. Lisa's foot found nothing where it expected to find the ground and down she went, tumbling head over heels down the mud and brush, slick with rain. On the bright side, maybe this way down was faster, but she landed with a thump at the bottom, crying out as her leg caught a sharp rock. She scrambled back to her feet, the pain and tiredness in her legs making them wobble beneath her. Forcing it to the back of her mind, she kept running, not caring where, just needing to keep moving, her injured leg now giving her a pronounced limp as she went. A wounded animal - easy prey for the pack. The howl sounded in unison as they closed in.

Was this how it had been for Talbot? For Mr Tull? Chased to exhaustion then torn apart. Was it a quick way to go?

By now Lisa was running in name alone. She felt more tired than she had ever felt, her limbs dragging like lead even as she urged them on. She stumbled forward like a zombie, a dead girl running, feet barely leaving the ground. Whether she tripped or simply ran out of strength, she was not sure, but down she went again to the muddy ground and lay there, lungs hollow, legs a mass of ache augmented by the sharp pain from where she had fallen. At the edge of hearing, beyond her own laboured breaths and pounding heart, she could hear the quick, approaching paws, drumming the ground. Desperately she strove to lever herself up, knowing that she could not outrun her pursuers but unwilling to give up so easily. But her arms would not hold her any more than her legs. Perhaps she would get lucky and pass out.

The world seemed to drift, though it was presumably Lisa's mind that was doing the drifting. The howls were on her, and, as much from fear as from exhaustion, Lisa blacked out. Her last memories were of a loud bang, and a flash of fire.

Chapter 11 - The Pack

When Lisa woke up, it was to someone shaking her and gently smacking her face.

"Wake up," said a heavily accented voice.

"...'m tryin..."

As she became aware of a sharp pain in her leg, Lisa's mind put together the last few things it remembered. The heavy cloak of unconsciousness shot back and Lisa started awake.

"I'm alive?" she checked.

"That is what I am trying to decide," said the old woman seated beside her.

Lisa would have thought that sitting up and talking were pretty compelling signs of life, but the old woman was apparently unwilling to take anything for granted.

"What happened here?"

Lisa winced as the woman jabbed a gnarled finger into a bloody gash on her calf.

"I fell down."

"You sure?"

"That I fell down? Yes. Very sure."

"Nothing bite you?"

Lisa shook her head. "Not unless it happened after I passed out. But that," she indicated the gash, "is from when I fell down."

The woman peered closer, screwing up her tiny, black eyes to squint at Lisa's wound. Finally she seemed satisfied. "Alright."

She took a bowl of water from a nearby table, delicately painted with intertwining flowers, dunked a cloth in it and began to clean the mud from the wound, making Lisa gasp.

"Thank you."

The old woman shrugged.

"My memories are a little sketchy, but did you by any chance save my life?"

"My son," the woman replied as she worked, "my eldest son - saw you running from the beasts. He shot above their heads to scare them away."

"Please thank him for me." It seemed woefully inadequate. She looked about the room by the light of the old-fashioned oil lamp that hung from the low roof. It was small and cluttered, every shelf was

112

filled, the walls were crowded with pictures, and bunches of herbs hung from the ceiling. The wooden walls were painted in a similarly floral style to the table, and the bed on which Lisa lay could be folded back into a cupboard for convenience. It was a caravan, and Lisa realised that it must be one of the gypsy caravans she had seen out on the moor when they were searching for Mr Tull.

That was where she had seen her saviour before! The woman cleaning her wound was the same who had spoken to Dr Bellamy that day. Lisa looked more closely at her companion. The old woman looked like every stereotypical gypsy fortune teller who had ever lied about the proximity of tall, dark strangers in a fairground tent. But somehow real. It was nothing Lisa could put her finger on, but the woman carried a built-in authenticity with her coloured headscarf, bangled arms, ringed fingers, hooped earrings, and the crocheted shawl she wore over her voluminous clothing. Her face was the colour of aged teak and the texture of a walnut shrink-wrapped in leather, framed by sparse tendrils of greasy, grey hair that poked out from her headscarf.

"I'm Lisa, by the way," volunteered Lisa. "Lisa Hobson."

"Maria Siniestro." The name rolled archaically in her non-specific eastern European accent. She finished cleaning Lisa's leg and dumped the cloth into the bowl, turning the water a ruddy brown. Reaching behind her she took a strip of cloth, torn from a blouse, and started to wrap it around Lisa's calf.

Stuck for something to say and finding the silence oppressive, Lisa looked about the caravan for inspiration, lighting on a picture of a handsome, gypsy man on the wall, white flowers twined about the frame.

"Is that your son? The man who saved me?"

"That is my youngest son." Maria's eyes barely flicked up from her work. "He died. In the old country."

"I'm sorry."

Maria grunted.

Lisa was about to ask 'how did he die?' but Maria's attitude did not invite further inquiry. "I can't believe there are wolves on the moor."

Maria knotted the makeshift bandage with a sharp tug. "There are no wolves on the moor, child."

"They looked like wolves." A group of escaped pet dogs

113

forming into a pack seemed more believable, but Lisa could not forget what she had seen.

"They do," agreed Maria, not very helpfully. "But they are not."

"You seem to know a bit about them," Lisa observed, wondering how long social convention demanded she make polite conversation before she could excuse herself and head back for the school. "You have them in your country?"

"My son was attacked by such a creature," said Maria, her black eyes focusing hard on Lisa.

"That's what killed him?"

A shake of the head. "I killed him."

Of all the things Lisa had expected her hostess to say, that she would not even have considered as a wild possibility. The phrase 'out of the frying pan and into the fire' flickered through her head as she realised that she was in a confined space with a woman who had just admitted to killing her own son.

"He was one of them," Maria went on. "He killed his father. After that, he begged me to take his life."

Lisa sat in cold horror at what she was hearing. "One of them?"

"A werewolf."

Lisa's first reaction was relief - for a moment she had thought this was serious. Her second reaction was realisation that the line between being stuck in a caravan with a woman who killed her son, and being stuck in a caravan with a woman who killed her son because she thought he was a werewolf, was a pretty thin one.

"A werewolf." She tried not to sound incredulous or as if she was humouring the old woman, but apparently did not succeed as Maria scoffed.

"You do not believe me. Of course you do not. And I wish that it was not necessary for you to do so. But this horror has entered your life. Now the pack has your scent, I fear they will not let you be." She flicked back a curtain to look out and up at the night sky. "Morning will be here soon. It is almost time."

As Lisa took one of those quiet moments in which you wonder how your life has taken you to a particular point, Maria got to her feet.

"Come."

"I was actually thinking I might head back to school," said Lisa, sitting up. "I'm already going to be in trouble for being out this late, I badly need a shower and a change of..."

"In good time. First there is something you must see. Come."

They left the caravan, Maria leading, Lisa following, still limping slightly. Outside, the caravans were arranged in a circle about a huge central bonfire, around which gypsies danced to the music of fiddle and accordion, as if determined to fulfil every cultural stereotype they could think of.

"Come," Maria repeated, leading Lisa back onto the darkness of the moor. The old woman seemed to have extraordinary night vision, strolling on without a qualm while Lisa stumbled and tripped in her wake. Up a steep slope they went, leading towards the peaks, ridges, ravines and gullies of the high hill range. The rain had stopped but the ground was still wet, and Lisa struggled to stay upright as the gradient got sharper and she was forced to use her hands to help her climb.

"Be silent," said Maria as they approached a crest. Lisa wasn't aware that she had been making much noise, but tried to at least not breathe so heavily.

Maria stopped a moment to lick her finger and hold it up, to check the wind direction before continuing. As they achieved the crest, the gypsy stooped low and loped nimbly forward to duck behind a boulder that had rolled down from higher cliffs during a rockfall. Lisa followed, staying close to the old woman, nervously agitated and wondering how much stress her system could take in one night. Turning back to Lisa, Maria raised a heavily ringed finger to her lips, then pointed out beyond the boulder, indicating for Lisa to take a look.

It was still night, and though dawn could not have been far distant, the full moon remained the only real light. But it was bright enough to illuminate the scene in the little gully beyond the crest. A stream ran through the gully, and arrayed about it, some standing, some lying, some drinking, some play-fighting, were several large wolves.

Lisa instantly pulled her head back behind the boulder, her chest tightening in fear at the sight. She had narrowly escaped these animals earlier and now this damn gypsy woman had brought her right back to them! And apparently bringing her here was not

115

enough. Maria grabbed Lisa's head in a strong grip and forced her to look out again.

There must have been around ten of them there, varying in size but all bigger than any wolf Lisa could recall seeing in a zoo - although she might have been mentally imbuing these with greater size and strength, because the ones in the zoo had not been out to get her. But, now she was forced to look longer and harder, it was not just in size that these animals differed from wolves she had seen in zoos or on TV. True, she was hardly an expert in wolves and for all she knew these were some sort of sub-species - which made sense given their presence here - but there was something about them that made them seem... unreal? Maybe that was the wrong word. They looked as if they had been designed by someone *trying* to design a scarier wolf. Like a Hollywood version of a wolf, where the teeth must be bigger, the eyes redder, the coarse, black hair shaggier. Everything was just that little bit *more* than was believable, and yet there they were. They moved with a slight awkwardness. Not that they were tripping over their feet, or anything else that might give Lisa the advantage in a foot race, but there was just something - what was the word? - 'clunky' about the way they moved. It was angular and deliberate, not fluid and natural as animals normally move. 'Not normal' was probably as good a summation as Lisa could find. There was something not normal about a wolf pack living on a moor in the north of England, and something not normal about the wolves themselves.

It also occurred to her that the white wolf she had seen silhouetted against the moon was not among them. She had a vague recollection that albino animals are often ostracised in the wild because they look different. Perhaps the white one was a wolf apart? Or maybe it was the one in charge and didn't go for a drink with its co-wolves after work.

The first narrow strands of dawn started to pick at the horizon, and Lisa heard a breath-like whisper from Maria, behind her. "Watch."

The coming of morning - though Lisa would still have deemed it the middle of the night - certainly seemed to have affected the wolves. Those lying down had got to their paws and were whining fretfully. They rolled on their backs, twisting as if in discomfort, pawing the ground or biting at their thick fur.

116

Then, one by one, their bodies seemed to be gripped by a series of spasms, shaking their heads and stretching their spines. Lisa clamped a hand over her mouth to stop herself from crying out as she saw their legs start to lengthen and expand, thickening as the black hair thinned, receding from them. Their bodies contorted into unnatural figures, before realigning themselves to something new and unwolf-like. Bones disjointed themselves and popped back in at an alien angle. Teeth seemed to crawl back into parent gums as snouts pulled in like stretched rubber. Fingers burst angrily forth from paws, flexing as their blackened claws became neat nails. Tails retracted into backsides like the wire of a vacuum cleaner. Skin shrank, shrivelled, filled, swelled, fluctuated, rippled and smoothed across the increasingly human bodies, that gasped on all fours, feet away from Lisa's astonished eyes. Finally, as if the change worked from the outside in, the growls and whines of the wolves went through a transitional period, like puberty at high speed, as vocal cords grated against each other, refashioning animal noise into human speech - mostly swearing at this point.

From start to finish the change took under a minute. At the end of it, Lisa found her overwhelming emotion to be one of ridiculous embarrassment as she stared out at the nude bodies of people with whom she went to school. There was Cristina, as irritatingly perfect naked as she was clothed; there was Zeffie, her curly hair more tangled than usual; Fay, her self-assured smile intact; Jane and Elena. There too were boys, who were the primary reason for Lisa's flushed cheeks as they were all naked and apparently quite unconcerned about it - which was at least a healthy body attitude. She recognised Patrick and Henry from her own year, as well as Anthony, a rugby star everyone said, and several others whose faces she knew, though the names escaped her. It was the bully group in its entirety. With one exception. There was no sign of Larry Glendon, and Lisa instantly knew why. He was the white wolf, the leader of the pack. He did not change with his subordinates. He changed in the mine.

Despite what their bodies had just gone through, the group seemed elated, wild eyed, laughing and whooping excitedly as they retrieved their clothes from where they had been stashed amongst the rocks. Did they know what had happened to them? Did they understand what they were? The whole thing seemed to be a game to

117

them – a shared secret in which they took a shared delight, a heady and forbidden thrill. A natural high.

"Come." Lisa had almost forgotten that Maria was there but obeyed her quickly.

They took a different route back, avoiding an encounter with the ex-wolves as they headed back to the school. Maria walked a little slower now, deliberately keeping pace with Lisa who stumbled, numb and dead-legged beside her.

They had gone some distance from the summit when Lisa spoke. "But… there's no such thing as werewolves."

"I'm sure you are right."

"But... but..." Lisa stopped for a moment, letting the previously defined borders of reality in her mind adjust to accommodate this new information. "They killed Talbot? Mr Tull? The miller - what's his name? Ralph?"

Maria shrugged. "I do not know. I only learnt of their presence here recently. We came from the old country looking for them."

"Your son. He was killed by one."

Maria shook her head. "I told you. I killed my son. He *was* one. We thought we could control him. Protect him. That he would have enough self-control, even in that state. We were wrong. He killed his own father. That was when he begged me to end his suffering." In the slowly increasing light of the early morning, Maria's eyes seemed to burn. "A silver bullet is the only way to put a werewolf to its rest. I did it. The next day we set out to find the wolf that infected my son with this nightmare. This is where the trail led. And when we find it, then I will kill again."

"One of the pack?" Lisa asked. They were still her schoolmates. Most of them she hated but...

"I do not know," Maria admitted. "Nor do I know how to find out. There have been times when I have been tempted to go up there one full moon and kill them all. But only one did this to my son. And I will not take a child from another mother. I have not seen any of them kill anything but animals. Sheep mostly." She gave a rueful half-smile in which there was no happiness at all. "Besides, I don't have enough silver bullets."

"What about Talbot?"

"I don't know who that is."

Quickly - or as quickly as she could - Lisa told her story about

118

Talbot, about Mr Tull, and about their arguments with Glendon before their deaths. The old woman listened. "Different people react to being a wolf in different ways. In the stories of my country, they say that a man who is already a wolf in his heart - a bad man - can control the wolf, use it for his own designs. But a good man has no control, and will become a monster despite himself. I do not know if this is true, but there is an old saying, '*Even a man who is pure of heart, and says his prayers at night, may become a wolf when the wolfbane blooms, and will tear your living guts out*'." She paused. "It loses something in translation. Some say the longer a person is a wolf, the more control they have when they are changed. Others say the opposite, that over time the wolf takes over. No one knows for sure. We do not study these monsters when we find them. We kill them."

"But you've let these ones live." Lisa wasn't sure if she was accusing or admiring.

"They're children," said Maria. "But when I find the one who killed my Bela, if it's this Glendon you speak of or any of them, I won't stay my hand. A man killer cannot be redeemed."

Lisa couldn't argue with any of that but a single thought burnt in her mind. "If you'd done something, you could have saved Talbot."

Maria turned to face her. "Yes. Perhaps I could. If I had killed them all I could have saved the one. I have to live with that. But it is not the worst thing I have to live with."

Lisa had never been fond of those hypothetical ethical puzzles that teachers sometimes posed, in which one innocent life sacrificed can save many others. She was not keen on the reality either. Perhaps there had been no 'right' thing to do, but that made the outcome no less unfair.

"This is where we part." Maria pointed a gnarled finger. "Keep going that way and you will reach the school. Your werewolf friends will be back already."

"They're not my friends."

"That may be just as well. Or it may be incredibly dangerous. One or the other."

"You're not particularly comforting," said Lisa.

Maria nodded. "So I have been told. Here." She reached into the depths of her shawl and brought out something wrapped in a brightly coloured cloth. It was heavy in Lisa's hand as she took it and unwrapped it.

"This is a gun."

"Well spotted. It contains a single silver bullet. I can spare no more. Use it wisely. Use it in protection."

Lisa stared at the weapon in her hand. She had never fired a gun in her life and would have been happy never to do so. She could go now and shoot Glendon, but... Even if she had proof that he had killed Talbot - and there now seemed to be a pack-full of suspects - could she be as ruthless as Maria? She put the gun in her pocket.

"What do I do now?" she asked, pathetically.

"Be careful," said Maria, as helpful as ever. "There is one night left of the full moon. Tonight." She walked away from Lisa with no further parting words

"I meant... In general, from here on in; what do I do?"

Maria continued to walk, not even turning. "I have no idea."

Chapter 12 - The Last Night of the Full Moon

'What do I do now?'

When she got back to her room, with only a few hours of potential sleep left and no chance whatsoever of sleeping, Lisa got out her diary and found herself completely incapable of writing anything beyond that one sentence.

It had been a long walk back to the school. Only then, with the excitements and fears of the night behind her, had Lisa realised just how bloody cold she was, how wet and how covered in mud. She snuck into the building, hoping she went unnoticed but happy enough to be caught as long as any potential consequences could wait until she was warm. As she stepped onto the dormitory corridor, her eyes lingered on doors behind which slept the girls whom she had seen earlier that night. Could it all be a nightmare? No, it had happened.

She took the quickest and most nervous shower of her life to get rid of the mud, constantly checking for anyone creeping in to disembowel her. Then she returned to her room to stare at the diary entry.

'What do I do now?'

Well, she had wanted to know what had happened to Talbot, and that mystery seemed solved. At least partially - the identity of his killer was still up for grabs.

'What do I do now?'

The police were out of the question. You could not go to the police with tales of werewolf bullies and expect to be taken seriously. If she had had her phone with her earlier then she could have taken pictures, and though Lisa had no desire to go out there again, there would be another full moon tonight, so she did have another chance. But would such evidence convince? It was extraordinary what you could do nowadays with a relatively simple computer program. It was the sort of thing people did all the time to post on YouTube - make a video pretending to depict real-life werewolves and laugh at all those falling for it. Might some of those actually be real?

So, the police weren't the answer. But who was? There was equally little point in telling a teacher. Best case scenario; she would end up under psychiatric observation (which she was starting to wonder if she needed). And who was to say there weren't werewolf teachers? She'd seen Dr Lloyd going out across the moor, the same night that Mr Tull had disappeared. And there had been that mysterious disagreement between them. As Lisa understood it - an understanding gleaned from movies and *Buffy the Vampire Slayer* - if a werewolf got its teeth into you then you were infected. At that point it could either leave you with this curse, or kill you outright, which was what had happened to Talbot. He had been spared the horrors of being a wolf. Which was no comfort at all. The point was; it was not so implausible to say that a teacher might have been exposed, or even that it was a teacher who had bitten the pupils. Who could Lisa trust?

Nobody.

There was no one she could trust and no one who would believe her. Her own family wouldn't even believe this sort of nonsense.

Would they? It was a sign of the distance that had always been a factor of their relationship, that it was only now Lisa thought of her brother. Might Oliver believe her? He always struck people as somewhat otherworldly, perhaps he would be open to such a thing. And having spent time with Glendon and the bullies, he might have seen something suspicious.

Either way, Lisa needed to speak to her brother sooner rather than later. He had pulled back from the bully group recently but was still in their ambit, and who knew what the requirements were for being initiated into the pack? Ollie might well be on the shortlist. She had not admitted it to herself at the time, but it had been a vast relief not to see him amongst those changing up in the gully on the hill. She had to get to him before it was too late.

Yes; that was what to do. If this was the last night of the full moon, then she had a month to come up with a more effective long-term plan, but tonight she had to protect her baby brother. Keep Ollie safe tonight, and tomorrow she could start figuring out her next step. And pray that it was only sheep that the wolves were after tonight.

If she asked Mrs Kerrigan, Lisa was sure she could get dispensation to have Oliver come to her dorm that evening. But rules were rules, and he would have to be back in the boys' wing before lights out – before the bullies headed for a convenient window, hopped the wall and made for the hills. She needed him to visit her in secret, so she could keep him in her room late enough that they would not be able take Ollie with them.

After breakfast, Lisa managed to grab a few minutes of her brother's time.

"I was hoping you could come to my dorm this evening?"

Ollie frowned. "Something wrong?"

"Just feeling blue." That was at least true.

"Sure. I'll speak to Mr Knowles."

"No." Lisa shook her head firmly. "I already asked Mrs Kerrigan and she said no."

"You want me to sneak over?"

"Can you? You know the way?" There was a well-established route by which boys visited the girls' dorms after lights out.

Oliver looked uncomfortable. "I know the way, I just... Is it important?"

Lisa hated to play the Talbot card but needs must. "I know time has passed, but it just doesn't seem to be getting any better. I thought it would and..."

"Okay." There was an odd tussle of emotions on Oliver's face, reflecting some internal battle. "I'll swing it. It'll be... It'll be fine."

"Great."

That was one less thing to worry about.

It was a strange day. Lisa felt as if the world had changed overnight, but in a way that no one else had noticed. There were people whom she had seen on a daily basis whom she now could not look at in the same light. She had never liked Cristina or her crew, and that night in the kitchen before Christmas had even made her fear them, but now she saw something different - and not just because she had seen them naked. Now she knew what she knew, Lisa wondered why she had not seen it before. Not that they were werewolves - that was not the sort of thing that you guessed - but the pack mentality. Of course, to a degree, all bullies are pack animals, deferring to their alphas and rounding on their weakest members for their own amusement. But now she knew what she was looking for, Lisa saw it all the more blatantly. At breakfast, Cristina and Jane reached for butter at the same time and Lisa watched Jane cringe back, almost in fear. Later, in a corridor outside of class, she heard Glendon make a comment about a boy, far bigger than him, and saw his pack bunch in around him, ready to back him up if necessary. When someone strayed too close to where the pack ate lunch, one of the younger members snapped at them, driving them away from the pack's territory.

It was a chilling observation. In their own way, they had probably all been pretty unpleasant individuals to start with - natural bullies - but the wolf in them still made its presence felt. They were acquiring characteristics, and Lisa could not help wondering if they were using the wolf to their own ends or if the wolf was controlling them. She recalled what Maria had said about people who were naturally wolfish being able to control the beast. Glendon and Cristina could have terrorised the three little pigs and eaten Granny for breakfast.

After class and after dinner, Lisa sat on her bed waiting, tension playing on her body. Would he come? It would be very much in character for Oliver to simply not bother and never even consider the other person's feelings.

But a tap at the window alleviated her concerns.

"Hi."

"Hi." Ollie returned as he clambered in. "I haven't done this before."

"Good. You shouldn't. But thanks for coming." There was no doubt that he had been more of a brother since the death of Talbot, and Lisa was grateful for that. He had seen that his sister needed him and his sympathy had been genuine and heartfelt. At times Lisa had thought he might cry himself when she sobbed gently on his shoulder.

"Is everything okay?" asked Ollie. He seemed nervous, uncomfortable in his own skin, but that was probably because he was somewhere he wasn't supposed to be.

"Well... you know."

"Sure."

"I just thought it would be nice to hang out."

Ollie smiled, though it was his vague, 'not quite there' smile. Sometimes he smiled like someone who had been taught to do so and was just trying to fit in.

"I thought we could have a midnight feast. Like when we were little."

This time Ollie's smile was more genuine. "Not sure I want to stay till midnight."

"Well, I don't think our midnight feasts were ever at midnight. It just felt like midnight."

"Good fun though."

"The best." Lisa found her own grin was natural too. These moments of shared history were when they were at their closest, back when they were little and the whole world was a plaything, before life interposed. Before she had become serious and Oliver had become 'special'.

Lisa had decided that tonight was not the night to tell him that his friends turned into monsters on a monthly cycle, ate raw sheep and might be responsible for a few deaths. That was not a good opener when she needed him to stay, late enough at least to ensure that he could not be dragged out for his 'initiation'. Tonight she would keep him safe. Then, at some point in the next month, she would talk to him about what she had seen, what she suspected, and anything that perhaps he might have seen that would bear out her suspicions.

This meant that tonight they could talk about whatever, which for any brother and sister in the awkward teenage years could be a stretch, and for the Hobson children was typically a disaster. Fortunately, things flowed more easily tonight, they chatted about school work, about upcoming holidays, and again Oliver proved a generous ear to Lisa's still raw emotions. The death of her 'maybe but not quite' boyfriend had brought them together in a way for which Lisa could not help being guiltily grateful.

It was pleasant. But it was also clear that Oliver would rather be somewhere else, and as the slamming of doors and calls of 'Goodnight' from the corridor indicated the arrival of lights out, Lisa noticed him checking his watch.

"You can stay a bit longer, right?"

He gave an awkward shrug. "I think so. No point in breaking rules if you don't do it properly."

But a point had clearly been reached. As they talked in lowered voices, now by torchlight, the easy chatter of before was gone. Oliver was checking his watch at regular intervals. He was tense, writhing in his seat in apparent discomfort, like a man on a job interview discovering the inexplicable presence of itching powder in his underwear. The minutes were clearly numbered, and Lisa

125

checked her own watch. It was late-ish, but later would be better.

"I think I should go," said Ollie. His voice sounded different, thick somehow.

Lisa played for time. "Could you just sit with me a while?"

Oliver's frown turned into a grimace of frustration. "For goodness sake Lisa, I've been sitting with you for hours. This is… This was a bad idea."

"What was?" Without answering, Oliver started for the window, but Lisa grabbed her brother's arm. "Not yet."

"Why not yet?!" The vehemence of his response seemed to shock even him. "Sorry." He sat back down. "I can stay. I can do this." He scratched his arm distractedly. "Not really a natural rule breaker am I?"

Lisa laughed. "I see that as a good thing. But I don't want you to feel bad. Just hang here a minute, there's something I need to check in the kitchen." She stood up.

"Lisa…?"

"Just give me a minute. One minute."

Ollie's fingers closed on his knees, tight enough to whiten his knuckles. "Okay. One minute. Could you get me a glass of water?"

Grabbing her coat - the heating in the building was woeful - Lisa darted out of the door and into the darkened corridor. She padded along quietly to the kitchen and crossed to the window. There was no cloud cover tonight, nothing to stop that damn full moon. Below her, hidden by the projecting roof of the lower storeys, was the garage, overlooked by the window of the third form locker room, where she had found Jane's wet footprints on that terrifying night a few months back. Beyond that she could see the perimeter wall of the school, and beyond that…

There!

They were trying to stay hidden, but there was no mistaking the blonde hair of Cristina as it caught the moonlight. She was followed by the other girls of the pack, running quickly across the moor, towards the hills for their appointment with the full moon. They vanished quickly into the darkness.

Lisa stepped back. Could she let Ollie go now? Chances were that the boys left at the same time, so there was no one there to make him go with them. Better to be safe than sorry though, if she could get him to stay a bit longer she would. She poured a glass of water and hurried back to her bedroom.

Ollie was pacing the room when she entered. "I brought you..."

"Lisa, I need to go."

"I know."

"I mean now. I thought I could do it, but this was a bad idea." Oliver stalked towards the window and Lisa blocked his way. He tried to go around her, then settled for grabbing her and throwing her onto the bed, the glass of water sent flying.

"Damn it Ollie, don't you want to know why I'm so keen for you to stay?" That would buy a bit of time, wouldn't it?

"No. Don't care. Have to go."

"Ollie..." She grabbed his arm again but Oliver wrenched free, shoving her back.

"I can't stay. I don't feel well."

"Stop making excuses, you feel fine." But as she said it, Lisa noticed that he was noticeably paler than a moment ago.

"I don't want to... I need to go. Now. I thought I could... I can't. I have to go."

"Ollie...?" The word hung on the edge of Lisa's lips before dropping as she watched her brother suddenly bend double, wracked with pain.

His head wrenched around to look at her, but there was no pain in his eyes, it had been burned away by anger. Not Ollie's anger, because they weren't Ollie's eyes. They were animal eyes, large, round and red. And she had seen them before.

"Oh no..."

As his teeth forced their way out, curving into fangs, Ollie's nose flattened while his face lengthened into a snout. He dropped to all fours, his body contorting and expanding, tearing the clothes from him as thick white fur burst from his skin.

Perhaps it should have occurred to Lisa much earlier that Ollie's 'initiation' into the pack had already taken place, even given his absence the previous night. But the thought had not even crossed her mind. Because this was her little brother. For all their differences, this was still the child she had played with from an early age, who had she had grown up with, whose joys she had shared and sorrows sought to halve. He couldn't be a werewolf. He certainly couldn't be the white wolf that had terrified her the night before. It wasn't conceivable. It wasn't fair.

But what did fairness have to do with Lisa's life of late?

As Oliver's transformation neared completion, Lisa snapped out of the trance in which she had been frozen and she rushed for the door, hurling it open and running out towards the stairs. She heard a growl behind her, followed by the voice of one of her neighbours asking who was snoring, and then the sound of paws on the hard wooden floor.

Down the stairs Lisa rushed, not sure where she was going, but confident that hiding was not a safe option. Animals could smell fear and she was leaving a trail of it that a blind wolf could follow. Outside she might be better off, in the dark. Perhaps once they were outside then her brother would forget about her and go join the rest of his pack. He had been brilliant at doing that for most of this year, his skills at ignoring his older sister honed through long practice, and just this once Lisa would give anything to be ignored.

The good news was that, on the stairs at least, she seemed to have some advantage, as the wolf slowed to navigate this alien territory, not designed for the four-pawed. If she could just keep ahead of him until she went outside, maybe she had a chance. She hit the bottom of the stairs running and turned right, leading the wolf away from the dorms full of sleeping children, and towards the chapel.

The big heavy doors had never felt lighter as Lisa ploughed through them and charged down the side aisle towards the main doors, leading to outside and maybe - just maybe - to safety. Not far now - she was so close.

"Lisa?"

The voice from behind her brought Lisa to a skidding halt, and she looked back into the interior of the chapel, only now noticing that someone had lit candles on the altar. Gwen was seated in a pew at the front. Unable to sleep again.

The conflux of circumstances met in Lisa's brain like cars at an intersection with malfunctioning traffic lights. No time to pick through the wreckage, she needed to act.

"Gwen, you've got to get out!"

"What? Why?"

A low, rumbling growl reverberated impressively around the ideal acoustics of the chapel, heralding the entry of the white wolf

128

that had once been, and presumably still was, Oliver Hobson. Shafts of glimmering moonlight, piercing the windows, criss-crossed in the darkness and made the wolf's fur gleam as it emerged from the shadows. It peered around one of the stone columns that supported the vaulted ceiling, taking in its surroundings, and gave an unimpressed 'wuff' before looking back to Lisa.

Gwen sprang from the pew, screeching in fright, tripping to the stone floor as she did so. The sudden movement caught the attention of the wolf and it turned its red-eyed gaze from Lisa to stare at Gwen, like a fox that had just seen a signpost to Watership Down.

"No! Me! Over here!" Lisa jumped up and down, waving her arms. "Ollie!"

But the wolf had picked its prey. With a pair of muscular springs it crossed the pews, its claws scratching the wood, to dominate the central aisle, blocking Gwen's escape as she scrabbled back towards the altar, white with terror.

All fear forgotten, Lisa raced down the aisle. She couldn't let Ollie kill Gwen, for his sake as much as hers. Grabbing the wolf's tail she yanked as hard as she could, drawing a vicious snarl of anger and a hastily flicked glance of rage. With a hind leg, the white wolf kicked back and sent Lisa tumbling, crashing into a wooden pew, knocking over a pile of hymn books and rolling to the floor, dazed. Something fell from her coat pocket, landing with a metallic clatter. The gun Maria had given her, loaded with a silver bullet. She'd quite forgotten it was there.

Lisa stared at it, barely even understanding what it was.

"Lisa...?" Gwen was backed up against the altar, the flickering candlelight highlighting the terror scrawled across her face. Her staring eyes never the left the wolf as it bore slowly down on her, savouring the fear of its prey. She screamed, her voice echoing about the chapel.

Lisa stared at the gun, then back to the wolf. It was Oliver. She couldn't. But if he killed Gwen...

Suddenly she understood how Maria must have felt. Her son had not been curable - he was cursed to kill again and again, and she had saved him the only way she could. Ollie's situation was the same.

But he was still her brother.

But she couldn't let him kill Gwen.

129

Maybe a shot to the leg wouldn't kill him? Lisa had no idea how silver bullets worked.

Up ahead of her, flanked by the rows of pews and framed by the apse, its fur burnished gold in the candlelight that broke the dark, the white wolf stalked forward, its broad shoulders squared, its claws scritching on the stone floor, a churning growl rumbling like an engine in its chest. Beyond it was Gwen, clinging to the altar in the hope of divine protection.

Without even realising she was doing it, Lisa had already taken aim, tears starting to stream down her face. "Please forgive me, Ollie."

Her finger closed on the trigger.

Chapter 13 – Two Months Earlier

[From the journal of Universal Agent Boris]

December 20th
Travelled to Naughton and took a room – *the* room – at *The Grey Boar Inn*. Made acquaintance of various regulars, a good source of local knowledge. C's disappearance (presumed death) a major topic of conversation.

Read C's reports on the train. Few and far between. Lack of phone and internet combined with C's dislike of admin. His personal notes may yield more when they arrive.

December 21st
Interviewed for caretaker position at Priory Grange School with deputy head, Dr Bellamy, under cover identity Stuart Rains.

A second night in the *Boar* chatting to locals. The house ale is called Naughton Gold. It is not to my taste.

December 22nd
Returned home. I will hear about the job after Christmas.

December 29th
Caretaker job confirmed and accepted. Will start in the new year.

January 3rd
Taken up residence at The Priory Grange (in the basement, with the mice). U has now received all of C's belongings, forwarded on by the school, including his private notes. Even allowing for C's hatred of paperwork, there are enormous gaps. This cannot represent all his investigation. No sign of his journal, and practically all salient facts and observations are missing, I must assume stolen. Unavoidable conclusion: someone found out who 'Mr Tull' was, and likely killed him. That someone must have had access to the school to be able to steal C's papers. I am likely living alongside the person who killed C, and who would just as readily kill me.

Will go to the *Boar* this evening to renew acquaintance with the locals. Their knowledge may prove valuable.

***

"Hello again. Got the job did you?"

Boris nodded. "I did. Just started today. So this is by way of a celebration if anyone'll join me in a drink."

The speed with which the regulars of *The Grey Boar* in Naughton village responded to even the suggestion of a free drink could only be measured in fractions of milliseconds, and pretty soon Boris was the most popular man in an Inn that he had only visited twice before.

"Mr Rains, wasn't it?" Stationmaster Lester Moncaster might be grown grizzled with age, but his memory was excellent when it came to people who bought him drinks.

"That's right. Call me Stuart," said Boris, in the West Country accent he had selected for The Priory Grange's new caretaker, the previous incumbent having left after enjoying a substantial lottery win.

Although the school had been in need of a new Geography teacher following the death of Curt Tull, aka Universal agent Creighton, it was decided that Boris would not apply for the role. Partly this was because the job had limited Creighton's flexibility in dealing with situations while maintaining his cover - it was a busy job. Partly it was because someone seemed to have discovered Creighton's real identity, so replacing him with another agent in the same position was foolhardy. Mostly it because Boris's knowledge of geography was on a par with his knowledge of Armenian independent cinema - it's a lively scene, but not one that Boris followed.

"This is my nephew Malcolm," said Lester, indicating the man behind him, currently occupying two stools at the bar. "Don't think you met him when you were up before Christmas. You'll remember Warren," Boris nodded at a beard which presumably was attached to a face, "young Frank," Boris could only guess how many years he had been 'young' Frank, "our Jessie," a silver haired woman with a broad smile, "Gertie," who saluted Boris with tankard the size of her head, "Harry," a younger man with a red face that bore testament to a life spent on the windswept moor. "And this here's Squire Montford."

"Simon, please," the young man said. "Squire doesn't mean much these days. Just one of you chaps, what? One of the lads." He raised a miniscule sherry glass.

Boris renewed acquaintances, met new faces, shook hand and bought drinks."You like the moor, Mr Rains?" rumbled Malcolm.

"I've never seen a better moor," Boris replied. "Not seen many, you understand."

"You'll be a bit isolated up at the school," said Lester.

"Funny types they are up there," added the beard that was hiding Warren.

"Now come along lads, they're jolly decent folk," Montford said.

"They don't drink much, I know that," said landlord George, morosely.

"Well I'll try to make up their shortfall," said Boris, raising his glass. He was not by nature an 'ale' drinker, but he was going to have to get used to it.

"Quite right," laughed George. "You don't be a stranger here."

"No danger of that, George. But don't none of the teachers come down?"

A montage of shrugs and muttered words of the 'too good for the likes of us' variety rippled about the assembly.

"They pops in from time to time," acknowledged Lester, as if were giving them the best of it. "But not what you'd call regular."

"That Mr Tull were in fair often," noted Malcolm, and Boris tried hard not to look interested.

"Not anymore?"

George shook his head. "I'd be worried if he did. Died on the moor last month. Taken by the mire, so they say."

"I told him how dangerous it was." The squire stared sadly down into his drink. "And he'd had a brush with it already. Bit of a 'rush in where angels fear to tread type'. I gave him a tour. He must have thought that was all he needed and went back by himself."

"Takes a local to know the mire," said Frank.

There was a general agreement in the room followed by a raising of glasses to the late Mr Tull, who, while a teacher, had not been such a bad sort at all that. Boris joined in, raising a glass to his late friend.

At the end of a pleasant evening, they tumbled out of the bar,

133

tripping over Malcolm's motorbike as they went – left propped outside on those nights when Malcolm had drunk too much to safely navigate it home. The locals went their several ways and Boris, his head light with Naughton Gold, headed for the moor, crossing the narrow log bridge which was the most direct route from village to school if you were on foot. It had been a useful evening, establishing himself as a friend, someone to whom, in the future, confidences and local gossip might be imparted. And it was interesting to note that Creighton had done the same thing.

Was it possible that one of the men he had just been drinking with had...? But it was too early for that sort of thinking.

***

January 5th

Pupils returned to school. No one notices the new caretaker.

[Note to self: thank Mrs Coombes for her excellent work at U. It is a hard and thankless job.]

January 7th

Identifying the WW must be my first priority (after safeguarding the children, but the two go hand in hand). Naughton does not have a large population but, for most of the time, werewolves blend in very well. It could be anyone. Had C known identity, he would have acted – potentially this is what got him killed. His notes refer to a list of suspects, but that list must be amongst the missing material. Only way forward, I fear, is to wait for the Full Moon and stake out suitable locations, then follow the wolf to identify it or, if necessary, kill it.

January 12th

First Full Moon approaching.

What remains of C's notes suggest an old slate mine as a possible point of interest – nothing specific, but the tone of the writing alludes to something specific written elsewhere in his notes; now lost/stolen.

Other place to consider: Naughton Mire. Again mentioned in C's notes, and locals seem sure it is where C died. Seems ideal spot for a werewolf to hide – assuming WW is local.

January 14th

On consideration, have decided to stake out mire tonight, given its association with C's death. Considered asking one of the *Boar* regulars to help - someone who knows the terrain - but still too soon; I might end up asking the WW itself. Will watch from high ground, if I am successful then will find a guide for the following night. Going armed.

January 15th

[Morning] Just returned. No sight of WW at Naughton Mire, but howling to be heard elsewhere on the moor. Impossible to pinpoint owing to geography - echoes, etc - but it did not appear to be coming from the mire.

This afternoon I will scout the mine before staking it out tonight. Going armed.

[Evening] I am writing this from a secluded spot, halfway up the hill into which the mine tunnels, waiting for the sun to set or someone to arrive.

Curious day thus far. This afternoon I walked out to the slate mine to take a look around before tonight. The mine entrance is in a short crevasse at the base of a hill, and has been out of use for many decades. It has an iron gate with chain and lock but neither was fastened (this is apparently normal). When I arrived, a dog was tethered up outside; far too friendly to be a guard dog. I surmised someone must be within; perhaps tourists. I entered. There is a single main tunnel, branched off at various points - these all seem to be blind; either sealed up or caved in. The main tunnel leads to a very large cavern, hollowed out by blasting.

Here I found the dog's owners, though they made a concerted effort to hide when I entered. Based on what I could hear, I guessed them to be a man and woman – possibly some elicit, romantic assignation. I let them believe that I had not noticed their presence. They continued to hide throughout my examination of the room – which I was not about to abandon to preserve the modesty of a subterranean 'hook up'.

Everything about the cavern leads me to believe this is the werewolf's lair. There are numerous bones on the floor, predominantly sheep, <u>certainly</u> no human (I checked most carefully).

135

Scratches on the wall compare favourably with pictures of known WW claw marks in UL archives. Slight acridity in the air cutting through the dankness (similar to that noted by Conrad, 20, UL1002-06). All indicators of typical WW lair; a place to change and to store food.

I left the couple to finish what they started (if possible) and exited the mine to assume my current vantage point, which gives me a clear view of the mine's entrance, while remaining hidden (relatively. The landscape does not provide much cover).

Some minutes later, a young man and a girl (late teens would be my guess) exited the mine. Contrary to my earlier supposition, they did not have the look of disturbed lovers. The girl I think I recognise from the school, though I am not certain (they all look alike to me).

As they untethered the friendly dog, I heard the girl say, 'He must have known that we were in there.'. Quite an astute girl. So perhaps I was mistaken in thinking she is a pupil.

The sun is now starting to set. With luck, I can end this tonight.

***

Night fell, and Boris strained his eyes against the darkness. Out here in the country you could really appreciate darkness. It felt like a real thing with weight being dropped over you. Back at the school, he had a pair of night-vision binoculars but he preferred not to use them on missions like this - while you were staring straight ahead, something nasty with fangs was always creeping up directly to your right. Still, it was one area where a wolf had the upper hand on even a well-armed agent. Werewolves had superb night vision. All the silver bullets in the world were little use if you couldn't see it, and it could see you. Was that what had happened to Creighton?

The question of what had happened to Creighton troubled Boris. A werewolf was a dangerous adversary, but a silver bullet was an effective weapon and his comrade had been a crack shot. If Creighton had known who the werewolf was then that should have been an end of it.

Yet Creighton was the one who had wound up dead.

Boris made a conscious effort to move on from this thought. It wasn't doing any good and it was distracting him from the task at hand. It was getting late, his quarry would surely arrive soon to change shape before going out on the prowl. But then...

The sound of a howl, caught on the wind that whipped across the moor, made Boris's insides contract. It had changed already.

Springing to his feet, Boris ran down the hillside. Where was the point in having a lair if you didn't use the bloody thing? How was he supposed to do his job if the damn werewolf refused to play the game?

Reaching the base of the hill Boris came to a reluctant stop. "Blast."

Charging out into the darkness and hunting for something that knew the terrain and could see in the dark, while he himself had neither of these advantages, was suicide. Irritating though it was, patience was the better part of valour in this situation. The wolf had not changed in its lair at the start of the night, but it might yet return there at the end of the night to change back.

He turned around to trudge back up the hill. It would mean a long wait, but it was his best chance of learning who the wolf was. The howl sounded again, as if the wolf was taunting him, seeming to echo and re-echo about the landscape, the hills playing weird tricks on the sound.

He was about halfway back to his vantage point when Boris heard a scream.

For all the danger of facing the wolf in the dark, in its territory, Boris didn't hesitate. He whirled about and sprinted back down, hitting the base of the hill and dashing off across the moor, gun in hand, nimbly jumping over and dodging around the obstacles that the moor threw into his path. But at the back of his mind was the unpleasant thought that, based on that scream, he was already too late.

He was.

By the time Boris ran up, the wolf was gone, and all that was left, revealed by Boris's torchlight, was a bloody mess spread across the damp ground. There was no point in checking for a pulse - there was no neck left in which to check for one.

A sound to Boris's right made him start and whip his torch about, startling the dog that had made the noise. The animal took off as fast as it could, though limping badly.

"Wait! Come back!" The dog was gone. But he had recognised it.

That meant these gory remains were of the man - barely more than a boy - whom he had seen coming out of the mine earlier that day.

"Shit." It took a lot to make Boris swear. "SHIIIIIIIIT!!!" Throwing back his head he screamed into the night sky.

That was stupid. It didn't fix anything and it just told the wolf where he was. But right at that moment, Boris didn't care. You had to develop a thick skin in this profession. People died who did not deserve to. Most of the cases Boris had worked had started with someone dying, and that person was seldom the last.

But he had been there. He had been on the moor and had staked out the wrong place. If he had only chosen better then...

As if to reinforce his sense of failure and frustration, the howl sounded again.

Boris stiffened. That hadn't sounded like an echo. That had sounded like two howls. Was that what he had been hearing? Forgetting how exposed he was, he stood still and listened. A few moments later, more howls answered the first two, joining together in lupine chorus.

A pack.

***

January 16th

[Morning] I do not think there was anything I could have done to prevent the boy's death. I used the best information I had, but that is of no comfort. No excuse. I should have been able to save him.

[Afternoon] The boy's name was Talbot Conliffe, son of a local landowner. I have also identified the girl he was with - who is indeed a pupil at the school - as Lisa Hobson.

[Evening] Difficult though it is, I have to refocus on the job in hand. The death of the Conliffe boy is a tragedy I will not forget. His name goes alongside those of Claude, Gibson, and the others I could not save. But I have to deal with the information last night gives me.

After I found the boy's body, I returned to the mine, but the WW never came. Why? The lair looked fresh and in regular use. I am forced to conclude that it changed its habits because of the kill.

138

That suggests Conliffe was targeted. Again; why? Because he visited the mine? If so, the girl, Hobson, is also in danger. The anatomy of the kill suggests a single wolf rather than the whole pack. Why? WW's are not supposed to carry personal grudges through the change. Is our information flawed?

Moving on...

There is a pack. A WW pack has been theorised (Sloan, 31, UL1101-82) but I am not aware of one ever having been confirmed. Possible this is how C met his end? A pack would be unexpected and a single man would have no chance against such an attack. Conjecture.

The lair only appeared to be for one wolf. The pack leader? The one who killed Conliffe? More conjecture.

My greatest fear at present: the instance of a WW pack occurring in the vicinity of a school cannot be a coincidence. Pupils are divided into houses, classes, teams, and divide themselves into peer and social groups. Werewolves are not pack animals but children are. Can that instinct survive the change?

I was sent here to protect the children. Is it possible I was also sent here to kill one?

Chapter 14 - The Leader of the Pack

[From the journal of Universal Agent Boris]

January 22nd

After nearly a week of searching I found the dog, still alive, though weak and thin as a rail, squeezed into a grubby hollow not far from the mire. It seemed pleased to see me and wolfed down the dog treats I gave it. Perhaps this is not the best use of my time, but until the next Full Moon it is hard to say what is. And I felt it the least I could do.

I have given the dog to Lisa Hobson, and their reaction on seeing each other confirms in my mind that this was the correct decision.

I have endeavoured to find out more about the girl since last week – perhaps out of guilt. Gossip suggests a romantic attachment to the dead boy, but she seems to have an interest in the mine that goes beyond its convenience for clandestine assignations. Interesting, but it may place her in danger. Or it may suggest that she is the wolf. A bad romance ending in blood? Wouldn't be the first.

[Later] It now occurs to me that C twice uses the abbreviation 'LH' in his notes, referring to someone I have been unable to identify. Possible???

January 23rd

The dog (Moose?!) is living in my basement while Hobson is away from school. It has made no dent in the mouse population and does not seem to be trying.

January 24th

Immediately prior to his death, Conliffe had an argument with a boy at the school named Larry Glendon. Glendon is the *de* facto leader of a nasty little group – 'bullies' is the only term. You don't have to be a werewolf to treat people poorly (if you did the world would be full of them), but this group does have the requisite pack mentality. Consider and observe.

January 25th

It would appear C also had an argument with Glendon not long before his death.

January 26th
 I need to learn everything I can about the other deaths in the area before the next Full Moon.

***

"Oh aye, the sheep." Lester Moncaster shook his head. "Warren could tell you more about that. Right, Warren? Them dead sheep?"

"Terrible thing," Warren nodded, draining his pint. "What happened to those poor animals. Terrible thing."

"When did it start?" asked Boris, ordering another pint of Naughton Gold. He was actually starting to enjoy it.

"September weren't it?" chipped in Malcolm from further down the bar, where he was taking up enough space for two and drinking enough for four.

That seemed to confirm Boris's worst fears. If the sheep killings started with the beginning of term then the pack was surely composed of children. One of them must have arrived bearing the curse, then inflicted it on their classmates.

"Nay," Lester shook his head. "Longer than that. Eh, Warren?"

"Aye," Warren started in on his next drink like a man with a quota to meet. "There's always been a beast of the moor."

"Always?" A glimmer of hope opened up before Boris.

"Well," Lester hedged, "not like it is now. Those massacres, they maybe started like the lad said; September time. But there've been sheep killed by some creature going back… How long Warren?"

"Ten year at least," Warren replied dourly. "Every full moon. Regular."

"Makes animals act crazy," judged Lester, as Boris tried to stifle his excitement. "The full moon. It's a dog or something living out there. Driven mad once a month by the fullness of the moon."

A werewolf that had been killing in these parts for the last decade?

Werewolves seldom reach any great age; they often commit suicide and are also prized targets for a particular type of game

141

hunter. Old werewolves had to be very clever to avoid hunters, and devoid of conscience enough not to take their own lives. Old werewolves were almost as rare as packs, and just as dangerous.

Could the school pack (assuming it existed) have been started by an elder werewolf? If so; why? A wolf of that age, which had managed to avoid killing people for at least a decade did not just start. There had to be a reason.

"You've gone all glassy eyed, Mr Rains," Lester noted.

"Just thinking," Boris replied. "Funny that the miller – what was his name?"

"Ralph."

The whole of *The Grey Boar* took this as a signal to raise their glasses to a departed friend. "Poor Ralph."

"That's him," Boris went on. "He died just as the sheep started to be killed in greater numbers."

Lester nodded. "You wouldn't be the first to notice that."

There was an unfortunate propensity in supernatural creatures for building armies of the undead with which to take over the world. What it was that encouraged people, who had been perfectly mild-mannered in life, to aspire towards megalomania after death, no one knew, but it was a condition Universal had long recognised under the name Blofeld's Syndrome.

A school, and particularly one as remote as the Priory Grange, was the ideal place to build such an army; stocked with an endless supply of raw material in the form of impressionable pupils who naturally banded together in hierarchical fashion.

But where did that leave the death of Ralph Matthews, which had first led Universal to send Creighton here? An accident? Or had he stumbled onto something that he shouldn't, and been taken care of by the pack or their elder?

If so, was it possible that Ralph had shared what he knew?

"What was Ralph like?"

"Poor Ralph." Up went the glasses again.

"Wouldn't have called him a talkative type," Lester continued. "Not a one for speeches. I don't know really. He was just Ralph. Why do you ask?"

Boris shook his head. "I've heard so much about him since I arrived yet I don't feel like I know him at all. Just wondered if he was the private sort?"

"I'd say that was fair," nodded Lester. "Same again, George. Kept himself to himself and his mind on his job. I always felt, since his wife left him, he were married to the Mill."

"And no one saw him out on the moor that night?"

"Not a soul."

"There was Miss Wotsit - from up the school." Malcolm spoke up. "She might have seen him."

"Miss Wotsit?" asked Boris, since the rest of the room seemed to immediately know who Malcolm was talking about.

"Aye. The headmaster - mistress I should say. What's her name?"

"Dr Lloyd?"

"That's the one."

"What makes you think she saw anything?" asked Boris, almost slipping out of character in his eagerness.

"I saw her, didn't I?" said Malcolm. "Walking across the moor, wasn't she?"

"Was she?"

"Aye. I was driving home from- now where would it have been?"

"Doesn't matter where, lad," chided Lester. "You were on the moor road, right?"

"Aye. And there she was, large as life, headed for the mill. And I thought, that's strange that. No business being out there that time of night, she might come to harm. Lucky she didn't really, with whatever killed poor Ralph about."

"Very lucky," agreed Boris.

"Did you tell the police any of this, our Malcolm?" asked Lester.

"No Uncle," Malcom replied, shrugging his massive shoulders seismically. "It's not like *she* tore him to pieces is it?"

Lester nodded. "That's true. Lady of class, that. Now if it had been my Ethel that'd been a different matter. Tear you limb from limb as soon as look at you. God rest her."

"Ethel." The drinks were raised again.

Boris raised his tankard and drank with them, but his mind was already racing.

***

143

January 27th

Amongst C's notes is an entry dated November 20th: '*L. seen crossing moor at night (FM) by LH. Direction of mill and mine.*'.

Assume 'L' is Lloyd and 'FM' Full Moon.

If an elder WW were starting a pack/army of schoolchildren, headmistress would be ideal cover. Dr Lloyd has been at the school more than ten years, long enough to account for historical sheep deaths. (Would be useful to check her background for visits to Eastern Europe, but difficult without internet.) All conjecture. Confirmation must wait for Full Moon.

January 30th

Hobson returned but the dog remains with me (still not eating mice, though it did bark at a spider around 3am).

February 7th

The next Full Moon in a week. What course to take?

Follow Lloyd? Conjecture. If wrong would miss real culprit.

Follow pack from school? More conjecture. My only evidence there is a 'school pack' is the rarity of packs in general. Not enough. No actual evidence. A pack of locals from Naughton village would be an anomaly, but is still possible. Again, I might miss them altogether, and for every wasted attempt I run the risk of another life lost.

The Mine? Went badly wrong last month but I am convinced that was bad luck. Lloyd and the 'school pack' I cannot be sure of, but I am certain the mine is a lair.

The mine then.

[Later] Is it possible that last month they saw or scented me and so did not approach? Waiting inside might yield better results.

Identifying the pack is no longer the priority. Stopping the pack is worthless if the elder goes free to start again somewhere else. Follow the pack; find the elder.

All seems simple when put like that. Going armed.

***

Arriving at the mine in late afternoon, Boris found a patch of mud and rolled about in it until he was as covered as he could be – werewolves had a powerful sense of smell. This done, he secreted himself in the cavern and settled down to wait.

The waiting ended with the sound of footsteps in the dark, and the noise was soon joined by a flashing torchlight. As cautiously as he could, Boris peered out. At first the torch swung about, illuminating everything but the person holding it. But then it was placed on a convenient rock as the holder started to undress. He turned as he unbuttoned his shirt, giving Boris the first clear view of his face. Larry Glendon.

The confirmation of his suspicions gave Boris little joy as he ducked back into hiding. He had held onto a hope that the pack might prove to be adults, the presence of Glendon strongly suggested otherwise.

When Glendon finished undressing there was a click and the torchlight vanished, plunging the cavern into darkness. For a few more seconds there was silence, and then the noises began.

Boris had never seen a werewolf change, but to hear one, leaving him with only his imagination, might have been worse. He heard the grinding and cracking of bone repositioning itself; the tortuous whine of stretched skin; claws on the floor, scraping and scratching. He heard the meaty tearing of muscles advancing and retreating. He heard the ragged breaths evolve into growls, wrenched up from Glendon's chest, and the clear, triumphant snarl at the end of it.

The werewolf Glendon gave a low snarl and ran back towards the entrance.

Switching his torch back on, Boris hurried after the creature, anxious not to lose it but wary of being seen. He needed it to lead him to the elder, and it wouldn't do that if it knew it was being pursued. Then, in the tunnel up ahead of him, Boris saw movement. But it didn't look like a wolf.

Lisa Hobson took one look at Boris and ran up the passage as fast as she could, fuelled by blind terror.

"Hey!" Boris yelled. How she had evaded the werewolf thus far he had no idea, but now she was running towards it.

As he dashed after her, desperate not to let another innocent get killed on his watch, Boris tripped on something on the slippery floor. "Rats!"

He tumbled to the ground, banging shin then hip and landing in an undignified heap before hauling himself back to his feet and running on. An iron clang echoed around the tunnel. What now?

Boris skidded to a halt at the entrance to the mine, his path blocked by the closed gate. He wrenched angrily at it but the girl had tied the rusty iron chain about the old fastenings. With his torch held in his mouth, Boris set to work freeing himself.

What the hell was the girl doing here anyway? Could she be one of the pack? Presumably not since she hadn't changed. All he knew for sure was that another opportunity had passed him by – there was no way he could follow the wolves now. Worse still, there was a girl out there in danger.

How the hell had he let this happen?

Finally managing to pull the chain free from the gate, Boris charged out into the night.

***

February 15th

[Morning] The best that can be said about last night is that no one is dead. Which, in the circumstances, I am happy to call a win. (Boots ruined – buying brand name was probably an error.)

Spent most of the night in futile search for Hobson girl, waiting for that tell-tale scream. She has now returned of her own accord. I have no idea where she spent the remainder of the night. Could she be a lone wolf? Not part of the pack? But she did not change when Glendon did. More gaps in our knowledge of WW.

But Glendon <u>did</u> change. If he is leader - and the fact he changes alone in his own lair argues strongly for that conclusion - the rest of his group are surely the pack. Therefore: 10-15 WW.

It is frustrating to know the identity of at least one WW, probably more, and be unable to act, but finding the elder must come first. If I move against the pack, I alert the elder, and he/she will vanish. A WW does not reach any sort of age without being a survivor.

Progress slower than hoped, but existence of school pack confirmed. Will therefore stake out school itself tonight. Plan remains the same: follow the pack, find the elder. And hope tonight is not disrupted by nosy children.

146

***

The day passed at a slack pace, which is often the case when you are the agent of an organisation specialising in tackling the living dead but are currently mopping floors and cleaning up after over-privileged pupils. As evening closed in, Boris made a surreptitious check on the location of Lisa Hobson. She was in her room – all was well.

As night fell, he dressed in his back-up 'moor clothes', having not yet had time to do his laundry, loaded his gun with silver bullets and placed it in his fitted shoulder holster. He noted 'Going armed.' in his journal, picked up his rucksack, then made his way up through the central school building to the attics where art was taught. The studio was silent save for the creaking floorboards that even Boris's cat-like step could not avoid. Selecting a key from the oversized bunch that is the birthright of every caretaker, Boris unlocked one of the skylights and slid it open. The cool, damp night air met him as he clambered nimbly out onto the roof. Leaving the window ajar, held open with a wooden block, Boris climbed higher till he had achieved the building's apex. The school fell away from him like a cliff, and surrounding it, spreading away like a vast, dark sea; the moor.

Boris reached into his rucksack, pulled out a pair of night vision binoculars and began to scan the area surrounding the boys' wing, keeping an eye on the windows, the wall, and the temptingly scale-able drainpipe. Logically, the children had to leave as humans and go somewhere to transform - people turning into wolves on school property would likely excite some comment. Then again, this was a school whose pupils seemed to make a positive habit of nocturnal excursions, so a lack of observation did seem to be endemic.

He did not have to wait long. Through the fuzzy red haze of the night vision, he saw a window open and a figure emerge. It was Larry Glendon - no surprise there - and he was followed by others. Boris counted six in all as they climbed down the drainpipe to a lower roof, along which they ran towards the wall surrounding the school. Turning one hundred and eighty degrees, he picked up a second group of children leaving the girls' wing.

If they had all been turned within the last six months, Boris

147

considered, then they presumably had no idea of what they were or what they did, beyond a few nightmarishly lucid memories. How did that square with this? Potentially they were acting on instinct - the wolf making itself felt in their blood, telling them to go out. But the truth was that Universal had some major blanks in their knowledge concerning werewolves. They spent most of their lives as humans which made studying them difficult. As did their high suicide rate. So much to learn. But right now, all that mattered was giving chase.

Moving fast, and as sure-footed as a mountain goat, Boris pattered down the sloped slate of the roof to the attic window. He dropped to the floor within, hastily locked the skylight and hurried out. The narrow, winding staircase that led to the attics ran the height of the building, and the walls were embellished at regular intervals with red signs instructing pupils not to run. Boris ignored these warnings, clattering down the hard stone steps, hitting the bottom running and hurrying out through the main doors into the night.

He was practically out of the gates when he heard a scream coming from the direction of the chapel.

For perhaps as long a second, Boris paused, mid-step. If he did not follow the wolves now then it would be a month before he got another chance. Screams coming from anywhere in the school were not that uncommon, a combination of the boisterous high spirits of youth, and the fact that children of that age are little monsters, devoid of humanity and intent on torturing each other.

But long experience told him that this was not that kind of scream. One thing you got really good at in Boris's line of work was identifying varieties of scream, and this one was a good, old-fashioned scream of terror.

Before that single second of immobility had the chance to tick over into the next, Boris had changed direction and was running towards the heavy, ornate doors of the chapel. He flung them open, went through the hall and entered the chapel itself, moving silently – something he did as a matter of habit.

The room was lit by candlelight, making it even eerier than a chapel at night already is. Against the altar, at the far end of the room, a smallish girl cowered in blind terror as a large wolf, its fur shockingly white, stalked towards her. Not far from Boris, facing away from him and towards the animal, was Lisa Hobson, pointing a revolver at the creature. She cocked the weapon with difficulty and, as a shard of moonlight from one of the high windows caught the outstretched gun, Boris saw the glint of a silver bullet housed in the chamber.

Chapter 15 - Tonight

"I'll take that."

The gun was snatched from Lisa's trembling hands just as her finger began to close on the trigger. Lisa whirled about to find the caretaker, Mr. Rains, standing behind her. "No, you don't understand!"

But Mr Rains wasn't listening. He had taken what looked like an extremely expensive pair of binoculars from his bag and, with a throw that would have guaranteed him a place on the school cricket team come summer, he brained the wolf between the ears.

"Oi!"

"Oh no..." Lisa's face drained of blood, as the wolf (Ollie, whatever) turned its shaggy head. Its eyes narrowed and its lips curled to a snarl.

"Good," said Mr Rains, suddenly much more well-spoken than Lisa remembered him being in the past, "now I have your attention. I think perhaps *you* should move away." Though the latter sentence was directed at Lisa, he never took his eyes from the wolf.

Lisa did as she was told - bravery was all very well but standing shoulder to shoulder with a man who heaved binoculars at werewolves was taking it too far.

The wolf issued a growl that Lisa felt in her bones. It did not like being hit over the head. Her eyes flicked back to Mr Rains and she saw him reaching into his bag again. He wasn't going to throw something else was he? The man had a death wish.

The wolf stalked towards the caretaker, anger making it move more quickly now. It would be on him in seconds and...

Suddenly its attention was elsewhere, the big head moving side to side, up and down, round and around in circles as it tried to follow a patch of light that skittered across the floor, between the pews, up the walls and pillars, onto the vaulted ceiling and back again. When the patch stopped the beast pounced, then moved its paws and looked bewildered to find it had not captured the light.

Mr Rains edged towards the door, twitching the powerful torch in his hand this way and that, holding the wolf's attention and drawing it after him. Lisa watched in quiet astonishment as the caretaker guided the creature out of the chapel.

With it gone, Lisa suddenly recalled Gwen and rushed to the

150

altar to hug her friend.

"I... I...." Gwen seemed unable to say anything else and Lisa quietly comforted her, holding her close until her breathing slowed and her tears dried. "What was that?" Gwen whispered hoarsely.

Lisa didn't know what to say. 'My brother' seemed likely to elicit some follow-up questions to which she had no answers.

A sound from the door made both girls look up sharply, but it was just Mr Rains returning, putting the torch back in his bag as he entered.

"Had a dog when I was a lad. Used to play the torch game for hours. Good times." His voice had returned to its countrified twang.

"Where's it gone?" hissed Gwen.

"Out onto the moor," Mr Rains replied. "Once it got outside it heard something that made it run off."

The howl? wondered Lisa. Had it heard the call of the pack?

"How did it get in here?" asked Gwen, her voice low and quavering.

Lisa thought she saw Mr Rains casting a glance in her direction, but he said. "The gate was open. There's been talk of a big dog loose on the moor, killing sheep. It must have wandered in. I don't think it would hurt a human. Probably more scared of you than you were of it."

"I really doubt that," said Gwen.

"Just making itself look scary. Don't think it would have done nothing."

"Lisa?" Gwen looked to her trusted friend for confirmation.

"No. I don't think it would have done nothing."

The flicker of a smile on Mr Rains' lips suggested that he had noticed the double meaning, but thankfully it passed Gwen by.

"When Dr Lloyd hears I left the gate open, it'll be me getting my guts spilled," muttered Mr Rains, contritely.

Now she knew it was an act, Lisa wondered how she had never noticed before. He might as well be tying his trousers up with string, tugging his forelock and calling everyone 'young master'.

"We won't tell, will we Lis?" said Gwen, as good-natured as always now that the danger was passed.

"Of course not."

"That's awful kind of you," replied Mr Rains. "Anything I can ever do for you, just name it. Now, you two'd better get yourselves

151

off to bed. Goodnight."

They watched him go and then Gwen turned to Lisa. "It was a *very* big dog."

"Probably got some Irish wolfhound in it."

"Did you have a gun?"

"No. You must have imagined it."

Lisa walked Gwen back to her room. She then went back downstairs. She made her way through the network of passageways to the main building and then turned down the basement staircase. At the bottom was a sky blue door, its paint flecked, with a sign on it that, for some reason, read 'Beware of the Leopard'. She knocked.

"Come in, Miss Hobson." Mr Rains was back to being well-spoken.

Lisa entered. "Hello Moose."

The dog bounded excitably up at her, delighted to receive a visit from its mistress.

"Take a seat," said Mr Rains.

"I'd sooner stand. Near the door."

Wordlessly, Mr Rains picked up the gun he had confiscated from Lisa and passed it back to her. "Now you have the advantage. Tea?"

He turned back to the little stove on which he was boiling a battered kettle. It wasn't just his voice, Lisa now noticed, he moved differently as well. He was in fact a whole different person, and, to her surprise, quite a handsome one.

"Milk and two sugars."

Mr Rains made the face of man who does not like to see the noble tea leaf treated in such brash fashion. "I think perhaps we should talk. Exchange information and so on. It seems as if we are both on the same trail. Something I frankly had not anticipated."

"How do I know I can trust you?" Lisa was desperate to trust someone, anyone. But there was a form for this sort of meeting and far be it from her to deviate from it. Mr Rains was now supposed to say 'You don't', but he did not stick to the script.

"I am - or I suppose was - a friend of Curt Tull."

Lisa felt a little clutch in her stomach. "Mr Tull?"

"I believe you knew him. In fact, I believe you helped him."

Lisa swelled with pride.

The kettle whistled and Mr Rains poured the water into a

teapot.

"If you just want to put the bag in the mug, I'm not fussed," said Lisa. But Mr Rains looked at her as if she had suggested, just this once, making it with rat poison.

As the tea brewed, he got out his phone, swiped a few times and showed the screen to Lisa. It was a group picture of some smartly dressed men and women wearing paper crowns.

"Office Christmas party," explained Mr Rains. He pointed to the screen. "Me... and Mr Tull."

There was no mistaking him, and Lisa felt suddenly weepy that she would never see that face again. This year had been hard on her, and tonight...

"Why did you take the gun?" she asked, consciously trying to keep to the point.

"Where did you get it?"

"A gypsy gave it to me."

Mr Rains nodded. "Eastern European. Of course. They told you about the werewolves?"

"They saved my life last night. Why did you take the gun?"

"Where did the wolf come from?"

The emotions that seeing Mr Tull had stirred up in Lisa shifted uncomfortably as the events of earlier came back to her. With all that had been going on she had been able to push the fact of Oliver's 'condition' to the back of her mind, but now she was reminded of it, and of what it meant.

"It was my brother." The tears came, even as she tried to hold them back.

Mr Rains breathed in. "That I did not know. I am sorry."

"So why did you take the gun?" Lisa snapped. "You know he doesn't... He can't be..." She couldn't say the words and apparently didn't have to, as Mr Rains held up a hand.

"I would not let anyone kill their own flesh and blood, however well-intentioned."

Lisa frowned. "You said you didn't know he was my brother."

"I'm not ready to let any of these children die yet."

A creeping hope, that barely dared make itself known, began to crawl up from inside Lisa. "There's... there's a way of saving them?"

"There *may* be," replied Mr Rains, stressing caution. "If you

153

kill a wolf's sire - the wolf that bit them - with a silver bullet, then those whom that sire turned will revert to normal."

Lisa felt a rush of light joy race through her, seeming to lift her up.

"But," Mr Rains continued, "if a wolf's sire dies in any other way, then that's it. If A is the sire of B, and B bites C, then killing B would cure C. But while killing A would cure B, C would be doomed to remain a wolf. You understand?"

Lisa nodded. "So, who 'turned' Oliver?"

"I don't know. I have my suspicions."

"Care to share them?"

Mr Rains poured the tea, added Lisa's sugar against his own better judgement, and passed her the cup.

"How about you tell me everything you know, and everything you suspect."

"Is Mr Rains your real name?"

"Call me Boris."

"Boris...?"

"Just Boris. Now, if you would..."

Lisa did her best to order her thoughts, knowing that her brother's life might depend on it, but the story still came out in a rambling and disjointed fashion. Boris sat and listened, mostly in silence as he sipped his tea, occasionally interrupting to clarify something.

"The white wolf you saw on the ridge – it wasn't with the rest of the pack?"

Lisa shook her head.

"It didn't pursue you when the others did?"

"I don't think so. It was Ollie. My brother is the white wolf."

Boris pondered a moment.

"What do you think that means?" Lisa pressed.

But Boris shook his head. "Continue with your story."

When she finally finished Boris was silent a moment longer, then said, "You're lucky to be alive."

Lisa hadn't stopped to think about it before but... yes, she probably was. Though that was not foremost amongst her thoughts. "Do you think you can save Ollie?"

Boris drew in a deep breath. "Somewhere in the region, I am convinced, is an older werewolf, building an army of wolves and

154

using the school as a source of raw material. If I can find them, then I hope to be able to save *all* the children."

"Including Ollie."

"Of course."

"What can I do?"

Boris shrugged. "Stop locking me in mines."

Lisa turned red. "That was you? You scared the hell out of me."

"I was trying to help."

"And you were in the mine before? Last month?"

"When you were down there with..." he paused. "Yes." He took a sip of tea and looked back up. "I did try to save Talbot, Lisa." It was the first time he had used her first name.

Lisa swallowed a gulp of tea, trying to cover her emotions. "Was it Glendon who killed Talbot?"

"I don't know."

"They'd had an argument."

Boris sighed. "Wolves don't remember... When Oliver was in your room, don't you think he would have left if he had known what was about to happen?"

"I suppose so."

"Chances are that Glendon and the others don't even know what they are." He paused. There seemed to be more he wanted say but was not sure if he should. "That said, it is possible that a hatred felt by a human may result in an unconscious hatred felt by a wolf. He may have done it. But the human can't control the wolf. Or at least," he hedged, "such is our current understanding."

"Ollie wanted to leave my room."

"Exactly. He didn't know why - just that he needed to go. The group has probably concocted some mythology of their own to justify it."

Lisa nodded, but her mind travelled back to the aftermath of Talbot's death and what Glendon had said to her, *'That's what you get when you mess with the big dog.'*. That sounded intentional, and unrepentant.

"How do you know about all this? About werewolves and that?"

Boris gave a light shrug. "Mr Tull and I work for an organisation that..." he tapped his spoon on the edge of his saucer,

155

searching for a word, "...looks into such things."

"This happens a lot?"

"Wolf packs?" Boris pulled a face. "No. This happens never. It's been theorised; they share so many traits with wolves, why not that one? But to my knowledge, this is the first documented pack."

It didn't seem fair. Why should something so rare, so unreasonable, happen to Lisa, to her brother, to her... Talbot?

"Why?"

"Why doesn't it happen or why has it?"

"Either. Both."

Boris sighed. "You ask large questions, Miss Hobson. Werewolves are not like vampires..."

"Vampires?!"

"Conversation for another night. Werewolves do not seek to propagate their species, they are lonely and sad. Though they possess only a limited understanding of what they are - at least when young - they seem to have some instinct not to inflict their curse on others. When people are turned it is by accident - a kill gone wrong. And those wolves do not band together. They seem to understand on some level that one hurt the other. The only way for a pack to form, is for someone to want it. Someone with malign intent. Someone without a conscience. Or," Boris placed his empty cup down as he contemplated the unthinkable possibility, "someone too young to have developed a useable one."

It made a horrible kind of sense. Lisa thought of all the things she had seen bullies do in one school or another, her fingers inadvertently seeking out the burn scar on the back of her hand. Children didn't need to be werewolves to hurt each other for no reason. They did it for fun, for attention, to make others like them. To belong. Teenagers band together as a matter of course out of a desperation to belong. They do not see the harm they do to others by their actions, or have the capacity for complex empathy. They gang up against each other because it's better than being the one on the outside.

"Mr Tull suspected the bully group as well." She was sure of it.

Boris nodded to himself. "Either the elder turned all of them, or he/she turned some and they started turning each other. Which would complicate matters."

"How will you know which is the killer?"

"Good question. Identifying a werewolf is never easy."

"Really? Seems like they should stand out."

Boris smiled ruefully. "In some circumstances; yes, it is easy. In others... It is a question of maths."

"Maths?"

"Throughout the better part of the month," Boris explained, "werewolves are completely normal. They only change at full moon, which means..." He did some mental arithmetic. Then gave up and got a calculator. "Assuming two full moons per month and a month of 31 days, and defining 'night' as eight hours, they're only wolves for 2.15% of their lives. Hardly seemed fair to judge them on that, but it is amazing what damage can be done in just that 2.15%."

Lisa stared. "When you put it like that, it seems amazing they ever get caught."

Boris shrugged. "By counterpoint, you know exactly when they are going to show up. And if you have a good idea where, then someone turning into a wolf (even if only for a statistically insignificant period) *ought* to stand out." He poured himself another cup and offered the pot to Lisa. "Werewolves are not subtle, and because they don't know what's happening to them – at least not at first – they are not cunning. But a pack..." He shook his head. "I said that identifying a werewolf is never easy. Finding one wolf among many - the killer amongst the victims..." He pulled a humourless grin. "Finding a needle in a wolf pack. One way or another this ends in blood. But if I kill the wrong wolf then all your schoolmates are destined to stay this way the rest of their lives."

The coldness of the statement made a chill run up Lisa's back.

"What can I tell Ollie?"

"Nothing. He might tell his pack and that might affect things. There is a chance that the elder stays in touch with the pack when they are human. One word out of place and she or he will vanish away, and those children are stuck as they are."

He stood and went to a cupboard beside the bed. "I'm going to give you something."

He handed the something to Lisa.

"I already have a phone."

"Does it work around here?"

"No."

"Then let's assume this one is better."

"It'll work on the moor?"

Boris hedged. "To a point. A very limited point. It's more like a walkie-talkie, except that you can use it to take pictures and send text messages as well. But it's only good for getting in touch with me." He leaned close to her. "If you see *anything*. Don't hesitate."

Lisa nodded. "So what do we do now?"

Boris stood, taking his and Lisa's tea cups to the sink. "Just to clarify; there is no 'we'. I cannot concentrate on what I'm doing while simultaneously trying to keep you safe. You have been immeasurably helpful, but from here on in you need to stop."

Lisa was not altogether surprised to hear that but was not sure how she felt about it. On the one hand, passing this whole thing over to a professional sounded ideal, on the other... it was her baby brother. The idea of not doing everything she could, when she knew the danger he was in, was appalling to her. But it would be best not to share any of that with Boris.

"What will *you* do then?"

"Wait," said Boris, as he began washing up.

"Wait?"

"I have some leads on which to follow up, concerning the elder werewolf. But, in truth, I have a month to wait until I can do anything useful."

Through the air-conditioning vent, that connected the basement to the outside, the sound of a distant howl carried on the wind. Moose whined and buried his head in his paws.

Chapter 16 - The Lovers

When Lisa had gone, Boris headed back to the roof.

Like most men who make their lives in a dangerous world, derring-doing where and when derring must be done, Boris was not given to introspection, because those quiet moments when you paused to consider the futility of existence were the ones in which something hideous crept up behind you, tore out your spine and turned you into a glove puppet. He preferred activity and, contrary to what he had said to Lisa, he had no intention of waiting as long as a month for his next action. He just needed to decide what that action ought to be.

She was an impressive girl. Boris knew women who could face down a werewolf and mutter something pithy and memorable (*'Smile you son of a bitch'* - something like that) before blowing its head off, but they were Universal agents, trained for that sort of thing. Lisa Hobson was a schoolgirl and the werewolf she had been facing down was her own brother. The gun might not have been very steady, but she *had* pointed it and Boris was relatively sure she would have fired. That took courage. Or possibly psychosis, but in this case it had probably been courage. So much potential.

That was part of the problem with this assignment. There was a school full of potential. Whether they were courageous like Lisa, brilliant athletes, peerless scholars, budding scientists, or indeed just decent people, they all needed protecting. Come to think of it, even if they were vile children with the potential to be nothing more than a horrible drain on society, they still did not deserve to be killed. They were just starting their lives and they deserved the opportunity to find out what they were going to be. Tracking down the elder werewolf was important, but keeping the children safe had to come first.

From his rooftop vantage point, Boris watched the children return by the weak light of the pale, morning sun, fighting its way up as if it had had a hard night and would really rather have stayed in bed. They were human now, which begged the question of what they thought when, twice a month they woke up far from the school with no memory of how they had got there. Did the amnesia of being a wolf extend into the first few hours of their being human again? It didn't seem very likely. Did they know what had happened to them?

159

Or was something else going on? Something that made them unconcerned. Had the elder wolf perhaps told them the truth and was preparing them for the task ahead? Children's minds were pliant and easily influenced.

Too many questions, not enough answers.

There, among the returning children, was young Oliver, wearing a jacket that someone had lent him and little else. There was a deal of laughing and joking around him, and Boris realised that while the others had left the building as humans and presumably stripped before changing, Oliver had changed in his sister's room, shredding his clothes. The others seemed to find it very funny. Oliver did not.

Boris recalled what Lisa had said about the white wolf not being with the rest of the pack. He was with them now, but not comfortably, looking like an outsider on the inside.

As the children snuck back to their rooms, Boris remained on the roof. If he was right, and if what he had gleaned from the remains of Creighton's notes was right, then…

There.

From the early morning mists that scudded low across the moor, a figure emerged. Even without his binoculars - broken by the werewolf's hard skull - Boris recognised the gait and general body shape. It was Dr Lloyd.

Flattening himself against the slates of the roof, Boris made himself as unobtrusive as possible - an elder werewolf would likely be more wary than the children. He watched the headmistress pass through the school gates and enter the building.

Well, that clarified his next action. If she had not already been at the head of his list of suspects, then Dr Lloyd had just leapfrogged her way there. From here on, Boris would be her shadow, trailing her as subtly as he could - which, he prided himself, was pretty subtly.

"Mr Rains?"

Or at least, he had thought it was pretty subtly. It was the following day, the first day of Boris's covert observation, and already that 'covertion' seemed to have been thwarted.

"Something wrong, Dr Lloyd?" Had she noticed that, wherever she had gone today, he was always nearby?

"My car, won't start. Would you mind giving me a lift into the village?"

Relieved at this vindication of his stalking skills, Boris nodded and led the way to the battered Cortina that he had picked up second (quite possibly third or fourth) hand, to suit Mr Rains' character. The Headmistress seemed unlikely to do anything incriminating with him sitting beside her, but he was not about to pass up the opportunity.

"So sorry to put you out like this," said Dr Lloyd, gratefully, as she got into the car - werewolves were quite capable of courtesy. "I was planning to walk but I left it too late and then the car wouldn't start."

"It's a fair walk," said Boris, careful to retain Mr Rains' guardedly taciturn way of speaking.

"I don't mind it," replied Dr Lloyd, looking out of the window as they passed through the gates and out onto the moor road. "You can't live up here and not embrace walking. Everywhere's a fair walk."

"Nice country though. Reminds me of Romania."

"Yes? I suppose. In its way."

She had been to Eastern Europe then. The area in which werewolves were found in their greatest number.

"If you could just drop me at the edge of town. Near the *Boar* is fine."

"Do you want me to wait for you?" Boris eased his inquiries forward with glacial slowness.

Dr Lloyd shook her head. "I can walk back. It's just that I have an appointment and I don't want to keep them waiting."

"It's no trouble."

Dr Lloyd managed a half smile. "It's very kind of you Mr Rains, but I would rather walk back."

Was she trying to get rid of him? Older werewolves retained full memory of both sides of their life. That was what made them dangerous; the wolf could think like a human and the human could plan the actions of the wolf. If she had worked out who he was then she might well lure him out of the school, out of sight of others, to deal with him. The deferential yokel shtick was not one of Boris's finest disguises and he was starting to regret picking it.

"You're relatively new to the school," said Dr Lloyd, as they drove. "Have you noticed anything out of the ordinary?"

Boris shook his head firmly - he would not condemn himself out of his own mouth. "No, Dr Lloyd."

161

"You know, when we're not around the children, you can call me Evelyn."

"Oh. Thank you."

In the village, Boris pulled up outside *The Grey* Boar, next to Malcolm's motorbike; indicating that he had drunk one too many the night before.

Evelyn Lloyd turned to him. "Thank you so much, you've really saved me."

"I don't mind hanging around."

She shook her head again. "That's quite alright. I'll see you back at the school."

"Well, now I'm here I'll pick up a few bits from the shop - so if you change your mind..."

"Thank you, but I won't."

They both got out of the car.

"Well, goodbye then." It was evident that Dr Lloyd was not going anywhere while Boris was watching her.

"Goodbye Dr... Evelyn." Boris walked off in the direction of the shop. As soon as he was out of sight, he peered back around the corner at the headmistress.

She hadn't waited about. Once Mr Rains was gone she had hurried off, not into Naughton, but back the way they had come, her heels clacking urgently on the road as she headed out of the village in the direction of the mill.

Taking the narrow alley that burrowed between *The Grey Boar* and the Post Office, Boris followed a path parallel to that taken by Dr Lloyd. Hopping fences and walls as he went, he ducked and covered his way through back gardens, delicately picking a path through vegetable patches and flower beds, ignoring the funny looks he received from snoozing cats and curious chickens. Reaching the outskirts of Naughton, he paused, looking for Dr Lloyd. There she was, walking at the same brisk pace along the exposed mill road, glancing at her watch more often than was necessary. Boris let her get a decent lead on him, then skidded down the steep earth slope into the ditch that ran along the right-hand side of the road. According to the archaeologists who descended on Naughton regularly to dig up bits of the village and its environs, it was originally Iron Age and had a lot of interesting features, but the one that appealed to Boris most right now was that it followed the road but made him invisible to anyone on it. Bent almost double, but eyes always up, he jogged silently along the ditch, his feet skidding and slipping in the mud. Occasionally he caught sight of Dr Lloyd's head bobbing along, keeping up its eager pace. That she was heading for the mill seemed in little doubt. *Why?* was the question that was currently exercising Boris's mind.

He had wondered why Ralph Matthews (poor Ralph) had been killed. Had it just been an accident that was bound to happen when a pack of juvenile werewolves were roaming the moor? Or had he found something out and been killed to keep his mouth shut? Was it possible that he had left some evidence of his findings that Dr Lloyd was now going to destroy?

At the sound of a car from behind, Boris flattened himself against the side of the ditch, the wet grass soaking his overalls. The car passed by and he heard it slow as it reached Dr Lloyd. The engine idled a while and Boris strained to hear the voices over it, but could not pick out the words. The tone sounded friendly enough. There was the slam of a door and the car started off again.

Clambering cautiously up the side of the ditch, Boris peered out along the road. Dr Lloyd had gone, presumably picked up by the car, which he could still see heading for the mill. Sliding back down, Boris continued his pursuit at a run.

The car was parked outside the mill when Boris arrived, its driver and the headmistress presumably within. Having heard nothing in the way of blood-curdling screams, Boris decided that whatever was happening inside required no urgent action on his part. It was the wrong time of the month for werewolf killings and he would learn more by letting events play out. He executed a circuit of the building - the mill and the adjoining house - keeping a safe distance, then secreted himself in the shelter of a willow that overhung the mill race.

After about half an hour, the door of the mill opened and Dr Lloyd emerged with a suited man carrying a folder of documents. There was a brief exchange of papers, of handshakes and of pleasantries before they parted, the suited man going back to his car while Dr Lloyd remained in the doorway.

Boris watched all this with bafflement. He had not been certain in any of his theories, but this backed up none of them. And matters did not get clearer as Dr Lloyd sat down on the stone doorstep and began to cry.

Boris's feet started moving before he was really aware of what they were doing and before he had had a chance to think about what he might say.

The headmistress looked up sharply at the sound of the garden gate opening, her eyes red from crying.

"Dr Lloyd?"

She relaxed as she recognised the school caretaker. "I told you to call me Evelyn."

"You also told me to go back to the school."

"And instead you followed me?"

"I'm a nosy person."

She seemed to accept this as a perfectly reasonable excuse and her gaze slid away from Boris, beyond the garden wall, the road and the river, to the beckoning vastness of the moor.

"I bloody hate it some days."

Boris seated himself beside her, not feeling the need to say anything or do anything beyond being there.

"That damn village is lousy with gossip," Evelyn said, eventually. "Last term I even caught a teacher asking questions about me behind my back. Ralph and I were both free, but there were still people who remembered, and liked, his ex-wife. And they have some funny ideas about the 'folk up the school'. Plus, it would have been awkward when he came to talk to the kids. Just seemed easier from every angle to keep it quiet, for the time being. I think we'd have come clean quite soon. Actually I think we'd have come clean sooner if we hadn't kind of enjoyed the sneaking about. It was fun. You know? At our age it was nice to be like kids again."

"How long were you together?" asked Boris.

"Just over a year. Not long really. Long enough to..." She sighed. "You reach a certain age and go through a certain number of what I guess you could call 'relationships', and you think; well, it's probably never going to happen for me. And you rather make your peace with that. And then you meet someone, and you don't even question why it didn't happen before because, who cares? It's happening now and you wouldn't change a moment of it. Until the night that you would."

"You went to see him that night." Boris did not elaborate how he knew, and Evelyn was so happy to finally talk about something

164

she had kept so long suppressed, that she did not notice.

"Our first date was a full moon so, however often we met up, we always met on full moons."

Boris tried not to let his reaction show. "I bet you still come out here most full moons."

"Every full moon. I lay flowers. I sleep in our bed and..." The tears were quick to her face. "But never again."

The scene he had witnessed earlier started to make more sense to Boris. "He left you the mill."

"Didn't have any family."

"And you're selling it."

Evelyn wiped away the tears. "It's the right thing to do. He loved this place and he'd hate to see it standing idle. A worthless monument to him and a keepsake for some dried up old maid, clinging to the memory of her last chance at happiness."

Boris placed a hand on her shoulder. "I don't think he'd have liked that sort of talk either."

He badly wanted to ask more about the night Ralph had died, but now was not the time.

As they drove back across the moor, Evelyn turned to him. "Thank you, Mr Rains."

"I had to go into town anyway."

"Not what I meant, as well you know, but thank you."

"Do you mind if I ask," Boris paced himself, holding off the questions that would make her relive that night, "you asked me earlier if I had noticed anything out of the ordinary at the school. What did you have in mind?"

"I..." Evelyn Lloyd paused and then deflated slightly. "I really don't know. I think... that is to say; I know that I took my eye off the ball where the school was concerned, and now... I feel like I'm coming back to a school I don't know. As if something is going on under the surface. Does that make any sense?"

It made a great deal of sense to Boris, but not to Mr Rains.

"I think there's some bullying amongst the kids."

Dr Lloyd nodded. "You get that in every school. It sometimes seems like the harder you fight it the worse it comes back. The sad truth is that if I expelled every bully then by the end of the week there'd be a new hierarchy in place to fill the vacuum."

"Children can be like animals."

165

"Not sure I would go quite that far. Although the fourth form at lunch could be narrated by David Attenborough."

"I meant like a pack," Boris pushed his luck a little. "Alphas and betas."

Dr Lloyd considered it for a moment. "Yes. Yes, I suppose I can see that." She shook her head. "But there's more than that at the Priory Grange at the moment. You know that feeling you get before a thunderstorm? Something in the air. Maybe if I hadn't been so distracted..."

"I don't think you can blame yourself for that."

"I might have been able to nip it in the bud."

They pulled into the school and Boris turned to the Headmistress. She knew nothing - he was as certain of that as he could be - but she might have seen something. Sensitivity would have to take a second place to expediency.

"Dr Lloyd, with all the people getting killed or going missing, I feel I've got to ask; did you see anything that night, when you went to see Ralph?"

Boris had expected her to become tearful again with the mention of that traumatic night, but instead her eyes narrowed with suspicion. "Why *did* you follow me, Mr Rains?"

"Seemed like the thing to do."

"Who are you?"

"I'm the caretaker," said Mr Rains.

"And no more?"

Boris held her eyes with his. "We all have our secrets, Evelyn."

For a long time, Evelyn Lloyd stared Boris down, before finally speaking. "I didn't see anything that night. The fog was in. But," she continued as Boris's shoulders slumped, "some other nights, when we went walking across the moor together. We saw something - someone, I suppose - out in Naughton Mire. Just a shape really, a silhouette of..." She paused. "A person, I suppose. It must have been a person, they were on two legs."

"You don't sound sure," Boris edged her on.

Dr Lloyd shook her head. "In the moor and the night and the fog, who can be sure? But... It was a very strange looking person. Almost... animal."

Chapter 17 – Naughton Mire

"Mr Rains!"

It was mid-afternoon the following day when Boris approached Naughton Mire to be met by Simon Montford, bounding across the undulating landscape like an unstrung marionette and thrusting out a welcoming hand.

"Good morning, Mr Squire," said Boris – it was quite good fun playing Mr Rains around the gentry. "Thanks for doing this."

"Oh it's a pleasure!" the young Squire exclaimed enthusiastically. "Anyone who wants to know more about the Mire is a good sort in my book."

"Well, it's more that I want to find this dog," lied Boris.

"Of course, of course. The dog. Happy to help, happy to help. Shall we?"

Montford led the way off the path and into the more vividly green surrounds of the marsh. Boris felt the ground giving uncomfortably beneath his feet, sucking at his shoes with every step.

"Step where I step and you'll be fine," Montford beamed, noticing Boris's anxiety. "Pretty much everywhere is soft underfoot. It's a question of how soft, what? There's soft, and there's up to your waist in mud, flailing around, screaming for help. Whole new meaning to 'brown trousers time', what?"

"Let's stick to soft," suggested Boris.

"Ha! Righto." The squire led on, weaving a careful path. "Now, I've given some thought to possible places a dog might hole up, as it were. There are a few. A lot of criminal elements have used the mire as a place to hide out over the years. A local highwayman with the wonderful name of Granville 'Twiddle' Helm made his base here. (I've a few stories about him if you're interested. Hanged of course.) But I have to say that, in all likelihood, any animal that wanders in will be damned lucky to get out with its life, let alone find a safe place to hide."

"Even something as light as a dog?" Boris wondered.

"I suppose it depends on the size of the dog," Montford shrugged. "But the problem is panic. If the ground starts to give under a dog's paws then it panics and that makes matters worse. So even if it was light enough to run through, its own panic will seal its fate."

Boris nodded. Thinking through his options yesterday, he had considered searching the mire on his own, without a guide. *How bad can it be?* he had confidently thought. It seemed that his decision to call Squire Montford (whose acquaintance he had made on evenings in *The Grey Boar*), concocting some story about a lost dog, had been a sensible one that might have saved his life.

"Now it does get a touch skooshy her," Montford rambled on. He narrated as he walked, but was pleasant enough company. Silence would have been oppressive.

Boris stepped forward and the ground farted beneath him, oozing brown muck about Mr Rains' steel toe-capped boots. What was he expecting to find? The lair was what he was hoping for. Even as recently turned a werewolf as Larry Glendon felt that lupine urge to make its home somewhere - a place that felt comfortable and safe, where a kill could be stored for later consumption - an older wolf was sure to have one. Although Universal had limited intelligence on werewolves themselves, their lairs were well-documented, going back hundreds of years. They were usually discovered after the wolf had been killed or taken its own tragic life. The moor presented any number of possible locations, but none was safer than Naughton Mire. Of course Boris had staked it out already, but that was before he had known what he was dealing with. An older and wilier wolf might have the sense to vary its routine. Also, it was in the mire that Dr Lloyd had seen something. It hadn't sounded like a wolf, but it was certainly worthy of a closer look.

"Now *this* is interesting," Montford stopped to point to the ground. "See that butterfly? For my money, this is a sub-species entirely unique to Naughton Mire. I'm not a lepidopterist, but I keep trying to get one to come up here and confirm it. Rather hoping they might name it after me. That'd be something to tell the grandkiddies, what?"

"Very nice." Boris watched the light brown butterfly, dappled with mud brown splotches as it flew off in that erratic way that butterflies have. "Could anyone else find their way around this place? You can't be the only one."

Montford laughed. "Rather wish I was. Imagine having all this as your private preserve." He surveyed the inhospitable green land around them and sighed. "But no. There's a fair few locals who can find their way around as well as me. Routes passed down from father

168

to son and all that. They don't come out here as often as I do, and I remain the authority on the flora and fauna of the mire, but there are certainly others who could walk across it."

If only there was a convenient list of their names to consult. They forged deeper into the heart of Naughton Mire.

"This way." Montford pointed in the direction of a series of hummocks that rose from the green carpet of the marsh.

"What's that?" asked Boris. The mire had its own distinct landscape of undulations - some large, some small - ornamented by occasional trees and bushes, but these did not fit in, they looked unnatural.

"Iron age barrow," explained Montford. "Burial of some sort. Some chieftain or other, I daresay. Archaeologists looked at it back in the fifties but found it had been used by too many other people in the interim. Anything iron age was long since turfed out by people like 'Twiddle' Helm using it as a place to stash their loot. If there was gold I suppose they kept it, but anything else - bones and suchlike - probably went straight into the marsh. Archaeological tragedy, what? No one goes there now, but it might be a good place for a dog to hide if it managed to get this far. The ground around it is more solid than pretty much anywhere else in the marsh – presumably why the iron age chappies chose the site. An island of safety in the middle of land that swallows you up. Might have had mystical significance to primitives. Always found it a bit boring myself. Rather lets the rest of the marsh down. Tell you who did like it though," he continued as they picked their way delicately towards the barrows. "That poor chap, Tull. Funny really; you'd think a geographer would have more enthusiasm for the marsh itself, but he had a good old root about."

"He find anything?" Boris tried to keep the tremor of anticipation out of his voice.

"Not to my knowledge. I did wonder if he came back out here on his own to look, and that's when he..." Montford made a roundabout gesture with his hand. "You know. Poor chap. But then why come out in the storm? Mystery, what?"

There was nothing specific to suggest that this island was what he was looking for, and yet Boris felt his pulse quicken as they approached. Creighton's had probably done the same. You developed instincts in this line of work and there was just something

169

about the place that screamed 'lair'.

As they drew closer, even Boris was surprised by the relief he felt when his feet found solid ground beneath them once more. Montford noticed his face and smiled.

"Ha. Yes, one does take ground for granted until one comes out to a place like this, doesn't one? First time I came out this way - Grandfather showed me - I could have kissed the earth."

Boris nodded in understanding. You got used to ground. The fact that it wasn't going anywhere was one of life's certainties, and the last hour of having it give uncomfortably beneath each step had been unnerving.

"Nice to be back on firmer *terra*." Not a very Mr Rainsian joke but Montford did not seem to notice.

Under Montford's careful supervision they skirted around the limits of the island, whistling and calling for 'Carl'. Boris wasn't sure why he had named the fictitious dog after his boss.

"Can't see any paw prints," mused Montford. "How long's he been gone?"

"Two days," said Boris.

Montford nodded. "The mire wouldn't hold prints that long. Usually oozes back after a few hours. Shall we check inside the barrow?"

"It's not locked up?"

Montford shook his head. "Why bother? It's right in the centre of the marsh." He looked out across the mire, the landscape fading into the greyness of early evening. "Let's be quick. The mist is coming in."

Boris nodded. The mist, that the moor seemed to attract, hung more heavily in the depression of the mire. It was at times like this with the white haze descending, curling spectral trails, wreathing the trees and bushes, that you could easily understand how so many had lost their lives here. Though not given to imaginative rumination, Boris could not help looking at the scene and imagining the mist as the departed spirits of all those whose mortal remains still lay beneath the surface, decomposing at the glacial pace dictated by the boggy ground.

"This way." Montford led the way to the central hump of earth. At one end of the barrow, a large stone had been sunk vertically into the ground, shielding the entrance behind it.

"I often wonder how they got this stone out here," mused Montford, absently. "How many must have died in the process."

Behind the main stone a pair of smaller stones, like guardsmen, stood in the entrance way. Montford slid his gangly body between them, and Boris followed into the cool dankness of the tunnel beyond.

"Always cold in here," shivered Montford. "Even in the height of summer. Have you got a torch?"

Boris nodded, and the powerful beam of his torch cleaved through the darkness of the tunnel.

"Good torch," observed Montford. "You seem like the kind of chap who would have a good torch. Do you own a tool belt?"

"Yes."

"Thought as much." He called down the tunnel. "Carl!"

Nothing. Which was to be expected.

"He might be hurt," said Boris. "Best have a look around."

"Right ho."

To left and right of them as they walked through the old burial mound, were small ante-chambers that had once housed... what? Something important certainly, but something lost to time. Treasure, perhaps? Practicalities for the journey to the afterlife? Animal sacrifices? Perhaps the bodies of the chieftain's family or those of his servants or enemies? Now, all empty.

"These are pretty small compared to the main chamber," Montford said as the tunnel trended downwards. "It's not Tutankhamun's tomb, but it's pretty impressive for what it is."

"Is that right?" Boris was more familiar with the tombs of ancient Egyptians than those of ancient Britons, but it was nice, for once, to be in a tomb where the occupant was unlikely to be up and about and bent on world domination.

"Through here."

It felt colder still as they entered a larger chamber, its doorway flanked by more stone guardsmen, the air almost frosty with chill, even alongside the heavy dampness of the marsh soil.

"I don't see a dog, but take a look around," said Montford, falling back a little, allowing Boris to experience the impressive burial chamber for himself.

"Thanks." Boris flashed his torch to the ceiling and around the walls, its bright beam cutting through the encompassing blackness.

In one wall was another doorway, to which a barred door had been added at some later date, leading to yet another ante-chamber – presumably a treasure chamber if it was this close to the chieftain's body. But all evidence that this had once been the final resting place of someone of importance - someone who might even have called himself 'king' - was gone, except for...

Except for the body.

A sharp chill shot through Boris as his torch illuminated the corpse in one corner of the burial chamber. For a moment his startled mind wondered if this was the body of that iron age chieftain, still preserved here by the cold and the properties of the marshland that surrounded it. But now he noticed that smell that, even masked by the damp earth, he should have noticed more quickly. This body was recent – not fresh, but certainly not ancient. It was also not complete. Both legs and one of its arms were largely gone.

Something had been eating it.

Though he was already certain of what he would see, Boris could not suppress a gag of horror rising within him as he allowed the torchlight to play on the dead man's face. It was Creighton.

All this, from the discovery of the body to the discovery of who it was, had played out in mere seconds, and despite the cold shock of finding his friend like this, Boris recovered himself quickly.

But not quickly enough.

As he started to turn, Boris felt a sharp pain on the back of his head, coinciding with a sickening thump. Blackness swallowed him.

At the same time that Boris was meeting up with Simon Montford at the fringes of Naughton Mire, Lisa was blowing off revision and coursework to head out across the moor with Moose by her side.

"You think I'm nuts, don't you?" asked Lisa, as she and Moose walked. "Not because I'm talking to a dog - I think that's probably fine - but because I'm doing this at all. You think I'm nuts."

Moose gambolled along beside her, ears flapping, tongue lolling, and doing everything in his limited capacity not to judge Lisa's actions.

Which did not stop her from trying to explain them. "I know Boris said to butt out – not in so many words, but that's what he

172

meant. I know it's dangerous *but* - big but - it's nowhere near full moon. So no danger. And regardless of what he said, I can't do nothing. And I think you agree with me on this." She looked at Moose, who looked back at her with that expression of confusion that some dogs maintain at all times. "If we didn't do our bit to find out who killed Talbot then what sort of friends would we be?"

Moose returned his attention to the moor ahead of them, which seemed to indicate that he was with Lisa on this one.

"I know what you're thinking," Lisa continued, in defiance of all evidence to the contrary. "If it's so safe, why did I bring the gun? Well, Boris seems to think there's some sort of mastermind werewolf in charge of all this and, I guess, he or she would be as dangerous as a human as they are as a wolf. And I don't know if werewolves in human form can only be killed by silver bullets or if that's strictly a wolf thing. There seem to be a lot of werewolf rules and no one managing them. The supernatural is very poorly organised. Anyway, if someone finds a gun in my dorm then I think it's an expelling offence - I'd be disappointed if it wasn't - so it's best I take it with me."

Moose snapped his jaws at a wayward crane fly as it passed, flying in that near suicidal way crane flies have, which makes even the most dedicated Darwinian raise questions about this whole evolution thing.

"So, why the mill?" It actually made Lisa feel better to talk this out with someone, and the fact that that someone did not answer was an added bonus. "That's a fair question, Moose, you obviously have a most penetrating insight into the whole affair. Firstly; if Mr Tull was killed because he was… whatever Boris is; and Talbot was killed because he messed with Glendon," she spat the name out, "then why was Ralph killed? Accident or design? He's the odd one out - no real connection to the school. I say it's worth having a look around. Secondly," she sighed, "where the hell else do I look? I've got to do something. I can't be just sitting around, knowing that all this is going on and doing nothing. And I don't know where else to go or what else to do. It'll probably be completely worthless but at least I'm doing something." She looked at Moose again, who was now chasing his tail. "You have a way of bringing the darkness out in me, Moose. Let's change the subject."

On their arrival at the mill in late afternoon, Moose once again questioned Lisa's actions as she jimmied open a window around the back of the property.

"I think we can all agree it's for a greater good. Stop being so 'by the book'!"

The mill itself and the house in which the miller traditionally lived were all one property, adjoining doors linking home to workplace on the ground and first floors. Lisa started by searching the mill, stealthily creeping about the wooden machinery that had stood silent since the death of its owner. That owner had been very proud of his work, and while it was for the moment inactive, at the throw of a lever, the whole edifice of interlinking cogs, wheels, cams, pulleys and other parts to which Lisa could not put names, would spring back to life. Ralph had kept it clean and well-maintained, neat and tidy and ready to go. The new miller would just have to move in.

As she looked around, Lisa's brain sent her vague messages that all this was familiar, and she sought her memory for a gothic novel that revolved around a mill. She couldn't think of anything specific (*The Mill on the Floss* (Mary Ann Evans writing as George Eliot) hardly counted as gothic), but then realised it was not a book she was thinking of, but a film. The climax of *Frankenstein* (the 1931 version) took place in a windmill. In sharp contradistinction to the book (Mary Shelley), she added to herself with a touch of literary snobbery. But although adaptations that stray from their source material were anathema to her, she could not think ill of that film. It had scared the hell out of her when she had ill-advisedly been shown it as a six year old, and the image of Karloff's creature peering through the moving spokes of a mill wheel was etched into her subconscious.

Finding nothing suspicious or suggestive in the mill itself, Lisa moved through into the homely cottage attached to the side of the building. Here too, all had been cleaned in anticipation of new tenants, but Ralph's belongings remained *in situ* for the present, to give the cottage that 'lived in' feel that apparently helps sell a property. The floorboards creaked reassuringly beneath Lisa's feet as she entered, making Moose, stare at the floor with head tilted to one side, wondering what monster lived down there and why it was making such a racket. The sofa in the living room was a faded green, heavily dented by years of use, the fireplace was laid, ready to be lit for an owner who would never return, and the scattered ephemera of everyday existence lay about the place, begging to be picked up, to mean something again. It was all quietly sad, and Lisa was overcome by a wave of melancholy for the loss of a man she had never known. There was something unbearably tragic about a home to which the owner had expected to return – the list of groceries that would never be purchased, the list of chores that would never be done, the muddy boots put to one side to be cleaned.

The search for something that would provide an adequate motive for murder ought to have given Lisa a good distraction from all this, but thus far that search was yielding nothing. Climbing up the stairs, Lisa observed the framed newspaper clippings - mostly local but a few national - about the mill, all with pictures of Ralph himself, bearded and beaming as he showed off his pride and joy. Upstairs, the bed was made, the toothbrush was in its cup, dirty clothes in a hamper waiting to be washed. None of which seemed like motives for murder.

What would happen to it all once the place was sold? Poor Ralph had had no family.

Heading back down to the living room, Lisa sat on the sofa and composed herself. Looking around here so soon after the deaths of Talbot and Mr Tull had clearly affected her in ways she had not anticipated. Maybe this had been a bad idea full stop. It was not as if she had found anything.

Moose moseyed over in his friendly, doggy way to nuzzle up against her cheek and Lisa scratched him behind the ears. Smelling salts are all well and good, but if you really need something to bring you back to reality with a jolt, then dog breath and a wet nose in your ear are more effective.

She looked up. And frowned.

On the table by the window were the limited family photos that poor Ralph possessed. There wasn't much to tell, but one of the figures looked curiously familiar. It could only be Ralph himself - the smile was unmistakable - taken before he had grown the thick beard that defined his face in more recent pictures, but that wasn't why it was familiar. It took Lisa a little time to realise who it reminded her of.

How about that?

Was it important? Probably not, but she took a picture of the photo with the phone that Boris had given her and texted it to him with the message; 'Ralph Matthews. Remind you of anyone?'.

It might yet prove important. It would be nice to think that this little excursion across the moor had not been a total waste of time.

She petted Moose a moment while looking about for anything else she might have missed.

"Shall we go?"

Moose barked. Which could have been yes or no.

"I think so too."

They left the way they had come, Lisa straining to lift Moose through the window while he barked excitedly at the novelty of the adventure. Closing the window behind them, and walking back to the front of the property, Lisa set out back across the moor with Moose bounding after her. It was later than she had thought; night was starting to fall. She had taken too long pondering the frailty of existence, the unfinished work it leaves behind, and the curious similarity that poor Ralph, when viewed without a beard, had borne to Squire Simon Montford.

Chapter 18 – The Barrow

The pain in Boris's head as he came around was sharp, but was as nothing to the shame he felt. For a Universal agent to be caught in so obvious a trap was... well it was pathetic. It was the sort of mistake that usually resulted in death, and perhaps still would. But Simon Montford was the least suspicious person imaginable, a bumbling and befuddled goofball. Which, now Boris came to think about it, was a perfect cover for a devious werewolf plotting world domination.

Had Creighton fallen into the same trap? If so he had certainly paid for it, and his fate was one which now awaited Boris.

"Awake, are you?" Montford's voice was different now, sharper, lower, less '*Yoiks! Jolly hockey sticks!*'.

Boris rolled over and took in his surroundings. The ante-chamber with the barred door made an excellent cell. The walls, illuminated by the light of flickering candles mounted about the room, were deeply scored by scratches that Boris instantly recognised from a picture in the archives of the Universal Library.

"Time was," Montford approached the bars to peer in at his prisoner, "when I locked myself in there every full moon, for fear of what I might do. I have more control now. That comes with age in my species. I assume. It's not like there's a rulebook or a social club where we share tips. In many ways it is a lonely existence."

"You'll forgive me if I don't have a great deal of sympathy," replied Boris, rubbing his head.

"Because I locked you up? Or because I killed your friend?" Montford even looked different now. He moved with a cold certainty, almost a grace, a far cry from his former gangliness. "You can hardly blame me. He was getting too close. As were you."

"You kept his body?" Boris still felt sick to his stomach at the thought.

Montford shrugged. "Most full moons I treat myself to a single sheep - though I have been cautious of venturing out these past few months - but I so seldom get to enjoy the taste of human flesh. The only way a werewolf reaches any sort of age - and I have been a wolf since my early teens - is to learn control. To lock yourself up during those early years and then, once you gain some self-awareness (or self-awerewolfness, as I like to call it) to keep a tight rein on those desires that course through you." His fists tightened as he spoke, as if he was feeling those desires now. "Werewolves don't *have* to eat human meat, but once you've tasted it..." his eyes widened manically. "To deny ones-self is a challenge." He shrugged again. "But one must be practical. If you kill humans (even just one or two) then the police get involved. Questions are asked and, before too long, people like you and your late friend start poking about."

Boris said nothing.

"You think people like me don't know about people like you?" asked Montford. "Ha. Anyway, my point was that human flesh is not something I get to taste very often these days. I pop over to Europe for snack when I can, but even that can be risky. I was over there not long ago and ended up turning someone I'd planned to eat. Got disturbed. It's the penalty one pays for being a long-lived werewolf. So, when necessity demands that I kill a human, I stash their body down here. The cold keeps it reasonably fresh," he glanced back at Creighton's corpse. "Fresh-ish. And I have a bit when I feel like it. I should really finish him up, he won't keep his flavour much longer and freezing does spoil it completely."

Boris strove to control his anger – it wouldn't help Creighton and certainly wouldn't help him escape. But when he did escape, this man was going to feel that anger in full and with interest. It was easy to feel sorry for werewolves - once bitten they had no choice over what they became - but Montford had clearly been a bastard all his life.

"I know what you're doing," said Boris. "Targeting the children because you can bend them to your will."

Montford scoffed. "I'll take responsibility for the Glendon boy, but 'children'? Plural? That was his doing. And surprised me. To form a pack? Quite something."

"You expect me to believe that you had nothing to do with it?"

"Why would I?"

Boris shook his head. "I've often asked myself that question. But the undead are always building armies, planning to take over the world and..." He broke off as Montford started laughing.

"*That's* what you think this is about? My dear fellow, we're not all supervillains. Some of us are just run of the mill greedy bastards."

There was a matter of factness to his tone that made Boris

178

believe him – he had no reason now to lie.

"My father, as you may know, died earlier this year." Though he was not a supervillain, Montford apparently shared their propensity for outlining their grand plans to prove how clever they were. "His will stipulated that his substantial wealth and holdings were to be divided between his children. An odd clause, I thought, since he had only one; me. I assumed - everyone assumed - that the will had been written at a time when he thought he might still have more children. Then, quite by chance, I discovered Ralph Matthews. I won't bore you with the details of how, but once I had found him, procuring a sample of DNA was no great trial. He was my elder half-brother; an unfortunate by-product of my father's somewhat rakish youth. No one else knew - not even Ralph himself - and perhaps I could have left matters at that, but," he smiled nastily, "I had no intention of sharing that money. One day, someone was going to find out. From the moment of my father's death, I was on a clock. Ralph had to die before his ancestry was discovered."

Montford crossed the burial chamber to sit beside the corpse of Creighton, quite at home in the company of the dead.

"In many ways I was lucky. I had the perfect means of killing Ralph and everyone would just assume that he had been killed by an animal of some sort. Every moor in Britain has rumours about big cats or beasts of some description, so Ralph would be just another victim."

"But you were worried about me," Boris spoke up.

Montford nodded. "And those like you. I'll admit, I know nothing about the organisation to which you belong. But you can't be an undead as long as I've been without hearing the rumours; that there is a group out there who hunt us."

"We exist to protect people," Boris interrupted.

"Where were you when I was turned?" asked Montford, sharply.

Boris let his chin sink to his chest. "We can't save everyone. And werewolves are the saddest of the creatures we have to face, because they have no say in what they have become. But here's the thing," he looked up again, targeting a venomous stare at Montford, "I know that young wolves have no control over what they do when they are in that shape. You do. And being a werewolf doesn't affect the kind of human you are – that's the tragedy. Even a man who is pure of heart and all that. You're not a bad werewolf. You're a bad person. And if you hadn't been bitten by the wolf then you'd have murdered Ralph some other way."

Montford met Boris's stare and then, as Boris watched, the squire's face broke into a smile. "Of course, you're right. Being a werewolf was not essential, it was merely helpful in avoiding the police. But, as I said, it might attract attention from your people. So I thought; if they're coming up here expecting to find a wild werewolf running about, why not give them one?"

The full horror of what Montford had done insinuated its way into Boris's mind. No wonder he hadn't figured it out, no wonder Creighton hadn't. What sort of person would do such a thing.

"You turned Larry Glendon into a werewolf just to create a scapegoat?"

Montford grinned. "And it worked far better than I could have dreamed. He gained self-awerewolfness far faster than I did. Really took to it, and started creating his pack. Basically duplicating his peer group around him. Imagine how I felt when I realised. I'd wanted a werewolf for you to find when you came looking for who killed Ralph Matthews, and Glendon gave me a whole damn pack of them. I couldn't have planned a better diversion."

"You doomed those children just so you could kill a man with impunity." Boris could still barely believe the cold callousness of it.

"Hardly," said Montford dismissively. "I did it for the money."

"Why Glendon?"

"From all I've learned over the years," Montford began, "the type of wolf you become is dependent on the type of human you are. I needed a werewolf that would create havoc. That would kill animals indiscriminately and maybe even a few humans as well. I've been to the school on numerous occasions to lecture and it was clear to me that Glendon was the biggest arsehole in the place." He shook his head in mild disbelief at his own good fortune. "Once he started killing sheep - in ridiculous numbers I might add - I made my move and killed Ralph. Irritatingly I had to leave the body, so it tied in with the sheep deaths. But it all worked out terribly well. Until our mutual friend," he patted Creighton's corpse, "started taking an interest beyond the school."

"What sort of interest?" How close had Creighton come to the truth?

"Same as you," said Montford. "Asking questions about the mire, about animals that had been seen there. I'd largely kept my distance since turning Glendon, but the rumours and old wives tales were still doing the rounds. When I met Curt Tull, he was waist deep in the mire. He'd decided to explore for himself. I saved his life." Montford smiled and shook his head. "After that, I kept a close eye on him, and it soon became clear that he wasn't buying my diversion. Unfortunately for him he rather fastened onto that headmistress as the one responsible (you did too; don't deny it). Asked a lot of questions about her in the *Boar*, which got him into hot water when she found out. Not a very discreet investigator."

Boris said nothing, but recognised Creighton's fatal impetuosity.

"It was only a matter of time before he discovered the truth," Montford continued, "so I decided to act. One full moon I phoned him at the school and told him I'd seen some sort of animal in my grounds and maybe it was what he was looking for. He came around - found nothing of course - and on his way back through the mire, I killed him."

Boris considered it. One man in dangerous terrain, hunted by a wolf that knew its way about the mire. Creighton had never had a chance.

"The following day," Montford went on, "the school was emptied to form search parties, and I took the opportunity to pop in and help myself to his notes. Alongside searching myself, of course. He was my 'friend' after all. I knew he'd be replaced, so I was on the look-out for someone like you. Just in case you've been beating yourself up about getting caught."

"What about the Conliffe boy?"

Montford stood up again. "Young Talbot? Nothing to do with me. My best guess would be Glendon. I suppose that any of his pack could have done it, but if I know anything about wolves then that boy wasn't a random kill, he was hunted. Glendon would do that. Though I can't say I know the other members of his pack – they are of absolutely no interest to me."

"The two of them - Glendon and Conliffe - had an argument earlier that evening."

Montford shrugged. "Seems to confirm it. The boy has advanced very quickly as a wolf and would be perfectly capable of

181

carrying that sort of grudge through the change." He approached the bars of Boris's cell. "Now, what am I going to do with you?" He shook his head, an ugly grin on his face. "Eating you is certainly my first choice, but if two of you go missing in the same area then your people are going to start taking a hard look. If you're to be killed, it needs to be by the pack. That should be enough to persuade any future 'meddlers' that the pack are responsible for all deaths." He moved back, away from the bars. "You can stay here while I make arrangements. I doubt anyone at the school will miss the caretaker like they did Mr Tull. No search parties for you."

Boris was about to speak, when the sound of a text alert came from under the table on which Creighton's body lay.

Montford frowned. "Is that yours?" He pulled out a wooden box from under the table. "Forgive me for going through your pockets, but- It *is* yours. How did you do that? There's no mobile service in these parts and we're underground."

He picked up the phone and a curious expression passed across his face. "Well, it seems we have another problem to deal with."

He held the phone up to Boris who saw the message; 'Ralph Matthews. Remind you of anyone?'. Accompanying the words was a picture; a framed photo of the young Ralph Matthews. The resemblance to the man currently holding the phone was striking.

"Father's damnable genes," muttered Montford. "Who sent this?"

"How about you let me out? Then I'll tell you," suggested Boris.

Simon Montford's face curled into a snarl. "Doesn't matter. Whoever it is they're at Ralph's." The snarl evolved into a smirk, which was equally unpleasant. "I think it's about time I used this pack, as long as it's here. I am the one who started it, after all. In a sense."

Boris smiled, pleased that for once he had the upper hand. "You're forgetting, Squire; it's not full moon."

The expression of mocking pity that Montford turned on Boris made him shiver in his cell. "Oh Mr Rains, one thing a werewolf learns as he gets older is that it's always full moon. Even if you can't see it, the moon is always there."

As Boris watched, the Squire's body was thrown into violent flux. His chest expanded, his arms lengthened, claws growing from his fingers. His shirt buttons burst and sleeves tore as his muscles expanded. Thick, black hair sprouted across his body and his legs reshaped into those of an animal. Yet he remained on his hind legs – not a wolf, but a wolf-man. The face that now stared at Boris was enough to make even the hardened Universal agent dig his fingernails into his palms to stop his skin from crawling off.

There had always been stories. That as werewolves grew older and more aware of the duality of their nature, so the creature they turned into changed as well, as if their human side influenced their body shape. Here was the proof. An older werewolf walked upright, only resorting to all fours when it gave chase; its paws became clawed hands, making it more dextrous; its chest broadened; its fore-legs became arms.

This was the shape Dr Lloyd had seen in the mire.

Jutting fangs protruded from a curved mouth, the nose had flattened while the face had extended to a short, blunt snout, the ears had lengthened and now twitched in the candlelight. But while it was a terrifying visage, fringed in black hair, it was the eyes that made the hairs on the back of Boris's neck stand on end. They were almost human, staring out of fiercely animal features, and yet something in those bloodshot orbs expressed more vile evil than any of the creature's more monstrous characteristics.

The werewolf let out a series of guttural, throaty noises, and Boris realised that it was laughing at him. Then it flung back its head and howled, loud enough that the sound echoed about the tunnels and chambers of the barrow and out into the night.

Boris didn't need to be told why it was howling. It didn't matter that Glendon was its only direct 'descendant'; it was the alpha dog in this region, and it was summoning its pack. The children might usually only change at full moon, but it was different when the Alpha commanded.

Chapter 19 - Flight

It was not late and certainly not night, but the heavily clouded sky had cut off the weak evening sun to make the distinction between evening and night a fairly semantic one. To make matters worse for Lisa, as she trudged across the moor, a heavy mist had blown in as if from nowhere. All she needed now was a low-cut dress (and a larger bosom to go with it) and she could be in a Hammer horror film. The presence of Moose, gambolling around her, sniffing things and snapping at moths without a care in the world, was a comfort as they headed back towards the school. Hopefully. She was relatively sure they were going the right way, but between the darkness and the mist (and of course she hadn't brought a bloody torch because it was daytime!), the major landmarks had vanished and she was now navigating on the principal of; *well, I started going the right way so I just to need keep going this way.* That was an ineffective principal at the best of times, and in amongst the uneven landscape of the moor, with trees and rocks and irregular bits of topography to be circumvented, it became next to useless.

"Do you know the way?" she asked Moose. "If I say 'home', you're just going to take me to the Conliffe estate aren't you?"

Moose chased his tail.

"Talbot didn't spend a lot of time teaching you stuff, did he?" said Lisa with a rueful smile. She ruffled the dog about the neck and Moose eagerly rubbed against her.

"Okay. We just keep going."

It was not full moon, but the idea of spending the night out here still made her shiver – and not with cold. She'd spent so much time recently with wolves on her mind that it was inevitable she started hearing things. The wind howled. *Just* the wind.

"There are no wolves out here." Saying it out loud made her feel better. Although even in the isolation of the moor she felt a little silly and self-conscious.

On she plodded. The boots, that she would forever associate with Talbot, were comfortable, kept her feet warm and dry, and were ideally suited for this sort of walking, but her jeans, T-shirt and woolly jumper left much to be desired, while her coat looked more wind-resistant that it actually was.

"Shit!" As she peered ahead to see through the thickening mist, she had stopped looking at the ground and taken a bad step. Losing what footing she had, Lisa tumbled down a slippery slope, smeared with mud, bashed by stones and her clothes plucked by brambles. She rolled to the bottom, sat up and swore more fluently. Moose trotted happily up and licked her face. "We're not in Kansas anymore, Moose." She looked about her. "Actually, for all I know, we *are* in Kansas."

She stood up, brushed off what mud and dirt she could and began to walk again in what she hoped was the same direction as before – though she had no memory of having climbed up so steep a slope on her way to the mill.

"I don't see how tonight could possibly get any worse."

The long, keening howl sounded on the wind before the sentence was completely out of her mouth.

An icy chill stole up Lisa's spine, spreading across her whole body. It couldn't be. It wasn't full moon.

Moose whined unhappily, pawing the ground, and somehow Lisa found that more terrifying than the howl. Moose was the happiest, daftest dog on the planet, worried by nothing. But he was scared now. He had heard that sound before; on the night his master died.

For a long moment, Lisa stood, frozen in fear and indecision. The school would be safest – there was safety in numbers, surrounded by thick walls. But she had no idea where it was. The mill was nearest (probably), she had only been walking for half an hour and if she ran then she could be back there in half that. But she had no idea where that was either.

Another howl carried to her through the mist and she snapped out of it. Backwards or forwards might be a tough decision, but either was better than standing like a lemon waiting to be eviscerated by her schoolmates. They were coming from the school, which meant the mill was the better of the two options.

Turning quickly, Lisa scrambled back up the steep bank down which she had just slid – there was probably a way around but she had no time to look for it. Reaching the top, she looked about her.

"Moose?"

But the dog was gone. She couldn't blame him. However scared she was, she had to imagine it was worse for Moose; the horrifying associations of that night, things he had seen but could not comprehend, had all come flooding back with the sound of the howl. He had run for safety and who could blame him?

When the howl came again it was no longer alone. As one sounded another joined it, then another and another. Lisa didn't pause any longer, she ran as fast as her legs would allow. Please God let her be running in the right direction.

"I'll be leaving you now," said Montford. He had changed back to human - something Boris would never be able to unsee - and put on fresh, unripped clothes, that he presumably kept here for just such an emergency. "I doubt anyone will ask, but I would rather have an alibi. 'At home reading a book on butterflies' may not be 'cool' but my housekeeper will verify it."

Boris nodded. "May I say something cliched?"

Montford shrugged. "I believe it is the done thing in these circumstances."

"You'll never get away with this."

"Feel better?"

"Not much."

"Ah well." Montford gave a little wave. "I'll be back when I've figured out how best to kill you. I think you and this other person dying on the same night might be overkill. Maybe give it a week. Can I bring you a book or anything?"

"Thank you," said Boris, as graciously as he could manage. "Nothing too long, I don't want to start something I won't be able to finish."

"Wise."

And with that, Montford left. In the flickering candlelight, Boris remained standing in the centre of his cell. To the casual observer he would have appeared entirely inactive but his brain was racing. Catching the werewolf was no longer foremost in his mind. He had to save Lisa. Why on earth had she gone to the mill?

Because she wanted to help. Because she was irritatingly brave. And because he had told her - *he had told her* - that there was no danger if there was no full moon.

He had to save her.

Which was easier said than done.

First things first: the cell door. Lockpicking was an art taught to all Universal agents and while Boris was by no means a prodigy,

186

the chunky padlock that hung from the chain on the barred door would present no great impediment. Sewn into the lining of Mr Rains' overalls were a few basic lockpick tools, and a minute or so later the lock clicked and the door swung open.

But Montford was no fool. He had probably known that the cell would prove little obstacle to Boris. The obstacle lay without, surrounding the barrow on every side. Naughton Mire was a prison that no lockpick could open.

Hurrying to the table in the corner, trying not to look at what lay on top, Boris reached for the box underneath and collected the belongings confiscated from him by Montford, and...

He paused. In amongst his own possessions lay a small handgun. It was Universal issue and loaded with silver bullets. Creighton's gun.

There were three bullets left, and Boris was oddly pleased to find that it had been fired. He had put up a fight.

"Thank you, my friend." He could not look at the corpse as he spoke, but pocketed the gun and hurried out of the barrow into the darkness that shrouded the moor.

There he stopped, frustrated and impotent, looking about him. Had it still been daylight then maybe - *maybe* - he might have been able to piece together the route that he and Montford had taken through the mire. At least he would have known where to start. But now night had fallen and the mist had descended, everything looked different. He didn't have a chance.

Which was a great pity since he was still going to try. What other choice did he have? He was going to save Lisa or die in the attempt.

Taking a deep breath, and relieved that he was not wearing his good shoes, Boris raised his foot to step out into the mire.

The sound of barking arrested his foot, which hung in mid-air as he peered through the mist, which his torch did nothing to alleviate.

"Carl?" he asked, in defiance of common sense.

A doggie shape emerged through the mist, weaving a path across the mire.

"Moose!"

On reaching him, the dog bounded up, agitated and whining, relieved to see a friendly face.

"You know your way through the mire?" Realisation dawned. "Your master showed you." Many of the locals knew the marsh, and Talbot was the type who would enjoy such exploring. The dog had run to a place where it instinctively felt safe, a place it associated with its old master. "Can you show me the way out?"

Moose stared back at Boris with blank incomprehension.

Boris grabbed the dog's head between his hands and eyeballed it. "Moose, I need you to understand; Miss Hobson - your new mistress - is in danger. I have to help her, and the only way I can do that is for you to show me the way out of here."

Moose licked his face.

Boris sat back on his haunches. "I suppose that was never likely to work. Moose, I'm sorry I have to do this."

He raised Creighton's gun in the air and fired straight up.

The loud report of the gun made Moose start in fear – even here he seemed to be in danger. Taking to his paws he ran back into the marsh, with Boris hot on his heels.

By now, Lisa had lost count of the number of times she had fallen. She was not sure why she had kept count in the first place, but that was human nature. The moor seemed suddenly more inhospitable than ever. It seemed to be out to get her, to trip her up and bite at her as she fell. It wanted to hurt her.

Her breath came in painful gasps. Her lungs burnt with effort, but every gulped breath was cold and wet with mist, mixing horribly in her chest so her gasps became guttural. Her legs screamed with pain, her face was flushed and sweaty, even in the cold. But she ran on.

The howls were still there behind her, and she knew they were closing in. '*Now the pack has your scent,*' Maria had said, and she had clearly been right. They weren't trying to sneak up on her, it was all a game to them and the fear they were inflicting was part of it. They enjoyed making their prey feel like this. Lisa's hand stole to the pocket of her coat, to find the heavy item that swung there, bashing against her hip bone with every pace she took. The gun, loaded with a single silver bullet.

If they caught her, which at this point seemed horribly inevitable, then she was going to take one of those bastards with her. As she ran, her panicked mind vaguely wondered if she would be able to pick out Glendon.

But for all that she hated him with a passion, could she actually kill him? He was still a man – still a boy really. Even when he was a wolf, would she have the ability to thrust a gun in his face and pull the trigger, knowing what she knew? The image of Talbot's father rose in her mind, his broken face and faltering words. Could she do that to another set of parents?

Glendon might have killed Talbot (though she didn't even know that for sure) but did that mean he had to die too? Where did it end?

It was an interesting debate, but this was probably not the time. Again, Lisa tripped as her foot caught a tendril of bramble, and she fell to earth, cursing the moor, the brambles, the wolves and pretty much everything else in the world. But as she struggled to her feet again, dragging her exhausted body back onto legs that no longer wanted to work, a sight met her eyes that made them well up with tears of relief.

The mill was only just visible through the mist, but it was unmistakable. Fresh strength flowed into her limbs, fuelled by hope, the howls of the wolves behind her suddenly seemed distant and unimportant.

She reached the window at the back of the building that had been her entry earlier, forced it open again, and clambered into the silent interior, tumbling to the floor, gasping and choking on her own tears. After allowing herself thirty seconds of self-indulgent sprawling on the wooden floor, she got back up and closed the window, locking it as best she could. She went for the light but then thought better of it – maybe if the lights were out the wolves would not realise she was here. It was a tough decision. In the darkness, the still, empty mill seemed even more like a horror film than it had when she had looked around that afternoon.

Putting her hands on her hips, Lisa bent double to get her breath back. If she got through this alive then she would take up jogging. Well… maybe not jogging, but some form of exercise. Something you could do in the privacy of your home without being judged by other people or wearing silly stretchy shorts that made your arse look enormous.

As oxygen made its way back to the deprived regions of her body, her brain began to work more lucidly and she remembered that

189

she was, at this moment, still being hunted. Where was safest?

Lisa looked up through one of the holes in the ceiling through which chains passed to work the sack hoist. Could wolves climb stairs?

Of course they could. They were wolves not Daleks. And if a dog could climb stairs then a wolf could. But the top attic, used for storage, was accessible only by ladder. Could a wolf climb a ladder?

Maybe, but it would be hilarious to watch. More usefully, a ladder could be removed, making the attic the most defensible place in the building. If they even figured out she was in the building.

Feeling a lot better than she had, Lisa made for the stairs. Things were looking up. The wolves might never find her here, and if they did she could surely hold them off till morning when they would all change back. At which point she would have some pretty stern words to say to the bunch of naked bullies she would be left with.

But as she reached the top floor, just below the attic, she glanced out the window, and her blood froze. There they were; slinking out of the mist. She counted ten of them but there might be more, moving slowly, casually, as if they were in no hurry whatsoever. Why should they be? It would not alter how tonight ended, so why not stretch out the game and enjoy it while it lasted?

They began to circle the mill, and Lisa ran from window to window, watching them as they padded around the building, penning her in, snuffling greetings to each other as they went, yapping in amusement. They could smell her fear, she was sure of it.

Lisa searched amongst them for the white wolf - for Oliver - but saw no sign. Well, that was a blessing at least. Perhaps he had been unable to get out of the school, or maybe he had even mastered this curse. It was the sort of thing Ollie would do, he always had to be better than everyone else and beholden to no one.

Apparently in charge was a large grey wolf, bullish in his treatment of the others, snarling at them and batting them with his paw if they did not do as he growled, so they flattened themselves to the ground before him or rolled on their backs, whining in submission. That was Glendon.

Lisa's hatred spiked, her fists clenched, a hot feeling itching inside her doing battle with her fear. She didn't want to be the victim here, like all the beaten-down heroines whose stories she had read,

190

waiting for some man to come rescue them. She wanted to be the swift and terrible sword of justice.

But as she thought this, the wolf Glendon raised its head and looked directly at the dark window from which she stared. He could not know she was there, and yet he seemed to. Throwing back his head, he howled and the rest of the pack, all around the encircled mill, picked up the cry.

Whether she wanted to be it or not, as far as the wolves were concerned, Lisa was the victim.

Once he was out of the mire, Boris took a moment to get his bearings and then hared off across the moor as fast as he could run. He was a good runner, and although the moor offered more obstacles than his habitual running route along the south bank of the Thames on a Wednesday morning, he took these challenges in his stride. Knowing that the girl, Lisa Hobson, was in danger, drove him on. His prime function here was to protect the children – that was his job and he would not fail. The pack was bound to have reached the mill by now - wolves ran faster than he did - but that did not mean Lisa was dead. She was a resourceful girl and Boris kept hold of the hope that she would be able to hold them off until he arrived.

At which point he would… what?

The plan in his mind was to draw the pack away from the mill, and he could certainly do that, but, as previously noted, the wolves were quicker than him, so he could only draw them away long enough for them to catch and eat him. Which might not be long enough for Lisa to escape, and had a few other points in its disfavour too.

Boris was not a man who liked to rely on luck, but he was a man who trusted his own ability to improvise as circumstances demanded. When he got there, something would occur to him. It had too.

Moose ran alongside him. It was hard to tell if the dog was running with him because it liked running, because it liked Boris, because it had overcome its fear and was hastening to the aid of its mistress, or if it didn't really do motivation and was just running, but Moose was always good company.

From up ahead came the sound of howling, and Boris pushed himself harder. Howling was probably a good sign. Werewolves howled when they were hunting, and if they were still on the hunt then they had not caught Lisa yet.

As he charged on, through the mist to his right, Boris saw a haze of light coming from Naughton village, illuminating the fog from within and making it look almost luminous. He wasn't far from the mill now.

But then he suddenly changed direction, skidding on the slippery grass of the moor and heading for the village with renewed purpose. An idea had popped into Boris's head and he was sure it would work. Relatively sure. He needed a couple of things to go his way and he was wasting time by going to the village first instead of straight to the mill, but...

As he crossed the log bridge over the river, Boris's eyes widened in delight. The first part of his plan had fallen into place. There ahead of him, leaning against a wall outside *The Grey Boar*, where he always left it when he was too drunk to ride, was Malcolm's motorbike. It might be an elderly thing that had seen better days, but Malcolm knew his way around engines well enough to keep it in good working order, and Boris knew his way around starter motors well enough to hotwire it. Most importantly, it was quicker than a werewolf.

Probably. One way or another he was going to find out.

The howl rang through the night again as Boris tore down the mill road on Malcolm's bike, as fast as the little engine could stand.

Though she knew that she should probably retreat to the safety (comparative safety) of the attic, Lisa found she could not tear herself away from the windows on the top floor. There was nothing outside that she wanted to see, it was more like the horribly compelling spectacle of a car crash or a really bad haircut, something that held your gaze even when you desperately wanted to look away. The circling wolves were now done taunting her - though they still howled from time to time, individually or as a group, just to remind her that they were there - and had begun to press in on the mill. They jumped at the windows, cautiously at first, like a cat playing with its reflection, and every bang of paws against the panes made Lisa start. They scratched at the doors, some trying the handles with paws and teeth – enough vestige of humanity remaining in them that they recognised this as the way in.

192

But these early efforts, testing the waters, swiftly gave way to more serious ones. The bangs against the windows became louder as the wolves hurled more weight against them; a thumping came from the doors as several wolves charged them at once. At the far end of the building where the wheel turned in the mill race, wolves boldly sprang onto the moving buckets, scrabbling up the slippery wood. A yelp and a splash indicated that they had not been successful, but with so many potential entrances it was only a matter of time.

Still Lisa remained at the window, gazing in wide-eyed horror. *This is really happening*, she tried to tell herself. But though she was certainly afraid, she did not think that her body had fully grasped the reality of the danger. Looking through the window it was easy to think of the whole thing like a movie – you were scared by a horror movie, but you knew it wasn't going to hurt you. It was important that she force herself to believe that this *could* hurt her. It could kill her. She listened out for any sign that one of the wolves might have got into the building, but so far nothing. She would stay at the window until then. That would still give her plenty of time to retreat to the attic.

The sound of breaking glass from beneath her clenched her stomach into a tight knot, and for a moment Lisa thought she might vomit in fear. Down below she saw the wolves converged on a window. One of them had blood on it and was being licked by its comrades, till the grey wolf, Glendon, came and barked at them: stop making a fuss, it's only a scratch.

They couldn't get in yet – the glass was broken but the small, individual frames of the sash window remained, and the wolves now took it in turns to rear up and punch their paws into the wooden spars. Though she was at too great a distance to actually hear it, in her mind's ear, Lisa imagined she could hear the wood creak and splinter beneath the onslaught. They had found their way in, it would not be long now.

So horridly compelling was the spectacle beneath her, Lisa did not at first notice a new noise or the approaching light, faint at first through the mist but getting stronger. It was only when the wolves looked up and around that she did the same and gave a choking cry of disbelief.

Riding out of the fog like a white knight on his charger - if you could picture a white knight in muck-stained overalls or his charger leaving a trail of noxious black exhaust behind it - was Boris on a motorbike. He didn't slow down as he approached the mill house, but crashed straight through the garden gate, sending shards of whitewashed wood spinning dangerously through the air. If that hadn't already got the wolves attention, he rode straight into the thick of them, knocking them left and right, kicking one or two as he passed, executing a brief, tight circuit of the garden before tearing out the way he had come, still going as fast as the little bike would endure.

But when he left, he was not alone.

As one wolf, the pack rushed after this interloper. Lisa might have been their target, but wolves are vengeful, and do not take kindly to being kicked in the face. They are also, at heart, dogs, and chasing something is like second nature. In the same way that Ollie, in wolf form, could not resist the light of a torch, even abandoning his prey to chase it, so the bully pack could not help themselves as they took off after the bike, scrambling over the garden wall in their haste. A wolf's got to do what a wolf's got to do.

Chapter 20 – The Frankenstein Moment

For a long moment, as she watched the wolves haring off into the darkness and mist on the tail of the motorbike, Lisa just sat. Eventually she had to remind herself to breathe. The hot sweat that had prickled across her, now cooled on her skin and her tense body slumped against the stone frame of the window.

They were gone.

Relief was not even the word. Nor was gratitude. Pleased though she was, she could not help wondering what might happen to Boris, who had saved her life yet again. He presumably had some sort of plan, he usually seemed to.

But it was quite possible that that plan was just to distract the werewolves long enough for her to get away, and she did not want to let him down. Pushing herself back up onto jelly legs, Lisa made her way for the steps leading down to the lower floors. The mill was as silent as ever, the creak of the water wheel, muffled by the thick stone wall, was the only sound.

On the ground floor, she paused to look at the broken window. That had been too close. The window was completely caved in, the wooden spars broken and shattered glass strewn about the floor. Boris had arrived just in time.

Lisa turned to go back out the window through which she had entered.

And froze as a low growl reverberated from the shadows in the corner of the room.

While her feet remained rooted the floor, Lisa turned, almost unwillingly, to look in the direction from which the noise had come. The eyes of the grey wolf glowed red in the dark as it slunk out from the deeper shadows, the darkness seeming to flow over its body, as if it could wear the night like a cloak. It was so much bigger than it had seemed when Lisa had looked down on it from the upstairs window, bigger even than Ollie had seemed in the confines of her dorm room. There was a powerful muscularity to its every step, the floorboards creaking beneath its weight. The Glendon wolf bared its teeth to snarl at her, and Lisa felt the sound vibrate in her guts, setting off a fear response that had been keyed into the human species since cave people had shrunk from wolves in the earliest days of man.

But no wolf back then had ever broken off its snarl, cocked its shaggy head and chuckled at the back of its throat. It was not an 'it'. It could not really be called a wolf. It was Glendon, and he knew damn well what he was doing.

The petrified fear in which Lisa had been frozen finally gave way to quick-footed terror and she leapt for the stairs, dashing up as fast as she could. At the same instant, Glendon sprang after her, snapping his jaws in glee. The game might have lost some of its players, but he still had the upper hand, and this was still only going to end one way. As he moved, his powerful haunch smacked against a wooden lever by the wall, and the mill sprang into life.

On the first floor, as wheels began to turn around her and the deafening noise of the suddenly active mill filled the air, Lisa ran for the next staircase. She just had to reach the ladder, just had to get to the attic, then she would be safe. The plan was the same as it had always been; safety was upwards.

She did not dare look around but could hear Glendon behind her, his paws pounding the steps, his deep, throaty breaths somehow louder than the roar of the mill machinery. On the top floor, Lisa scrambled for the ladder and started up its rungs, two at a time.

But not quite quickly enough.

Glendon's snarl made Lisa jump as his paw swiped at the ladder, balanced against the lip of the trapdoor into the attic. The ladder fell and Lisa screamed as she hit the floor with it, rolling instantly onto her back and bringing the ladder with her, holding it out in front of her like a shield. As Glendon slashed his claws at her, she thrust the ladder towards him, blocking the blow which reduced the ladder to kindling. She rolled away again, still grasping a broken bit of ladder in each hand, scrambling back to her feet as Glendon advanced. Blindly she swiped the wooden shards out before her and got in a lucky hit, whacking Glendon sharply on the nose and making him pull back involuntarily with a whine of pained fury.

It wasn't much, but it was long enough for Lisa to dive out of reach, putting the rotating column at the centre of the room between her and Glendon. They eyed each other through the moving bars of the cogged wheel that turned the grinding stones far below. This was it, Lisa thought, this was the *Frankenstein* moment, the moment that had haunted her from youth, suddenly made real. And whenever this part of the film emerged in her nightmares, as it still did from time to time, she always ended up dead. The monster always won.

Glendon started to his right, swift and agile on his paws, but Lisa managed to keep the column between them. How long could she keep this up? Till morning? That seemed unlikely. Wildly, she wondered if she could throw a stick for the wolf and it might go fetch it. But no. That might have worked on one of the other wolves, but not on Glendon. For whatever reason, he had more awareness than the others, he would not be fooled so easily. He also had the necessary smarts to cover the stairs.

Lisa tried hard not to look at the stairs; she did not want to telegraph what her next move might be, and did not want to look away from Glendon. He moved so fast, she could not give him a micro-second.

"Why are you doing this?" Maybe it wasn't going to get any response, maybe it wasn't going to make any difference, but perhaps it would give her a little extra time. And if there was any shred of humanity in Glendon, then perhaps she could appeal to it. The problem was, she wasn't sure he'd had that much humanity when he was human.

The wolf Glendon cocked its head to one side and its mouth drew back in what could only be described as a grin. Wolves are not designed to smile, but the sense of the grin was there, albeit ugly and twisted. There was an irony of sorts to the fact that it was when the creature was at its most human, that it seemed most monstrous.

"Larry," Lisa began, and observed a slight start in the wolf – it had not realised that she knew who it was. More importantly, it *definitely* knew who and what it was. "You don't want to kill me," Lisa tried, edging as subtly as she could toward the stairs. "Don't get me wrong, I think you're about as low as a human being can go. At least for your age." There was no sense in sugar-coating or pretending that they liked each other. "But there's a big step, Larry, between being a total ass who picks on smaller kids, and killing someone in cold blood. I don't think that even you would be able to live with that."

A snort of derision and a toss of the head.

"You think you can." It had not been the purpose of this line of questioning, but now Lisa felt she had to know – this might be the only chance she got to ask the question that burnt in her mind. "Or perhaps you know you can."

If it was possible for a wolf to look smug then this one did.

"You killed Talbot."

The wolf nodded.

There was no misinterpreting the gesture. There was no misunderstanding it. Nor was there any mistaking the leer that expanded across Glendon's lupine features. He had done it, he had enjoyed it, and he would do it again.

White hot rage seared through Lisa, of a kind she would never have thought herself capable. Every other moment of anger and hatred in her life paled next to it. The fury seemed to steam from her skin and blister beneath it. She reached into her coat pocket.

"Not so damn funny now, is it?" she said, as she levelled the gun at Glendon.

There was a moment of awkward uncertainty on the wolf's face, but then it seemed to dismiss this threat as the hysteria of a panicked girl. Summoning her courage, Lisa grasped the unfamiliar weapon tightly in sweaty palms, remembering the smile on Talbot's face when they had met, remembering the horridness of their last moments together – a hurt that could never now be healed.

Suddenly, Glendon feinted left. Lisa followed but the wolf sprang back right and lashed at her outstretched hands with a large paw. The gun slipped free and sailed through the air, smashing the window as it hit it and falling to the earth far below.

Lisa watched it go. So did Glendon. But he watched it for a split-second longer.

Legs fuelled by adrenalin and panic, Lisa rushed for the stairs. She didn't bother with the steps but just jumped down the steep flight, tripping, falling, rolling back to her feet and hurling herself towards the next one. The crash of the wolf's heavy weight on the floor behind her drove her on, but as she reached the top of the stairs to the ground floor she heard it spring and felt heavy paws at her back. Glendon pushed her forwards with all his weight, sending Lisa tumbling down the next flight, hitting every step as she went, till she landed at the bottom a bruised ball of pain, whimpering softly.

It would be so easy to stay like this. To curl up here and wait for the hurt to stop. Or just to die here if that was what was going to happen. And yet there was a stubborn streak in Lisa that she had learnt from the best heroines of the books she read – she would always be more Marian Halcombe than Laura Fairlie (*The Woman in White*, Wilkie Collins). Even when it hurt just to raise her head, she would not lie down. Even when the end was inevitable, she would not give up.

With an effort, she brought her battered head off the floor and stared back up the stairs to where Glendon stood at the top, looking down at her. He pulled back, and then leapt.

At the best of times, riding a motorbike across the humps and bumps of a moor is a hazardous exercise, especially for a man who plans on fathering children at some future date. Doing so at night, in the mist, on a bike that, while well-maintained, was mostly held together by prayer and habit was downright insane. But in Boris's view, life needed a little insanity from time to time, it made the world turn around.

This second part of the plan had come to him while he was riding the short distance from Naughton to the mill, and if the bike could hold out and his sense of direction was on the money, then he was confident it would work.

His eyes lit up as the lowering shadow of a hill emerged through the mist. At its base, he could just see the narrow split that led to the mine. Boris headed straight for it. He had to admit that the next part of the plan was a little bit dicey, but so had every other part been and it had all worked thus far.

He chanced a look back over his shoulder - a dangerous game on this uneven ground - and saw the pack, still hot on his heels, tearing after him, snapping and growling as they went. The bike was faster, but not by much.

Heading for the split, and wondering briefly if the gate was open, Boris did not even slow up. The noise of the motor echoed in that narrow crevasse and then boomed about him as he rode straight into the tunnel, the headlight cutting a path through the darkness before him. Moments later, the deafening noise of the engine in that confined and yet limitless space was joined by the echoing of the wolves' raised voices. If they had any anxiety in entering the lair of their pack leader, then it was lost in the heat of the hunt.

Boris grinned manically as he rode – the plan was working. It was still nuts, he reminded himself as the bike's back wheel skidded on the slippery floor of the mine, but it was working. And it was reaching its conclusion not a moment too soon; the bike's engine was starting to make a discomfiting choking noise, as if it had developed a bad cough.

The character of the echo changed again as Boris rode into the central cavern, finally daring to touch the brakes, allowing the pack to close in on him as he led them across the uneven floor of the mine and around the towering column that held up the roof. He couldn't have gotten away with this with people - or even with more evolved werewolves - but these wolves had all the reasoning capacity of dogs, and it never occurred to them to cut Boris off as he led them on a circuit of the cavern and back out again, hitting the accelerator once more, and hard. This was the key moment – the race for the finish.

The bike's engine screamed, whined and hacked its guts up as Boris gunned it for all he was worth, back down the long tunnel to the entrance. Just a little longer. He could see the opening up ahead, a patch of vague, misty grey against the slabs of blackness surrounding it. He could hear the wolves on his tail, still close, but falling back a little as exhaustion began to tell.

As he burst forth out of the mine, Boris jammed on the brakes, leaping off the bike as he went and letting it skid away from under him as he scrambled back towards the entrance, ignoring the scuffs and scrapes on his arms and legs. The wolves were almost there – he could hear them and see the bright reflective circles of their eyes as they charged towards him. Grabbing the rusted gate, Boris hauled it closed and twisted the chain around the bars.

A heartbeat later, the first wolf hit the gate with a yelp, followed by more yelps as its pack cannoned into it from behind.

As they lay in the mine entrance, whining and groaning, Boris checked that the chain was fast – yes; no paws were going to untangle that. He stepped back, placing his hands on his hips and breathing deeply. It had worked. Lisa was safe, and when the sun rose again he could deal with the fall-out.

But just as he was allowing himself a moment to enjoy his victory, he heard a horribly familiar sound floating across the moor from the direction of the mill. The howl of a wolf.

"No…"

Had he lost a wolf along the way? Had another shown up from the school, late to the party? Worse yet, had Montford decided to take matters into his own clawed hands?

It didn't matter and Boris didn't waste a moment wondering.

200

Dragging the bike back to its wheels, he leapt on and the kicked the starter.

The bike wheezed briefly and died.

"No."

Boris tried again and again.

"No!"

But it was not good. With no other options left to him, Boris took off running towards the mill, forcing his worn-out body on. But it was a long way, and the howl sounded again.

Glendon leapt, and Lisa tensed herself against the inevitable. She seemed to see in slow motion the arc of his powerful body coming towards her, clawed paws outstretched, jaws bared and salivating, eyes burning with red ferocity.

Then suddenly, from nowhere, a white blur sprang across Lisa's vision, taking Glendon out of the air and knocking him to the floor of the mill with a crash. It was Oliver.

Lisa stared in shock as the two wolves, the white and the grey, twisted on the floor together, tearing at each other. Oliver had the element of surprise, he had landed on top of Glendon and latched his jaws onto the bully's neck. But Glendon was bigger, stronger, and more dominant. He batted Oliver away with a fierce blow to the white wolf's head.

The pair rolled apart, snarling and eyeing each other as they got back to their paws and began to circle slowly, facing off. Then, without warning, they both sprang forward and clashed again, fur flying as they snapped and scratched at one another, going up on their hind legs as they met. Again it was Glendon who got the upper hand, pushing Ollie back, slashing with his claws till Ollie was pinned to the wall. Lisa saw Ollie's eyes turn to her, and in them she saw, not the wolf, but her brother, telling her to run while she had the chance.

"Hey!"

It probably wasn't the smartest thing Lisa had ever done – Ollie had saved her and she was throwing away the chance he had given her. But there was no way she would let her little brother be treated like this. Maybe they hadn't always got along, but Lisa loved her brother, and you did dumb things for the ones you loved.

Grabbing a bag of flour from a table by the door - part of a display for tourists - Lisa hurled it at Glendon. The bag hit the grey wolf's head hard and exploded, showering both fighters in a cloud of wholemeal powder.

"Leave my brother alone!"

Shaking his head free of flour, Glendon fixed Lisa with a look that said he was more than happy to leave Ollie alone – *she* was his focus. He started towards her but was immediately yanked back by Ollie pulling on his tail. Glendon turned to snap at Oliver and Lisa hurled another bag of flour, infuriating the big wolf.

Torn between brother and sister, Glendon finally launched himself in full-blooded attack at Oliver, recognising him as the one who might be an actual threat, and smart enough to know that Lisa would not abandon her brother, so he could kill her afterwards.

Lisa screamed as Glendon grabbed Ollie by his throat and took him to the floor, pounding his chest with heavy strokes of his paws. Ollie wriggled to get free but was caught in a tight grip, that just seemed to get tighter. He desperately kicked up but Glendon was too strong, and as the grip on his throat tightened, Ollie whimpered and howled in pain, his eyes rolling back into his head.

Grabbing a chair in both hands, Lisa rushed forward to bring it down with brutal force at the big wolf. Glendon dodged at the last moment, releasing Ollie and snarling at Lisa as the chair shattered on the floor where he had been. Brandishing the broken wood in her hands, Lisa snarled right back at the wolf and swiped the air in front of her. She would not back down.

But she could be taken down. Glendon moved like a streak of furred lightning, leaping forwards faster than Lisa could swipe, his paws on her chest, knocking her to the floor and pinning her there. His snout was barely an inch from Lisa and terror flooded into her as he bared his teeth, his drool dripping onto her face, his eyes burning with bloodlust.

But in the next moment, Glendon was distracted by a growl from beside them. To her left, Lisa saw Ollie stumbling back to his paws, beaten and bruised but still standing and as intent on defending his sister as she was on defending him. Ollie attacked again, but Glendon kept a firm paw on Lisa, keeping her where she was, struggle as she might, as the frenzied wolf attack raged above her. She tried to cover her face as jaws and claws, snapped and tore in close proximity.

Even with his attention split between the siblings, Glendon remained the alpha, the master of the situation, and Ollie was slowly forced back, desperately defending himself from his own pack leader. Perhaps that inbuilt lupine subservience prevented him from going all out.

But Lisa had no such restriction. Summoning what reserves of strength and courage she had left, she beat at the wolf's chest from beneath, then brought her legs into play with a vicious kick, right where Glendon, human or wolf, would feel it most.

It only distracted Glendon for a moment but that moment was long enough. Ollie charged forward again, knocking Glendon back and grabbing his sister to drag her free from the big wolf's clutches. Lisa felt a stab of pain in her arm as Ollie tugged her loose, but easily dismissed it as she scrabbled back to her feet and, with Ollie beside her, ran for the broken window.

Brother and sister leapt out into the garden, rolling as they hit the grass. But they did not get far. With a powerful spring, Glendon was back on top of Ollie, driven by fury.

Lisa screamed as she saw blood tainting her brother's white fur, and cast about desperately for some weapon she could use against Glendon.

And there was one. Lying in the grass, where it had fallen from the top floor of the mill, was the gun with the silver bullet.

Glendon's claws slashed across Ollie's snout, making the white wolf howl in agony. Pinning his prey to the ground, Glendon raised his head to deliver the killing bite.

The gun shot echoed across the moor.

Boris pulled up in his running. Had that been what it had sounded like, coming from the direction of the mill? If it had indeed been a gunshot, then what might that mean?

He ran on.

Chapter 21 – The Wolf-Man

Lisa helped her brother to his feet, taking his weight on her shoulder
and trying not to look at him too closely because, even in such
desperate circumstances, sisters don't need to see their brother
naked.

"You're hurt." Which was an understatement. Claw and bite
marks peppered Oliver's pale skin, blood seeping from the cuts,
scratches and gouges.

Her brother looked up vaguely. "What happened? Where am
I?"

"You saved my life." Maybe she had saved his too.

Ollie shook his head. "It doesn't usually end like this."

"What doesn't?"

Ollie looked down at his feet. "You won't tell Mum and Dad?"

It was rare to see Ollie like this; contrite and concerned what
other people thought. Especially Mum and Dad. Where they were
concerned he had always been the golden boy who could do no
wrong.

As the pair seated themselves on the garden wall, Moose
trotted up, looking slightly sheepish, and nuzzled against Lisa, who
petted him automatically. "Tell them what?"

"We've been going on 'trips'." He used finger quotes to make
it clear that he did not mean an excursion to Margate Sands.

Lisa frowned. "Drugs?"

"I…" It was Ollie's turn to frown. "I suppose so. I never
remember that bit. Or the bit in between. Just some amazing dreams.
And waking up on the moor."

"Twice a month?" suggested Lisa.

"I tried to quit."

"After Talbot died."

Ollie nodded. "Yeah. I… I'm not sure why. It just…" He
frowned again, straining to make the feelings of the wolf coalesce
into the thoughts of a human. "It felt wrong. Now…" He looked at
his wounds. "What happened to me?"

"You got in a fight with a wolf."

Ollie shook his head again. "Maybe I'm dreaming now.
There's always wolves in my dreams. Did I win?"

For the first time, Lisa allowed her gaze to drift back to the body of the grey wolf, lying still on the lawn. It had remained a wolf. For which she was very grateful.

"You've been hurt too." Ollie pointed to a cut on Lisa's arm.

"It's nothing." She looked up sharply. "Someone's coming."

Relief poured into Lisa as Boris, puffing and panting, jogged up out of the fog. Her white knight had lost his charger, but was still there to, if not save the day, at least make the remains it of it easier to handle.

Boris smiled as he caught his breath, looking as relieved as Lisa felt. "Everyone alright?"

Once Ollie had been dispatched inside to find clothes he could borrow from poor Ralph, Lisa brought Boris up to speed. He listened in silence and then, wordlessly, put out an arm. Lisa collapsed against him, unable to hold back the tears any longer. She hadn't even realised she'd needed this. Boris held her until the sobbing subsided.

"Feel better?"

"Not much."

Boris nodded. "You had no choice." He didn't have to elaborate, and Lisa was glad that he did not.

"What now?"

"Did Mr Matthews have a landline?"

"I think so."

"Then I shall make a few calls."

The calls Boris made were to people who were sympathetic to this sort of situation (whatever this situation was) and promised to yield medical attention, as well as someone to deal with the dead wolf, release several naked bullies from an abandoned mine, and concoct a believable cover story.

"I think Dr Lloyd will understand," nodded Boris. "Or at least accept a lack of complete understanding. A very intelligent woman, Dr Lloyd. Now if you'll excuse me."

"You're leaving?" Lisa felt panicked again.

Boris nodded. "I'm sure Moose will look after you and the relevant authorities will be here shortly. I have to pay someone a visit, to ensure that this never happens again."

It did not feel right to Boris to steal two vehicles in one night, but time was of the essence and poor Ralph had no use for his car.

As Boris drove, he tried to force down some of the thoughts and feelings that thrashed about inside of him. He was going to face a dangerous adversary, and doing so in this emotional state of mind just made the encounter more dangerous.

But Montford had killed his friend, Creighton. He had killed Ralph Matthews, ruining the life of Evelyn Lloyd. He had deliberately turned Larry Glendon who now also lay dead. Maybe Glendon had been an unpleasant character but that did not mean he deserved...

And what had Glendon done? He had killed young Talbot Conliffe, he had given a bunch of his friends nightmares that might last a lifetime, and he had forced Lisa to do something that would live with her till the day she died.

Then there was Lisa's arm...

But that was for another day. The point was that all these things were to be laid at Simon Montford's door and the man seemed wholly unrepentant. It was very hard, even for someone as experienced as Boris, to keep anything like a level head in this situation.

The car roared up the driveway of Montford Hall and came to a skidding halt in a spray of gravel. Boris leapt out and strode purposefully towards the doors. As he did so, the door opened and Simon Montford stepped out with a suitcase in his hand. He froze at the sight of Boris and rushed to slam the door. But Boris was too quick, hurling his weight against it and forcing his way in to the grand hallway of the Squire's country residence, resplendent in dark wood and dusted with antiques.

"Fleeing somewhere?"

"How did you get out of the mire?" hissed Montford.

"Had help. It's over Montford."

Despite his cowering position, Montford still managed a sneer. "Over? How? What are you going to do? Tell the police that Ralph was killed by a werewolf? You think the solicitors are going to change the way they handle my father's estate because of the ravings of a man crying wolf?" He barked out a laugh as he finished.

Boris listened and shook his head. "That's not how we work in my organisation. We prefer to keep the existence of creatures like you secret. The good news for you is that we've long wanted to learn more about werewolves, so you have the option of coming with me and living a long life – albeit in a small cell. Which, I think we can both agree, is a deal better than you deserve."

"And if I refuse?"

"You don't really need me to answer that do you?"

Montford met Boris's stare. "Aren't you forgetting something, Mr Rains?"

Montford was running for the stairs even as he started to change. Boris pulled out Creighton's gun's and fired but the wolf-man was too quick and the silver bullet slammed into the stairs. Stupid; he should have waited until he had a clear shot.

Now fully shifted into wolf-man form, Montford turned at the top of the magnificent stairway that dominated the hall, and sprang. Boris barely had time to dive aside as the wolf-man landed, cannoning into a side table and sending several thousand pounds worth of china smashing to the carpet.

Struggling to his feet, Boris tried to aim but the werewolf moved like lightning, bounding towards him and knocking the gun from his hand. It roared into his face, curved yellow teeth lining its wide open jaws.

With a crack, Boris brought his elbow around into beast's jaw, then stamped on its foot. He dived sideways, going for his gun but Montford recovered quickly, clawing at his legs and dragging him back. Rolling over, Boris kicked Montford repeatedly on the snout then jerked his leg free. Both man and wolf-man dived for the gun and it was Montford's clawed hand that closed on it and hurled it away across the room. With a snarl of triumph, he grabbed the struggling Boris and tossed him into display cabinet that proudly showed off a selection of hunting trophies.

Smashing through the glass, Boris felt tiny lacerations all over his body. He crashed through the cabinet shelves to the floor, landing on broken glass and with silverware tumbling down heavily to bury him. An ominous creak from behind made him roll aside, just in time to avoid the cabinet itself as it too crashed to the floor.

Looking up through a haze of disorientation and blood, that trickled down his forehead and into his eyes, Boris saw the wolf-man loping towards the door, intent on escape.

Not bloody likely. Not while there was still breath in the Universal agent's body.

Leaving the various aches and pains on the floor behind him, where they belonged, Boris launched himself forwards, leaping onto the wolf-man's back just as it reached the door.

"No you damn well don't!" He brought his elbow down between the creature's ears into its skull with all the strength he had left in him. "That was for Creighton." He smacked both fists into the sides of the werewolf's head. "That was for Ralph and Dr Lloyd." He raised his hands again. "And this is for- oh shit…"

The angry Montford grabbed Boris's leg and threw him to the floor. Winded, Boris struggled to get out of the way, but this time was too slow as the wolf-man slashed its claws at him. The pain seared across Boris's back, but he still manged to roll away, scrabbling on the floor to get back to his feet before the werewolf could attack again.

Fortunately, the creature seemed less interested in him than it was in escaping, and Boris was left hurling a silver cup (won by Montford's paternal grandmother for Best Dressed in the Naughton Hunt), which hit the door as Montford charged through it.

Boris didn't wait. Bloodied and beaten, he staggered on after his quarry. He was going to stop that creature or die in the attempt. He would *not* allow this to happen again. As best he could, he ran out the doors.

And was brought up short.

The wolf-man stood in the middle of the gravelled courtyard outside his stately home, illuminated by the burning torches of the men and women who stood about him in a circle, that closed just as Boris came out. They were gypsies by their clothes, and they looked on the beast in their midst with stern, fearless expressions. Boris could not shake the feeling that he had walked in on some ceremony in progress.

For the moment, Montford seemed to be so taken aback by all this that he had quite forgotten himself, and simply stood, regarding these bafflingly unafraid people with confusion. He soon recovered himself however, and roared his defiance at them. It seemed to have no effect, and he rushed at the circle. But instead of running, the gypsies closed in, thrusting fiery torches into the wolf-man's face, forcing it to back down, snarling.

Backing away, Montford tried another part of the circle but got the same response. For whatever reason, these people weren't afraid of him, and dangerous though a werewolf was, fear was a major weapon in its arsenal when it was outnumbered to this extent.

As Boris watched, still not quite sure what he was seeing, the circle parted at the far end, just enough to let through an elderly woman. It closed up behind her, sealing her in with the wolf-man. It didn't look like a fair fight, until you saw that in her hand the woman clutched an old pistol. Though he had no way of knowing, Boris would have bet every penny he had that there were silver bullets in it.

Clearly Montford had the same idea, he growled sharply and darted at the fringes of the circle, slashing his claws at the gypsies, testing their mettle, trying to find a weak spot. But everywhere he went, he was met by grim faces and the torches thrust at him.

The old woman raised the gun, her hand as steady as steel, tracking the wolf as its movements became more and more frantic.

Suddenly, the wolf was gone, shrinking in a series of hasty spasms back into Simon Montford, his clothes tattered, his eyes pleading.

"Please don't hurt me."

The old woman spoke. "Did you listen to the pleas of your victims?"

Montford's panicked eyes flicked back to Boris, standing at the front door. "That man up there? He works for an organisation that studies people like me – *victims* like me. If you let me go then I will go with him. They'll keep me locked up. I'll never be able to hurt anyone again. You – tell them."

Boris shrugged. "Everything he said is true."

"There!" Montford turned a desperate stare back to the gypsy woman. "I'll never harm another living soul."

"It is not your future victims I care about."

If Montford did not know exactly *who* this woman was, then he could guess at *what* she was. A grieving relative.

He dropped to his knees. "Do you think I don't regret what I've done? If you knew what I feel when I look at myself in the mirror in the morning. If you knew the guilt that wracks me every day."

It was a good act, and the gypsy woman's impassive face left Boris unclear as to whether or not she was buying it.

"It's not my fault," Montford continued, raising his hands towards the gypsy. "A werewolf cannot help what he does when the curse is upon him."

For the first time, the gypsy woman's expression seemed to change as she said, "I know that better than anyone."

The pistol cracked. Montford fell.

It was, Boris felt, a thoroughly unspectacular death. But it would do. Creighton, Ralph, Talbot, and who knew how many others, even Glendon; they had all been avenged.

The gypsy woman tucked the gun away, in amongst the folds of her shawl, and looked up at Boris. She gave an almost imperceptible nod, perhaps the acknowledgment of one professional to another, or perhaps just saying, 'Clean this lot up, would you?'. She turned to leave and the gypsy troupe fell in behind her. There was nothing triumphal about them, it was more like a funeral cortege.

Boris watched until they were out of sight, then went back inside to retrieve Creighton's gun and make another phone call. He yawned as he went. It had been a very long night.

Epilogue

"It would have been in November, I guess."

Oliver sat up in his hospital bed, his various wounds bandaged, his face pale. Beside him, Lisa sat. A hundred and twenty questions bubbled in her head but she held her tongue. Let him talk at his own pace – there was stuff he was probably better off not knowing.

"Larry asked if I wanted to go on a trip one night. I guess I misunderstood, but I said 'yes' and then just sort of went with it. There was a bunch of us. I was the youngest. I guess I was flattered to be asked."

That surprised Lisa. She'd never thought her brother cared about stuff like that, about being accepted.

"We climbed out the dorm window, Larry leading, down the drainpipe, then over the wall. It was exciting." He couldn't help grinning. "It was cold too," he added. "We walked up into the hills, and then..." Ollie paused, trying to remember. "That night wasn't the same as the others. I woke up with a sore head and punctures in my arm. I guess, needle marks."

Bite marks, thought Lisa.

"I thought they'd just played a trick on me. But the next night, we went out again. We stripped off our clothes and..." the grin returned, "and it was a magic. I can't tell you how it felt, like I was running in the wind. This thin, wild thrill. Primal. Visceral. I don't have the words. When we woke up, lying out in the hills, I could still feel it, rushing in my veins like mercury. Fizzing in my brain. From then on, twice a month we'd go out. Sometimes Larry would lead us, others... I don't know; he was just... there." Ollie paused again, reliving those wild nights. "I've never felt so alive."

"Then why did you try to stop?" asked Lisa, not wanting to press, but desperate to know more.

"I..." There again was that look on Ollie's face, like someone with dementia searching for an answer they know they have but are unable to find. "I didn't want to hang out with those guys any more. It was... It was wrong somehow. I mean, obviously we were doing something wrong but I never felt it until then."

Until Talbot died, thought Lisa. Then, without knowing why, he had pulled away from the bully group and away from his pack. The knowledge of what Glendon had done had not remained, but the sense of it, and the guilt by association, had.

"What happened the night I was in your room?" Oliver asked.

Lisa shrugged. "You just left. Went out the window. Don't you remember?"

Why torture him with things she could not explain, and which he would probably never believe?

She thought back to when she had first seen the white wolf, the night she met Maria, when he had been apart from the pack. Had he been warning her? Had he been running to defend her? She would never know, but she liked to think so.

Lisa took her brother's hand and squeezed, and could not help smiling when she felt him squeeze back.

The assembly on the dangers of drug addiction, given two days later, was agreed by pupils and staff to be one of the best assemblies ever. Lisa scanned the rows of attentive faces staring up at 'Mr Rains' as he spoke, and saw none of the cynicism that this sort of speech would normally bring. Partly that was because Boris was an excellent public speaker. Mostly it was because rumour travels fast in a school, and about twenty different versions of 'what happened that night' were doing the rounds. None of which bore any relation to the truth. As her gaze wandered through the audience, Lisa lighted on the remaining members of the bully group, looking pale but otherwise none the worse for their adventures. Cristina wore an expression that Lisa had never seen on her face before, one of almost desperate attention. No one was listening more closely than she and her friends – they weren't quite sure what they had been doing, but were damn sure they didn't want to do it again. An expression of fervent relief passed across all their faces as Mr Rains announced that parents would not be contacted in this instance, as he and his colleagues with the UK's drug enforcement taskforce, wanted to build trust between them and the children they were trying to help. The relief of the bullies (*former*-bullies Lisa corrected; girls like Gwen would be safe from here on in) was mirrored in that of the teachers, who had been mentally editing their resumés. Perhaps, Lisa considered, that relief was the reason that so few people were questioning why a drug enforcement officer had felt the need to go undercover as a caretaker at a remote public school; a tactic for winning the war on drugs that really required closer examination.

212

People's willingness to believe whatever suited them really was amazing.

As Boris finished, Lisa thought she saw a look pass between him and Evelyn Lloyd. The headmistress might not know the full story, but perhaps she knew that her lost love had been avenged.

"So," said Lisa to Boris, later that afternoon. "When I shot the wolf," she could not call it Glendon; that remained the darkest shadow of this whole affair, "the curse was lifted from all the others."

Boris nodded. "Montford never planned to turn more than one wolf. All the others were turned by Glendon himself, recreating his human 'pack' in wolf form."

"Consciously?" asked Lisa, tentatively.

Boris sighed. "I'm not sure we'll ever know how conscious Larry Glendon was of what he was doing. As it stands we simply don't know enough about werewolves. It should have been impossible for so young a wolf, but from everything he did and from everything you've told me, I think we have to assume that Glendon retained a deal of control over his actions when he was a wolf. That he did everything deliberately."

"Maria said that a man who was already a wolf in his heart, someone bad, could control the wolf."

Boris shrugged. "Maybe." Or maybe that's what we would both like to believe, he added to himself. Early that morning he had trekked across the moors looking for the gypsy encampment, but they had moved on, taking whatever knowledge they had with them.

"And the only way to turn Glendon back would have been to kill Montford?"

"Yes," acknowledged Boris. "But then your brother, and all the others, would have been trapped as wolves forever. There are seldom happy endings to werewolf stories. This one… Perhaps it is as happy as could have been expected." He did not mention that, after Montford had been killed, Glendon's lupine corpse had changed back to its human state. That seemed one gruesome detail too many.

Lisa felt sick in her stomach just thinking about what had happened, and wondered if the feeling would ever go away. Seated beside her, Moose lapped at her hand and she scratched him behind the ears, her thoughts turning to Talbot, and wishing that the 'happy ending' of which Boris spoke could have made her feel better, or at least afforded some kind of closure.

"How is your brother?" asked Boris, making conversation.

"They've patched him up. He's leaving hospital tomorrow, after our parents have gone." There had been tremendous fuss over Oliver. Which was reasonable. He had suffered a number of injuries while she just had a cut on her arm that was easily bandaged. There were always good reasons to fuss over Ollie, and Lisa, as always, felt guilty for resenting it. "He seems..." she sought for words. "I think he and I are going to be closer after this. For a while at least. Maybe we're too different to ever be... But better. And I don't think he'll be hanging around with bullies anymore."

"Always a silver lining."

"He saved my life, but... afterwards, it didn't seem like he knew what he was doing."

Boris shook his head. "I wish I had more answers. You're Oliver's sister. That bond may have been strong enough that it still motivated him after he changed."

Lisa could not help remembering Maria's story – it did not always work that way.

"It's a mistake to think of the supernatural as a science," Boris continued. "The 'rules' aren't clear cut. With werewolves especially they can seem vague and nebulous."

Some rules, maybe. But others were absolutes.

"Boris, when Ollie was getting me out of the mill..." Lisa saw Boris's body stiffen, as if he knew what was coming. "It was an accident, but..." She touched the bandage on her arm.

She had tried to tell herself that the cut was from broken glass or Glendon's attack, but she knew these were fantasies. When Ollie had dragged her out from under Glendon, he had done so with his mouth and, in his haste, his teeth had drawn blood.

"That is..." Boris tried to find the right words, "unfortunate."

Lisa gave a rueful smile. "Yeah. 'Unfortunate' was the word I was going to use."

"Do you have plans for what you want to do when you leave school?"

"You mean, do I have some burning, unfulfilled desire to live my life as a lab rat for your organisation?" She was only half-joking.

"I hadn't, but I guess my options just became pretty damn limited, so…"

"No." Boris held up a hand as he shook his head. "I was wondering if you'd be interested in a job?"

Lisa stared.

"Universal needs people like you," Boris continued. "And I don't mean people like you are *now*. I mean brave, intelligent, *special* people."

Lisa laughed. "There's nothing special about me – or at least there wasn't. Now Ollie…"

"I would not be making this offer to your brother," said Boris firmly. "And the fact that you are a werewolf - we may as well call a spade a spade - is, as far as we are concerned, the least special thing about you. Hopefully we can learn something about the curse as well, but that is *not* why I am making this offer."

"So I would be like you and Mr Tull?" Lisa wondered. "Constantly in danger of being torn apart, making life or death decisions about other people, always having to rescue idiots like me."

Boris gave a small smile. "It has its compensations. You meet the most interesting people."

When Lisa had caught up with Boris, after the morning's assembly, he had been on the phone. He had hung up with a frown and she has asked what was wrong.

"Apparently I'm going to Romania tomorrow."

Was that a life Lisa wanted? She had spent eighteen years as an also-ran, wondering if she could at least be happy with the mediocre future fate seemed to have in store for her. This offer was…

"I guess I've finally got something to write my first book about."

Boris held up an admonitory finger. "We would frown on that."

"But I could write about someone who lost their first love."

"Yes," Boris admitted, "you could do that."

Lisa stared out across the moor. For all that had happened, all that she had lost, she still loved it – the emptiness, the isolation. What was up with that?

"We offer an excellent education," Boris continued, "if you

215

intend to pursue your studies. And a wide variety of plausible excuses to tell loved ones. We're not asking you to cut anyone out of your life, we're asking…" he looked down at Moose, nuzzling into Lisa's lap, then back up to follow her line of sight out across the windswept tussocks of the moor. "We're asking you to help us make sure that what happened here, happens to as few people as possible."

Lisa looked back at him. "You should have opened with that."

The End

About the Author

Robin Bailes lives in Wiltshire and has been writing in one capacity or another for the last twenty years. Outside of these books his fondest achievement is the 6-part comedy/drama web-series Coping, which you can find on YouTube (if you look hard enough). Robin's interest in old films began with a book about Lon Chaney that belonged to his Grandpa, which led to a lifelong passion for cinema, particularly the horror movies of the 1920s and 30s. That passion has also led Robin to volunteer at London's Cinema Museum (where he can be found serving coffee at most silent film screenings) and to the creation of weekly web-series Dark Corners...
@robinbailes

Dark Corners

Co-created by Robin Bailes and Graham Trelfer, Dark Corners Reviews began as a bad movie review show on YouTube and has grown into a sprawling collection of videos celebrating the best and worst of cult cinema. With bad movie reviews every Tuesday, streaming movie reviews every Friday, and monthly specials about classic films and franchises, the show has a loyal following of movie fans from all over the world, people who share a love of cinema and a sense of humour. The success of Dark Corners directly gave rise to The Universal Library...
@DarkCorners3

The Universal Library

The idea of a series of books featuring characters from horror's golden age initially came when the movies themselves were being re-booted, and while those reboots have now gone in a very different direction, the books remain a tongue-in-cheek, but respectful, take on the classics. Hopefully the series meets with the approval of horror fans, film fans and neophytes alike.
Facebook – The Universal Library

Made in United States
Troutdale, OR
10/10/2023

13581047R00137